Rescue Me

Rescue Me

a love story

Gigi Levangie Grazer

POCKET STAR BOOKS
New York London Toronto Sydney Singapore

This book is a work of fiction. Names, characters, places and incidents are products of the author's imagination or are used fictitiously. Any resemblance to actual events or locales or persons, living or dead, is entirely coincidental.

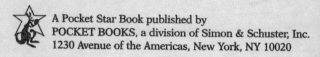

A Pocket Star Book published by
POCKET BOOKS, a division of Simon & Schuster, Inc.
1230 Avenue of the Americas, New York, NY 10020

Copyright © 2000 by Gigi Levangie Grazer

Originally published in hardcover in 2000 by Pocket Books

ISBN: 0-671-04280-7

First Pocket Books printing August 2001

10 9 8 7 6 5 4 3 2 1

POCKET STAR BOOKS and colophon are registered
trademarks of Simon & Schuster, Inc.

Cover art by Lisa Litwack
Photo credits: © Bill Brooks/Masterfile, Tony Stone Images

Printed in the U.S.A.

Acknowledgments

First, I wish to thank my "team:" Jennifer Rudolph Walsh, Stephanie Davis, Ruth Pomerance, and Sylvie Rabineau; I also wish to thank my editor, Marysue Rucci, and my publisher, David Rosenthal. Many thanks, as well, to the ladies of the Wednesday night writers group who listened patiently to chapter after chapter: Amy Schiffman, Laurie Horowitz, Roberta Grant, and Candy Haskell. I am indebted to my friend, Doug Lane, not only for his enthusiasm, but also for his tireless accounting of grammatical errors.

I am very grateful to my family: my father, Frank Levangie, my mother, Phillipa Brown, my sisters, and all the children in my life, for their continued support and love.

Last, thank you to my hometown of Los Angeles, where far more stories are born than can be written.

For Brian,
whose heart and energy inspire

One

To some it would be a distinctive scent, picked up on the breeze of a stranger. To others it would be a familiar smile, the crinkle of a nose, the slope of a peculiar walk. To Amanda Cruz, née McHenry, Encino mother of two (the Valley, yes—however, significantly, 2.5 blocks south of the boulevard), it was all about sound.

This hazy evening, with air heavy as an old woman's drapes, the deafening and insistent drumbeat of a Ninja 2X900 motorcycle shifting into first gear caused Amanda to drop an entire tray of stuffed Cornish game hens, rush outside to the curb, past the newly planted pink and violet hydrangeas and the (hideous) sandstone Labrador retriever, and back indoors, charging into the sanctuary of her separate bath to relieve herself in the cool waters of her recently installed imported brass-and-Italian-marble bidet.

Which, in turn, sent her little one, Tildy, yawling in terror at the sudden noise, to the stringy, Nautilized arms of her daddy; which sent her husband, James Cruz, rushing into gibberished explanation in front of the dinner party, teeming with various yet entirely similar corporate attorneys and their spouses.

Only Maddie—Madison, her son, her brother's son—did not get upset, taking in his adoptive mother's antics and his stepfather's overreaction with a bemused and exotic eye. Even at ten he'd lived too much to overreact to anything, except maybe death or the loss of a stolen skateboard with narrow glow-in-the-dark racing wheels.

Amanda sat in her bidet—yes, sat (she had no shame at the moment)—and lit a Marlboro cigarette, the real, no-bullshit, take-no-prisoners kind, the ones she kept hidden in the linen closet or behind the toilet or underneath the shiny brass sink.

She sucked in the shame-laced tobacco, exhaled its smoke slowly, and watched her reflection, covering her face in the gilt-framed antique mirror secured on the peach-colored, sponge-textured wall in front of her, her mind tearing away the days, like the images of a flip book, into her past.

As James banged on the bathroom door, yelling through gritted teeth, embarrassed and frantic over his loss of standing before his befuddled guests, who were well finished by now (it was eight-thirty, for crissakes) with their crab-meat rolls and feta cheese canapés, Amanda exhaled. The air came out of her like a death rattle, she thought ruefully. She took a moment to smile at her juvenile behavior.

And then she remembered. And the water rushed over her.

She took another puff, inhaling as deeply as she could—as deeply as her pink, overaerobicized lungs would allow (this sometimes takes a minute)—and leaned her head back against her peach-colored sponged wall. She closed her eyes.

"Amanda—you can't do this to me!"

Unfortunately, she could not close her ears as well.

"I'll be out in a sec, honey!" she yelled back at him, as though dropping twelve tiny corn-bread-and-mushroom-stuffed birds and running off like her heels were on fire were normal, everyday behavior.

"We lost the game hens! Jerry loves game hens!" James's voice was getting higher, more hysterical.

"We have cereal," Amanda replied, and then jumped as James threw his fist against the door to her bath. Amanda could tell he hurt his hand (she heard him swallow his yelp) and could feel him dancing about the bathroom in a rage he could not voice adequately in front of his illustrious guests.

Amanda almost felt bad for him. James could not shake the chip from his shoulder. Though he had wrestled down the American dream, though he drove a Lexus (just as good as a BMW, he told his aging frat-boy friends, without the sticker shock) and his wife an entirely too large SUV, though she shopped for his clothes at Neiman Marcus and no longer at JCPenney, though they had the house with the pool *and* cabana, he was still, in his heart of hearts, the poor immigrant boy who would never stop having to prove himself to the establishment. Even if it meant voting Republican.

And then she remembered why she was here

in the first place, sitting in this bidet, in this home, in this tract, in this valley.

And Amanda shuddered.

"I was just wondering what would have happened," she said to James in hushed, secretive tones, "if we hadn't killed my brother."

James paused, sucked in his breath. "Okay. This is not funny. You know you are never to bring that up. Never!" he hissed.

"Would I be sitting in this million-dollar prison . . . fretting away my days, sweating over the correct canapés to serve pompous, forever-dieting Century City lawyers?"

"You're acting nuts—you crazy bitch!"

Amanda stifled her laugh. When Jimmy was this angry, his Latin accent would come out in full force. He sounded like Ricky Ricardo on diet pills.

"Okay, okay. Any woman would trade places with you. There's a million women, good-looking women—"

"Please, Jimmy, invite them over. I'll have a little girls' luncheon, nothing fancy, serve my famous Louisiana crab cakes, the mini ones, you know, with the pepper flakes."

"You'd better come out right now!"

Amanda turned the bidet on higher.

"Amanda? What the hell do you think you're doing?"

Amanda reached over to the toilet paper roll and proceeded to stuff her ears with quilted triple-ply, no dyes, no scent.

And she allowed herself to drift.

She pictured herself sitting in an old porcelain sink with a cold gray metal faucet in an early 1920s dank two-story house in what used to be one of the finer neighborhoods in Los Angeles, when the city was new, when movie stars did not consider east of La Brea to be the real estate equivalent of contracting an embarrassing disease, a cold sore on an upper lip. Someone with a strong, sure hand is bathing her in lukewarm water in the old cracked sink. She is not a child. She is a woman of twenty-three, old enough to enjoy a good cleaning. She grabs the hand, covered in soap suds, and looks at it, stares for a good long time. This, she thinks, belongs to a man who would not force her to be someone she was not; this belongs to a man who has pride in her solely because of who, not what, she is; this hand belongs to a man who would not slam doors in her face when she did not feel well enough to attend a business function, or pull her arm into a party crowded with people who never remembered her name.

She has never been happier and will never be this happy again.

Amanda brings herself back. Her smile drops. And she asks herself the inevitable: Will she go with him when he does ride up, his 2X900 purring, cutting into her heart like a new razor? Will she be that brave? Because she knows—as well as she knows the words to Tildy's favorite Raffi song, or Madison's fifth-grade girlfriend's last name, or where to find James's lost black Calvin Klein cashmere sock on the morning of a very important meeting—she knows he will come for her eventually.

TWO

Summer 1985. Laurel Canyon. Raymond Chandler had given this run-down bohemian enclave a sexy, dangerous edge. Amanda had read every one of his novels, searching for the Laurel Canyon she knew so well—the cramped, spidery streets with names like Amor Road and Sugar Hill Drive, winding up to nowhere; the dirt roads that remained unnamed and forgotten; the decaying concrete walls soaked in green moss; the skinny, wild-eyed coyotes; the weary hills littered with old Colt 45 cans and grafittied boulders.

The canyon she knew was a place of dreams gone awry, of beautiful young men and women who grew old and ugly in this muddy hiding place, amid promises of a bright future. There was an old grocery store on Laurel Canyon, a couple of miles above Sunset. More than once, among the stacks of frozen TV dinners, Amanda had spotted a familiar face that had long ago lost its youthful sheen under a web of lines or layers of mottled flesh. More than once the face would turn away as quickly as it had been spotted.

Amanda McHenry grew up in these tangled hills. When kids at her junior high would ask where she lived, she replied, with a hint of impatience, "The hills." She knew most kids lived in the flats. In Hollywood, the flats consisted of apartment buildings with thin walls, or 1940s Spanish-style duplexes filled with people whose languages could not be gauged by any of the public school teachers. Some were "lucky" enough to live in one-story bungalows, dreary save for a patch of well-tended red and purple poppies and the snarl of the usual ancient Chihuahua.

The truth was, though—and Amanda felt this every time she replied to the inevitable question "Where do you live?"—her implied exotic, upper-middle-class life in "the hills" was nothing but a flat-out lie.

To be sure, there may have been cool houses in Laurel Canyon; Amanda's wasn't one of them. As a child she'd never invite her other friends who lived in the hills over—the friends whose fathers went to offices and had secretaries, the ones whose mothers stayed home and painted or smoked pot and took pottery lessons—for one simple reason: her house was a dump.

The outside of the dilapidated two-story structure was brown. It had been brown since her first memory and it remained brown; it had never been painted, not through years of mildew, not through hot, dry summers, not through several floods and earthquakes. Painting a house was a waste of good money, according to her mother, and since there was no father around (the divorce had taken place when she was a baby), there was no one to do the job anyway.

Inside, the wood was rotting. The sweet, sickening smell licked Amanda's nostrils every time she opened the front door. Plus, occasionally, her mother would allow her or her older brother, Valentin, to have a pet. Inevitably that pet would take a dump on the worn hardwood floors. Inevitably the dumps would leave both a new pungent odor and stains, stains that would not respond to detergent, to bleach, to tears, to plutonium.

Amanda's mother happened to be a collector,

as she put it. Mountains of newspapers would grow, awaiting the pledge of recycling, holding the promise of new change in a torn pocket. There were dusty glass apple-juice jars filled with coins, mostly pennies, a few lonely nickels (as Amanda and her brother had stolen the prized quarters and dimes when their world was young). There were old peach cans overflowing with pencils with no tips and pens that had stopped working long before the earth had heard of Jimmy Carter or puka shells. Open a drawer and you might find bunches of rubber bands that would crumble at a touch. Open another to find balls of string, of all sizes, saved for no reason at all.

For young Amanda there would be no invite-the-whole-class birthday parties. There would be no answer to "Why don't you have your friends come over here sometime?" Amanda couldn't remember what her first emotion was when she thought of her childhood, but she was fairly sure it was utter and complete embarrassment.

At age twelve Amanda had taken matters into her own hands. She dumped the papers, cleaned out the drawers, forced her will upon her mother to such an extent that their roles reversed and would remain so for all time. Amanda became the woman of the house. She paid the bills (her mother, a secretary at an insurance firm, would hand over one check every month to her preteen daughter), she cleaned, she scrubbed, she potty trained whatever stray her brother brought home (even if they were human).

Sometimes, if the gods were smiling—if her mother wasn't too hysterical and her brother too surly, and the smells of the old house had died down—she invited a friend over.

Jimmy Cruz, dangerously armed with the impatience of youth, pumped away on his girlfriend's naked body on her creaky, familiar, decade-old bed in her family home in the hills above Laurel Canyon, imagining she was enjoying every moment, every second of this, their last encounter before he left L.A. for the year.

Harvard Law was beckoning. The thought made him so excited he came too fast. He kept going a few seconds longer to satisfy his longtime girlfriend.

He listened to her sharpened breathing, her soft moans. Listened closely. Decided she was done. He rolled off, stared at the pockmarked ceiling, mesmerized by the turns his life was taking. Harvard Law School—Jesus Christ and fuckin' A! Every cell in his body screamed out in ecstasy. He hugged Amanda hard. He knew she took this to mean he cared about leaving her behind. He knew she took this to mean he was heartbroken over the changes before them.

He wasn't. He was trying to keep himself from yelling at the top of his lungs, celebrating his righteous fortune.

He heard the undergrads at the sister schools weren't too bad. From good families, too. Old *Mayflower* families. Families with Anglo-Saxon names. Names distinctly unlike his. Families with money. Families from exotic places like Greenwich, a word he pronounced like "sandwich." Families who could do something for him, the immigrant boy made good.

Amanda rolled on her belly, stared at him with her dark eyes. James looked into them. Sad eyes.

"Are you okay?" she asked him. She sounded concerned. She was. About her lack of orgasm. She wished to God that she at least had had an orgasm for this, their last time together for at least six months.

James shook his head slightly and bit his

tongue. Attempted a pained expression. His high
school acting class, the one he took to impress
that soap opera star's daughter, was proving use-
ful after all. "What is wrong with me?" he
thought to himself. James knew all too well his
dark side, but was he really such a pig? Where
was his love for this little girl who had caught his
eye and his heart long before he ever knew the
correct words to tell her so?

"James. Look at me." Amanda propped herself up on her elbows. James looked away. He
was finding it hard to look into her trusting eyes
for longer than a second.

"You're going to have such a great time.
Boston is amazing. I mean, it has everything, all
those schools, culture—"

"Culture? It's fucking freezing. Very bad for
Latin blood. We don't like cold weather."

"Well, then you have to come visit us undered-
ucated Left Coasters—thaw your Latin butt out."

"I hear the girls have hair on their lips."

"I'm sure that doesn't affect more than, oh,
eighty-five percent of them. And how would they
stay warm?" Amanda liked when James was
playful. She liked being able to cheer him up.

"The other fifteen percent are lard-asses.

That's what Con told me." Conrad, James's friend who was also heading to Boston, had said nothing of the kind.

"Poor little Jimmy. Poor, poor Jimmy! Not lard-asses!"

"I'm just sorry I'm leaving, Amanda." Oh, James liked to go in for the kill, make it sound sincere.

Amanda tut-tutted, smiled. "You have to go. It's your future." And then added, as if following a prewritten script ("Does this sound right?" she wondered), "Don't worry about me. I'll be fine."

"You won't see anyone else?"

She played with his chest hair. "No. I'm not even thinking about anyone else." It was the truth. She wasn't thinking about another man. She may have been thinking about the baby in the next room.

He held her tighter against the truth. "Me neither."

Amanda searched for his hand, squeezed it. Sighed. And thought, "Liar. You fucking liar."

But that was okay. Because Amanda loved James. The kind of love that begins on the first day of sixth grade when a boy pulls your hair and calls you a name in a romantic language you can't understand. The kind of love that goes on because, to be truthful, you can't picture your life without this man—what would you be without this man? You've never known yourself without this man.

He had loved her when she was chunky and her teeth crooked; he had loved her as her limbs grew long and her teeth, magically, straightened. She would never forget that he had loved her first, long before another boy would ever look in her direction.

Someday, as James had told her again and again, they would get married. There would be plenty of time for good sex. They had had good sex at one time. He had given her her first orgasm, hadn't he?

She closed her eyes, put her head back against his chest, comforted for the moment in his familiar feel. She enjoyed his lithe body, athletic, with long, stringy muscles, yet acquiescent to her touch. Amanda often thought he had the body of a ballet dancer, but would never tell her Venezuelan-born boyfriend with the olive skin and golden curly hair. He fancied himself as being too macho for the comparison; James preferred b-ball shorts and soccer cleats to a pair of tights and ballet slippers.

In the real world, though, James was more

girl than Amanda. He was more concerned with his weight, the minute layer of fat around his middle ("Does my stomach look bigger?" he would say, anxiously tugging at an imaginary fat cell). Concerned that his nose was slightly crooked from a soccer injury ("Should I have this fixed?"). Concerned about the particular way his sneaks would match his shirts. Amanda was burdened with none of these feminine peculiarities. She had an ass that expanded or contracted in response to various external stimuli; happiness made her ass bigger, sadness or anxiety made her ass smaller. If she wanted to know how she was feeling, all she had to do was get a look at her backside in the mirror. It was an amazingly accurate measure.

The deafening roar of motorcycles pulling up in front of the house ended their moment. Amanda was now thinking about her new job this summer: carrying out her first job after graduating from UCLA with a major in English lit and a minor in political science. James was busy contemplating smart, rich, possibly even blond pussy.

Amanda looked at James, just opening his eyes. She gestured toward the window, the engines outside. "Val," she said as if it were a sentence. "We'd better get dressed."

"Can't your brother just leave us alone?"

Amanda looked out the window. Valentin, romantically named after the holiday on which his birth fell, with his jet black hair, thanks to Miss Clairol Black Velvet #51. His girlfriend, Patrice, bad news, usually high on something, but good natured and a stone cold beauty. And a third, his helmet still on. Big guy. Big bike. He took his helmet off, turned. And looked straight at her.

Amanda shut the blinds. "No, he can't." Why was her mouth dry all of a sudden? "You know he loves torturing you."

"Criminal."

"Someone in my family has to make money," she joked ruefully. She hated what her brother did to make a living. Not only did she hate it; it had the added charm of also scaring her.

Amanda stepped out of bed, got into her oldest pair of cutoff Levi's shorts, which hadn't been washed in a week and therefore were the perfect fit, and a T-shirt. Thought briefly about her lack of chest as she appraised her looks in a cheap full-length Kmart mirror.

"Don't even think about it," James said, knowing what Amanda was thinking. "You're just right." Off her look. She knew better. Amanda was a firm 7.2—okay, 7.0—on the official and worldwide beauty scale of 1–10. Attractive. Almost girl-next-door, but with a dark quality. Something too ethnic in the eyebrow and nasal-passage categories.

She thought of her looks like this: a beauty contestant in certain very tiny, Slavic, third-world countries; but in L.A., well, she was the attractive, funny girl boys of all ages felt comfortable talking with about other girls—though they'd like to sleep with her as well. Which was better than what she used to be—the girl boys wouldn't sit next to on the bus, she being fat, uncoordinated, the target of chubby jokes in those bright days of childhood.

Thank God for vertical growth.

"Your butt is perfect."

Perfect? Amanda turned to get a good look at her butt. It was of average size now, for her—padded but not full. Obviously, by her scientific method, she was happy enough, satisfied, but not ecstatic. But then, who was ecstatic?

Amanda smiled gratefully at her boyfriend's compliment and remembered what it was she liked about James. Most of the time, James was self-consumed, too bright for his own good, narcissistic, and always ready for a fight; his temper was notoriously bad—their last semester in high school, James went through three windshields in two months, breaking them with his fist. But from the second they met, James was the one person on the planet Amanda could turn to at any time for help. In grade school James found money to mend her old cat's leg after a bad episode with an erratic lawn mower (Amanda always figured he "found" it in some unsuspecting person's wallet); later on he protected her in her increasing conflicts with her out-of-control brother. Even as an adult Amanda could count on James for anything, from getting her mother's transmission fixed to drying her tears after a particularly hairy econ exam.

James had steadily made his way into her life, made himself the one necessity she didn't know she needed until he was there. He had become, over the years, her best friend.

A brief thought flitted into her head. "Why am I fucking my best friend? Shouldn't I be shopping excitedly for that sexy Friday-night dress for that someone who makes my heart palpitate, the chubby inside of my knees sweat, my tongue heavy with—"

"A-man-da!" Singsong. The voice of her tormentor. Val was about to cause trouble.

Amanda rolled her eyes and gave James a little wave, stepped outside her small, pale bedroom still furnished with childhood things, into the hallway.

She touched a wall where paint was cracking. Someday, she thought, she'd paint this place. This decaying, decrepit house only the Manson family could love. She'd make some money and actually paint the whole damned thing.

Or torch it. She laughed. "I wish," she said out loud, her voice cracking as badly as the paint. The house was worth nothing, bought by her cleaning-lady great-grandmother in the 1930s for the amount of money she had stashed, over the course of twenty years, under her mattress. But the land was now worth something. Her mother, who had taken a leave of absence from her job, her life, her children (well, grown children) two months ago, was threatening to sell.

Voices were coming from the kitchen. Someone was moving pots and pans. She thought about her lasagna, the one she had made for James's car trip to the Land of Oz. The one that was sitting out on the kitchen counter.

It seemed like a safe enough idea at the time.

"I'm going to kill Val," she thought. "I'm really going to kill him."

Amanda rushed into the kitchen, just in time to see Valentin diving into the lasagna with a spoon she had used to feed the dog with the purple tongue, a stray that would inevitably run off again.

Patrice was next to him, bending over the playpen, a lollipop in her hand.

At the other end was Madison. Grabbing at the lollipop. Six months old. Patrice and Valentin's baby.

The day Madison was born, the first day Amanda looked into his little piggy eyes, Amanda had made a solemn promise to protect him. She didn't know exactly from what; there were too many things in his hours-old life that could go wrong, but she knew the child would need protection.

The big guy was not here, Amanda noted, surprising herself with her disappointed observation before she turned her sights on Valentin.

"Get the fuck out of my lasagna."

Valentin stuck the dog-licked spoon in again.

He never bothered with clean silverware. Having never washed a dish, he probably had no idea how to open the dishwasher. He took another large scoop.

"You are such an asshole," Amanda continued, almost amused. Amanda loved her brother, but he was getting worse. They had always fought, but at the same time she could count on him for protection from the *cholas* at school who wanted to beat her up, the reason being she was, number one, fat, and number two, white, and number three, she didn't know when to shut her mouth. Other times she could count on Valentin for an extra ten bucks, or for those special overalls she was dying for in the seventh grade that only made her look fatter than she ever was. And then there was the time he surprised her with a pair of red suede Adidas when it wasn't even her birthday . . .

He smiled at her. Valentin, the jerk, with his olive skin and large green eyes, long sable lashes, was better looking than Amanda. He was smacked with the beauty stick upon entering this world. His monopoly of the family attractiveness quotient only added to her rage when Amanda was angry with Val. Amanda was the smart one, yes, but not perfect. Because of an unfortunate series of genetic events, Valentin was Warren Beatty to Amanda's Shirley MacLaine.

"Is that what Mom sent you to college for? To come out with that mouth?" Valentin spoke too fast. His mouth twitched.

Amanda mouthed the words "Fuck you" to Valentin as she grabbed the casserole dish and turned away, too quickly.

The dish slipped from her hands, crashing to the floor.

Patrice looked up slowly. This is the only way she moved. Slowly. Always on downers. Ate quaaludes when they were readily available on any street corner in Hollywood, by the handful. Still owned a tight, frayed Rorer 714 T-shirt and wore it all the time (her breasts perfectly suited to a frayed white T-shirt, unfortunately). It was hard for Amanda to look at those breasts every day. They only got better after the baby came. Amanda took this to mean God hated her for some unapparent reason; why else would he give such magnificence to a drugged-out Def Leppard fanatic who ate Raisinets all day long? Amanda took half a quaalude once and forgot her own name. Then slept for twelve hours straight and missed Eddie Murphy's final *Saturday Night Live* performance.

The first time she smoked pot, she was barely twelve. But then, that's what you get when your older brother is the major drug supplier at the local high school. Popular, good looking, athletic, Valentin had it all, except money—until drugs came into the picture.

Now he paid the second mortgage on the house and made Amanda's mom laugh (before she went on her extended trip to find herself), and that was enough for everybody.

Valentin looked down at the mess adorning the tacky plastic red-tile floor, then back at Amanda. He gave her his crooked smile, revealing the small dimple in his left cheek. This was his way of apologizing. Amanda only had a small dimple on her left thigh, which no amount of exercise could annihilate.

"Needed more garlic, anyway. You're too shy with that garlic, Junior."

Valentin's pet name for Amanda. Junior. She had once liked it, when she liked him more.

Patrice forgot about the baby, went to sit on Valentin's lap. They started making out, their sucking sounds serenading Amanda as she sighed, disgusted, and bent over to clean the floor.

And that's when she saw the man's hands.

Some women notice a man's eyes or teeth or hair. Amanda noticed a man's hands. Jimmy's hands, for example, were lovely. They were pianist's hands. Long, lean fingers, clean. No calluses to speak of, even after years of playing street basketball with the Venice Beach crowd. No nails; always filed and clipped and scrubbed clean.

But these hands.

Dark compared to her own, but really a light brown color. Umber? Amanda tried to recall the names of her Crayola crayon collection from childhood. Tried to recall the name for this particular shade. Tried not to stare too long. Tried to act as though she were in deep concentration, pondering the cheese-and-tomato-ravaged floor.

They were the exact color of the light brown M&M's. Her favorite M&M. She truly believed they tasted different from the rest. Smoother.

These hands were large. Not scary large. "This is corny," Amanda thought, even as she thought it: "Manly large. Marlboro Country large."

Every finger was strong, knew its purpose, and knew how to follow through. There was a tinge of grease, grease that had been washed off time and again but would not budge, underneath the short, blunt nails—nails that had never met a file. These hands were not dirty, merely used.

And here's the other thing.

They were helping her. They were helping her pick up a messy, broken, somewhat (according to Valentin) garlic-deprived lasagna mixed with shards of deadly Pyrex. She was also aware of two other things at that moment: that James had come into the kitchen, busying himself with his traditional postcoital gulp of milk straight from the carton, and that Valentin and Patrice had moved their tongue derby to a more convenient location upstairs.

Amanda knew James so well. She could feel him behind her, checking the date on the carton, poking his sharp Errol Flynn nose for a check-in smell before finally lifting the carton to his delicate bow-shaped lips and chugging like every cow in America had suddenly ceased to exist.

Amanda was aware of all this and more as she looked up from the hands to their owner. And fell in love.

Okay, okay. She knew. You can't fall in love just like that, on the basis of someone's hands. C'mon!

But it's true. Amanda studied these hands, then looked at their owner's face. Maybe it was just lust. Amanda felt a wave of nausea, her face got flushed, her hair stood on end, her stomach rumbled.

"Oh, man. What'd you do?"

Amanda scowled. Who dared break her REM state?

Who else but Jimmy? Standing behind her, wiping milk off his thin, sensitive lips with a Kleenex. Softer than napkins.

She looked at this man in front of her. There was something familiar in the feral nature of his greenish brown eyes, but she couldn't quite place it. She finally answered James.

"I dropped it."

"What a mess," James replied. Distant. Amanda thought he sounded like someone she didn't know at all. He added—a sweet afterthought—"Need help?"

His thoughts centered again on the cool blonds at Harvard that Conrad told him about, populating every floor in his new dorm. A cool blond, that's what he needed.

"We got it covered." The man spoke. Low. Soft. Not hostile and not cowed. Matter-of-fact.

Amanda wished there had been more lasagna.

She thought about throwing a few more plates on the floor and wondered about what kind of mess the leftover minestrone in the refrigerator could make.

She wanted to stay on this floor, her knees red from the patterns in the tile, her hands sticky with tomato sauce. She wanted to stay on this floor, grab this man, and take him—

"I have to leave, honey."

Amanda closed her eyes to her fantasy. She found her bearings, grabbing the counter. She stood. She felt the man's eyes on her.

"We're done."

"'Cause, you know, I've"—James glanced toward the stranger—"I'm on a tight schedule."

He lowered his eyes. Sad. Very sad.

Amanda merely smiled. Seconds ago she had been feeling nauseous, if only at the loss of a confidant. Now she was elated. One door closes . . .

"'Scuse me." The man stood. He was in his mid-twenties maybe. Over six feet. Six two. Short, tightly curled hair, light brown. Almost the same as his skin. Almost shaven. No mustache, no beard.

The shoulders—

Amanda caught her smile before James

looked up to acknowledge the stranger. But Amanda thought the man knew. He must know. She felt she was radiating pheromones. Whatever it was in the animal kingdom to let the male of the species know today was his lucky day! Yep, let's go to it!

The man had turned and was gone. His scent hung between her and James. She hadn't noticed until he left the room—he smelled like a man. There were no two ways about it.

James looked back at Amanda. He took her hand. They walked toward the front door in awkward silence.

After all these years together, Amanda was psychic about James's thoughts; she knew he thought she was devastated.

"Go. Go, go-go-go-go!" Amanda's brain shouted. *"Go! Arrivederci, Roma. Bye-bye, Sayonara. Later. Hasta la vista, Babeee!"*

They stopped at the door.

"Okay, okay," James said suddenly. When he was nervous, he said "okay" twice. It was the first English word he had ever spoken.

"Okay," said Amanda.

"I'm going to call you. I'll call you when we stop tonight." It was going to take at least three days to get there. Conrad wanted to stop in Chicago along the way, but James wanted to push straight through. He couldn't wait to get to Boston.

"You have to call me—otherwise I'll think you're dead, and that's not the best thing."

"And I'll write you the first day I get there."

"You won't have time. . . . Write me the first *night* you get there." Amanda had an odd compulsion to joke to break the onerous weight of a serious moment. Sometimes James appreciated her humor, sometimes he didn't.

"I love you," James said. And meant it.

"I love you, too," Amanda replied. And meant it, as well. And then her brain, her mortal enemy, added, "But now I have to fuck somebody else.

"Oh God, Amanda," she thought to herself. "The man standing in front of you is the right one! The one who knows every nook and cranny of your shabby, warped soul. The one who knows which shoes go best with your one good, slightly ill-fitting suit (stolen from your mother and blamed on the dry cleaners). The one who knows when to take the Chips Ahoy bag from your sweaty, grasping palms. The one who makes sure you floss every single night so your teeth don't fall out of your head at the age of thirty. The one you'll end up married to in a ceremony in some rich law partner's backyard in front of a not-a-wet-eye-in-the-house business crowd.

Amanda coughed. She hugged James. Kissed him. Tears sprang to her eyes, but she didn't know what recesses they had come from. Sadness at his leaving? Happiness at his leaving?

She watched him take off in his cheap old English sports car, the kind young men in L.A. without funds buy to maintain some semblance of cool.

And she waved, seeing his license plate fade. The license plate an old girlfriend, a magician's assistant from West Covina, had given him as a birthday present during a four-month period in which James needed time away from Amanda because he was so consumed by their relationship.

"Aha," Amanda had thought at the time. "The boy wants strange pussy. Without the guilt." She was hurt by the breakup, but the devastation James was expecting, the desperate late-night phone calls, the tear-stained missives, never emerged. Amanda had been too busy studying and figuring out what to do with her life.

Amanda used the break well. She studied her ass off; she discovered she had a knack for short-story writing, in a creative writing course she took on a whim; she rested well, stretching her body out fully on her single bed; she flirted with cute boys with no accents; she walked instead of ran; she averted natural disasters at home. She was almost disappointed when James returned, tail firmly held between his firm, newly shaved legs (beneficial for his most recent hobby, long-distance biking; James had also found a two-week period to date a big-boned Swedish triathlete, until he found out she could bench-press more than he). Amanda took him back; she had missed him, but more than that, he had chosen the right look to woo her—baggy running shorts, a plain white V-necked T-shirt, curly golden hair perfectly mussed, a tan to match, a sorrowful, hangdog expression. And a box of See's candies. Besides, frankly, four months without getting laid was feeling like an eternity.

The magician's assistant, whose intellect had, surprisingly, been found wanting, desired to celebrate James's "uniqueness," so she tried to buy a license plate that would spell it out for the whole world. Amanda had been positively giddy the first time she read it.

YOUNIK.

She had congratulated James on the gift and dashed away quickly to swallow her laughter before he witnessed her tear-inducing convulsions.

Amanda remembered, shook her head, smiled to herself, and walked back into her mother's old house to face the rest of her life.

The baby was crying.

Amanda hightailed it back inside and over to the playpen. Maddie looked at her, his face cherry red. She picked him up, the solid little man, patted his back to soothe him.

The playpen was strewn with torn books. Books she had left in there to be ripped to shreds and eaten, if that's what he liked. She wanted Maddie to be comfortable with books.

Madison made grunting sounds. He was starting to calm down now. Amanda bent over the playpen, looking for a toy. She brushed his blankie aside, his bubbe, and saw a piece of candy. The lollipop top his mother was playing with had fallen off into his crib.

Patrice, the narcoleptic moron, had dropped a choking hazard practically into her child's hands.

Amanda shook her head in disgust. Looked at her brother's baby. A cross between Patrice and

Valentin, Maddie was the kind of baby strangers said should be in commercials. The kind of baby mothers always assumed was a girl. He was that pretty.

"Honey," she said to Madison, "I'm afraid your parents suck."

She heard steps upstairs. Valentin and Patrice, and maybe that man with the animal eyes, were on the deck. The old redwood deck, decayed. "This whole house should be condemned," Amanda said to Madison.

"I think it's a nice house." There was that voice again. Matter-of-fact. Amanda took a deep breath.

Amanda looked up at the man. "Thank God," she thought, "thank God I have the baby in my arms."

For his sake. Without the baby, there would have been nothing between them except his scent.

She didn't say anything. The man walked past her.

"Val said I could get something to drink. That okay?"

Amanda shrugged. "Sure."

He stopped, looked closely at the baby, touched his head, his cheek. Not the sort of touch men do to impress a woman who's holding a child. The sort of thoughtful, interested touch.

"Can I hold him?"

Amanda's eyes widened. She didn't say anything, just handed Maddie, now quiet, staring, over to the man. He took him in his arms, this tiny baby, and put his hand over the baby's belly.

"You're good . . ." Amanda didn't know what to say. She gestured toward Maddie.

"I love babies," he said. And it was the truth. She could see it.

Amanda turned and opened the refrigerator. "What would you like?" ("Please, God, let it be me," she thought.)

"Water'd be fine."

"Sure?"

"Sure."

Amanda took a glass from the cupboard, turned on the tap, held the glass under it, wondering what she would tell James, her mother, or anyone else who wondered why a normal girl like herself ran away with a complete stranger.

"I can't believe this is Val's baby. He's so sweet."

Amanda looked at the man. He wasn't looking at her. His eyes were taking in Madison.

"Yeah, well." ("Yeah, well?" Amanda screamed at herself.) She held the water out. There was an awkward moment, the trade of water for baby. The man took the glass in one hand and handed Madison over with the other, handed him over as though he were a softball, but the most precious softball of all time. Their skin touched during the pass. Amanda wondered if the rest of him felt like that, soft but strong, muscled underneath.

He stood there drinking his water slowly, looking at her and the baby. Amanda wondered when he would leave her alone. For the first time since the floor incident, she felt something different about this man, toward this man. Fear.

"I have to—" She heard herself speak.

"You don't like this house?" He cut her off.

Amanda became flustered, defensive. "It's not that I don't like it."

"It's comfortable." He sipped his water. He wasn't going anywhere.

"You don't live here." It sounded snottier than she meant it, but Amanda really wanted him to leave. She herself did not have the strength to pee, much less make it through the kitchen door into her bedroom. The baby, playing with her necklace, was beginning to get heavy, very heavy.

"No." Pause. "But I still think it's nice." More sips. His full mouth on the lip of the glass. Standing there. Why won't he look away?

"Well, if you like rotting wood, paint peeling, earthquake damage, cracks, mold, mildew, a deck that's due to snap any second . . ." She walked over to the playpen. How she found the strength, only God knows. She felt his eyes on her. She became conscious of every move, every hair on her body, regretted the condition of her toenails. (Why couldn't she be a girl for once and spend ten bucks for a lousy pedicure!)

"Thanks for the water."

She turned quickly but he was gone. She heard his steps, solid and steady, unhurried. She wiped a tiny bead of perspiration from behind her knee. She finally breathed.

"Oh God," Amanda thought, "I want to bear this man's children and I don't even know his name."

Three

Gabe Williams sat back on his king-sized bed, in the dark bedroom tucked into a corner of the second story of the tired wood-frame house on the east side of town, just half a mile above the freeway, and thought of the girl. He had been doing this for several days now. Several nights. She had seemed so nervous with him; he wondered why. She probably didn't recognize him, he thought. He had grown a lot, had filled out. He didn't look like the boy, the long-armed string bean, he was in elementary. Taller than anyone in his class, with a reputation as a kid you didn't mess with. He could still hear kids whispering in the halls, eyes averted, stepping to the side as he walked out of the principal's office for the third time in a month and passed them by, walking tall, with a small, cocky skip masking the pain in his stomach, just below the rib cage, a small hot pinprick. "Gabe Williams," the kids would whisper. "He's bad. He'll kill you, man."

He took a second puff on the joint. Held it, filling his rounded, hard chest. Two light-colored scars crisscrossed the left side of his chest, thick scars. He peered down at them, pursing his lips in a frown. Old friends. War buddies. Every scar he had, and Gabe had more than his share (if he counted, head to toe, he could do double digits, easy), told his story. Broken toes, a broken ankle—these were from childhood, from kicking at a locked door, from jumping off a three-story building on a dare. The knees, lumps of scar tissue inside and out, told of his life as a teenager on the verge of becoming a man, the years when sports became his escape, the focal point for his anger. Gabe was only a freshman in high school when he made varsity by breaking a kid's leg on a tackle. The skewed way the boy walked from that day on, his femur broken in half like a pencil, reminded everyone, including Gabe, of the awful power of his strength.

Gabe's immense, raging body had caught up with his reputation—he had transformed,

Hulklike, over a summer. It was never lost on Gabe that his first real feeling of belonging, of acceptance, the first slaps on his back, came at the price of a boy's leg.

Gabe remembered that day, etched as clear in his mind as if it had happened two hours ago.

"I'm sorry!" Gabe had screamed when he heard the snap, like a gunshot. "I'm sorry!" Beneath his helmet, Gabe's tears came heavy and streaked with mud—this boy couldn't have known he didn't stand a chance against Gabe and his past. Gabe pushed past the coaches and the players and the stares and ran and did not stop running until he reached his home and could cry in seclusion. He did not come out of his room for three days, despite the pleadings of his father.

The scars on his chest came later, after Gabe's reputation preceded him in every club, every dive on Hollywood Boulevard, every dingy coffee shop on Sunset. Kids seemed to come out of nowhere, out of darkness, to taunt him, to force him into a fight: Mexican gangs, Armenian tough guys, young black men who were a little older than he was, a little more desperate. The knife came at him at the hands of a wiry little Mexican dude, allegedly Thirteenth Street–affiliated. Gabe had stepped out of a falafel place on the boulevard, into the parking lot. It was after five, and the sky was hazy with smog and diminishing sunlight.

"Hey, *ese*," Gabe heard the guy's voice. Tinged with a practiced *cholo* accent. "I know you," the guy said.

Gabe turned around. Looked at this guy. A hundred and twelve pounds, maybe, after a big meal, and short—five five in shoes. He didn't pay him any mind. "Yeah," was all Gabe said. He just wanted to get on his bike, his first, a dinky little Honda, and head home.

He should have known. He'd watched enough kung fu movies growing up. Bruce Lee was an idol—even had a poster of the little fuck on his wall. He should have known that the meanest, toughest dogs in any fight are the smallest ones.

All Gabe saw was a flash of metal, and then there was blood. And then, much to his chagrin, Gabe fainted as the footsteps of the little guy serenaded his fall, running off in triumph to tell his friends. "Aw, shit." Gabe heard his voice as he slumped to the ground. Beware the little guys, Gabe would tell his kids someday. Beware the little guys.

*　　*　　*

And then her face shoved its way into his mind again. He thought about her hair. The color. Reddish brown? What was the word? She looked like his own mother. But his mother's skin was even more pale, almost blue. His father had told him how his mother started and finished fights all up and down the chitlin circuit; his mother didn't take no guff from anyone who didn't like the fact that a white girl from a small town in Virginia had married a black saxophone player from the big city of Chi-ca-go. His mother didn't take guff off nobody.

"What color is my blood, Mom?" a six-year-old Gabe asked, coming home from his new school, already confused.

"'Scuse me? What color do you think your blood is, my baby?" His mother always liked to put the question back to him; Gabe looked back and knew his mom was trying to make him think. Before she walked out of his childhood, Gabe felt he was the luckiest boy in the world, having such a beautiful, smart mom.

"Red?"

"That's right. It's red, like my lips, when it hits

the air." She paused, thinking. She liked to think. "But it looks kinda blue when it's inside your body." She looked at her young son, all big eyes and curls, and pursed her lips. "Why're you asking?"

"Because this kid said my blood isn't the same as his."

Gabe's mom knew what this meant. The outside world was encroaching, and it was coming fast. She sat Gabe down to cookies and hot tea and an hour lecture on what kind of people there were in this world (good people and bad people) and how Gabe was to avoid the bad people and hang out with the good people, but still feel sorry for the bad people, because the Lord God made them too, after all. He just "fucked up a little." Her words. And when she was done, Gabe watched as she made her famous peach cobbler, put her favorite hat on, her lucky hat, and marched down to the offending kid's house, hips tossing this way and that.

"The best way to fight fire," she said to Gabe, "is with food."

The kid never said another word to Gabe about blood.

*   *   *

Gabe smiled. He knew all about Amanda McHenry. He knew she had been a chubby little thing at one time, but cute. Always cute. And smart. Even skipped a grade in school. A hard look crossed his face; intense pain that was gone as soon as it appeared. Gabe had been held back a grade. Twice.

Gabe inhaled again, letting the sweet aroma relax his tired body. His body was always tired, even at his age, twenty-four. He looked at his weary arms, big from lifting engines day in, day out. It was a good job, union pay, and Gabe knew he was lucky to have it. He knew how many men stood in line for one of these jobs, sometimes over a thousand men, standing in their best blue jeans—their baseball caps shielding their faces from the angry Valley sun (knowing they'd be waiting a good long time, three, four hours), or politely held in their hands—praying for one opening. Gabe had seen their faces watching him, sad and angry and bitter and hopeful. He walked by them, gruff, out of respect not wanting to look them in the eye. He knew he should count himself lucky. He knew this. But still, it was hard, backbreaking work. And every once in a while Gabe—at his worst moments, when sweat was pouring down his face and arms and the engines were coming too fast and his legs were unsteady—at his worst moments he'd look down the line and see the black faces working the same job, drowning in the same sweat, and he'd think about how this was no different from picking cotton, a paycheck's difference from working on a chain gang. He was a body, not a mind, doing the same physical labor his ancestors had done. Same thing, just more money. He thought about the new football league he read about in the sports pages. Two years ago he had tried out for a walk-on with the Canadian League. He still had some speed in his legs, had made the first cut; then the second; Lord God, the third—had called his father from the pay phone at the stadium. Then he slipped on the fourth.

He called his father back. And found he had no voice. He breathed into the phone, the smoggy Pasadena air too thick for his overtaxed lungs, his heart beating into his throat.

"Pops," he croaked. He was afraid to say anything more.

"It's okay, son" was all he said.

Gabe Williams was an engine lifter at the GM plant in Panorama City, California, on the dry, hot edge of nowhere. And that was what he would always be, until the day he wouldn't even be that.

Gabe bit his lip. He shook his head, shaking the cobwebs out, as his father would say. He shouldn't think bad thoughts of the job; he heard the big automakers were moving to Mexico and Taiwan, places like that. Cheap labor, cheaper than his $10.50 an hour plus, that's for sure.

Gabe swung his legs over the side of the bed, walked gingerly across his bedroom, turned on the stereo. A Marvin Gaye song was playing on the station that played Rick James and Ice-T during the day, slow grooves at night. Usually Gabe listened to the daytime stuff, the sounds that kept him going at work, kept his rhythm up. But tonight he would listen to Marvin Gaye.

He stepped over the sleeping pointy-eared Doberman with the chain choker, the tough-guy dog who never barked, never had to (like his owner), and looked at himself in the smoky mirror leaning against the thick plaster wall, hiding a fist-sized hole. He didn't look at a mirror very often or for very long. He searched his reflection without pretense. That was the way he did everything. He liked what he saw. He wiped a thin layer of dust from the mirror's surface and continued, his mind drifting to the girl with the red hair. Could she ever love this man?

He unwrapped the towel from around his waist, threw it over the mirror, and walked naked to the small stack of magazines he kept under his bed. Here he was, twenty-four years old, and still embarrassed that he looked at pictures of naked women. Worried that his father might come upstairs looking for something, God knows what, and find his girlie stash. He sat back on his bed; it shifted underneath him as he slid under the purple and burnt orange velveteen bedcover. A masculine choice, he had thought, when he purchased it. A man's bedcover. His mother, who had made one of her occasional appearances into his life, had playfully teased him about it at the time. He wished she were around to tease him more.

He opened one of the magazines, his favorite, from two years ago, and looked at the pictures. Sometimes he would reread a letter or something, but he was usually so drowsy at night, especially after a toke, he couldn't concentrate.

He looked at the blond girls with their big tits and big hair and big blue eyes, and after a moment, after nothing happened, nothing stirred, he tossed the magazine to the floor. And thought about the girl with the small breasts and dark eyes. And that was all he wanted.

He awakened later, his head throbbing, and removed the gun from under his pillow and went back to sleep, hoping his headache wouldn't worsen. He couldn't take tomorrow off. Not for a migraine, not for anything.

Amanda woke with a start. She had been dreaming—a bad dream, she knew that much, but couldn't recall it. Her chest was sweaty, the bed damp. It was still early. She got herself up out of bed, thinking that she would at least go check on the baby. She hadn't heard anything from him all night.

She wrapped a robe around her body, still shaking not from cold, and stepped out into the hallway. The house was silent. Her bare feet caused the floorboards to moan slightly as she moved down the long hallway to Valentin and Patrice's room. They must have come in very late last night; she hadn't heard them, and she usually did. They saved most of their arguing for night, when they were tired, defenses down, inhibitions at rest. Amanda had recorded the litany in her brain; she knew their arguments better than she knew herself: Patrice was doing too many downers, Valentin was doing too much coke. Patrice was a whore, Valentin was an asshole. Patrice sucked somebody's cock while Valentin was making a sale, Valentin fucked some girl in a bathroom at a party when Patrice was outside vomiting. It went on and on. Amanda had eventually gotten used to the rhythms of their eighteen-month-long relationship (a lifetime for Valentin the lothario), even found a certain sick comfort in it—at least they were communicating, even if they were defecating on each other. And she found amusement in it, too. What would they come up with next? What new insult? What new turn of phrase? The last one she had heard out of Valentin's mouth, who was always good for a toilet shot, was "wigger." Which, as Valentin explained to Patrice in less than dulcet tones, stood for "white nigger." Which is what he claimed she was. This sent Amanda into a fit of giggles. But Patrice had screamed at this ultimate insult and, judging from the shaking walls, had jumped on him and tried to strangle him. Ever since the baby came, Amanda had become less amused, more afraid, and a light sleeper, awake at the slightest sound, always on call. Her services were open to Madison twenty-four hours a day.

She opened the door the slightest bit. It brushed against the shag rug that had long since lost its brightness and now could be said to be no color at all.

She tiptoed in, careful beyond human experience to not wake the sleeping bodies in the twin bed slammed against the wall. Her mission was clear, her goal focused. (Every time she performed this stunt, Amanda felt like a Russian spy in a James Bond movie.)

The crib was pushed against the far wall, a gift from Amanda's mom to the happy drugged-out couple. (Her mother, when she was there, chose not to see the vials in the kitchen trash can, not to notice her grandson's mother falling asleep, snoring, in her Froot Loops, not to care that her son woke up just in time for lunch. Amanda felt her mother's denial kept her from having a nervous breakdown; Amanda thought maybe her mom was a genius.) The crib was far too expensive and far too frilly for its environment. It stood out like a beacon of purity and goodness in putrid surroundings. She tiptoed silently across the room.

She looked in, peering over the edges of the crib excitedly, as a child stands tall to look over the kitchen counter at the chocolate cake his mother is icing for his sixth birthday.

Her heart dropped. The crib was empty. Amanda spun around and looked at Valentin's bed and realized her eyes, accustomed to seeing two, had tricked her. Valentin was alone.

Where was Patrice? Where was the baby?

Amanda rushed out of Valentin's room and down the hall, into the kitchen. The playpen, empty. She looked outside, front, back, which was ridiculous—what would Patrice be doing standing on a muddy slope holding her heavy little boy?

Amanda ran upstairs. Their mother was gone, had been for the last two months on a Spanish-speaking tour of Guatemala with a younger boyfriend who sold cars for a living at the highest-selling Toyota dealership in North Hollywood (you couldn't drive down any freeway in L.A. without seeing the obnoxious yellow license plate with the black letters MILTON LANE TOYOTA).

Nowhere. Maybe Patrice was sleeping in her room. Maybe she was out on the deck. Maybe she too had gotten up early and decided to change her ways, to get up early with her child every morning, to not be lazy, to not do drugs so that someday, maybe with the next child, she would be able to breast-feed . . .

Her mother's bed was empty. Amanda's mother had locked her door (her mother still didn't get that her son, Valentin, had criminal leanings that could manifest in the knowledge of how to unlock a two-bit locked door with a, strangely enough, stolen credit card), knowing that Amanda might use her clothes, or the worst thing, Valentin and Patrice would have sex in her queen-sized bed (which they did, as often as possible, often leaving traces of their exploits, from guitar picks to hot-pink colored pubic hair, thanks to Patrice's recent experiments in the world of hair color). They did not, however, leave empty condom packets, as they were still using the handy withdrawal method, which had worked quite well for Patrice over the years. She had only gotten pregnant four times since the age of thirteen, once to full term. Quite a few of her friends had done worse.

Amanda ran, sprinted out onto the cold redwood deck, splinters slicing into the softness of the bottoms of her bare feet, not yet thickened by summer.

Panic set in. Tears flowed in an instant. Her breathing shortened. She heard herself panting. Would Patrice take the baby away?

Amanda ran down the stairs and back into Valentin's room.

"Val!" Amanda shook her brother, crying out, "Valentin!" taking his bony, pale green shoulders (had he lost weight?) in her hands until he mumbled and then swung his arm out at her, his eyes still closed, leaving a mark on her arm. This made Amanda furious, and no longer afraid.

"Where is the *baby?*" Amanda screamed in her brother's ear, up close, noting the smell of cigarettes and pot and Patrice's men's musk cologne, and also noting the tight, unaffected state of his pores. The smell made her dizzy and disgusted and she sat back on the floor in her robe, legs splayed open as if asking forgiveness, when her brother screamed back at her, his voice too hoarse to scare her.

"We had a fight, okay? The bitch'll be back! Now get the fuck outta *my room!*" Amanda took a step back. Valentin sounded and looked like a twelve-year-old kid, as Amanda remembered, always sleeping late, voice hoarse and appealing to girls, eyes unfocused, the hair a mop of blackness. He turned his back to her, rolled back into his petulant slumber.

Amanda sat back on the floor as if a weight had fallen on her, then stood, slowly, like an old woman. She had aged fifty years in one sad morning. Valentin, on the other hand, was already snoring; he'd be up at the usual time— one in the afternoon. And he'd wait awhile. He'd turn on the TV with its pilfered cable box, stare at MTV, and think he could be on there, too, if only he had time to learn to play guitar, to sing. Then he'd switch to the Playboy Channel and realize with deep disappointment that it didn't start until eight P.M. Finally, an afternoon Western would be on, a John Wayne movie or maybe even a Gary Cooper film. And that would keep him still, keep him from rocking in his chair, from pacing. He'd go through a couple of cereal boxes' worth of Corn Chex or Rice Chex (he thought of them as being healthy) before he'd run roughshod through the Corn Pops, all of this dry, no milk, dairy being bad for you, clogging up the system (unless one used it to repair chemical damage to the sinuses by snorting the white liquid, restoring the mucus membranes, enabling yet another night of powder surfing). And he'd wait until he couldn't stand it anymore. Then he'd call around. Call Patrice's girlfriends, who were just like her, looked just like her, the same long skinny legs and perfect noses, did her same drugs, and who would take her place with Valentin at word one. And then he'd call Patrice's ex-boyfriends, this being no small feat, taking half the day, threatening them, threatening their families, screaming back and forth, until the ex would say he needed a dime, and Valentin would make a smooth turn into business. And the matter would be lost.

Patrice used to disappear before the baby. Every six weeks (give or take) she'd be off to parts unknown yet easy to find. Someone's single apartment in Los Feliz, a gay friend of hers from high school living with his Hispanic lover in a stucco building with a cracked swimming pool that people in the apartment building would lie around but never, God, never wade into, not with that ten-year-old crusty green mold growing around the pale blue tiles. Or a girlfriend from

Catholic school on the way to Palm Springs for a weekend with a band, a famous band, blowing its not-so-famous and not-so-attractive drummer in the hopes of attracting the lead singer. Or to take first prize in a wet T-shirt contest held in front of a drunken mélange of college students and jobless Eurotrash and long-haul truckers and gas station attendants with precious little extra cash (the college students always being the most obnoxious, the most sexist, the meanest, and the most flush with cash, thanks to Daddy and Mommy), winner takes five hundred bucks.

But Patrice hadn't taken off since the baby. Hadn't really been anywhere with the baby, tell the truth, except the Ralphs on Sunset, where rock bands hoping for a shot at the Whisky or the Troubadour or the Rainbow bought saltines and Doritos and Velveeta macaroni and cheese and Clairol hair dye and dark red lipstick in dollar containers like their mothers used to buy in the fifties. Patrice liked to show off the baby, but only for about twenty minutes at a time, which fit perfectly with the rare grocery trip. Most of the time, she neglected to buy anything except for the occasional carton of milk, and always Raisinets in the large box, the kind they sell in movie theaters. The colors in the grocery store confused her, she said. Made her forget what was on the grocery list she forgot on the kitchen counter by the phone at the house.

Amanda would have laughed at that, again. She laughed at Patrice a lot, especially in the beginning when Valentin brought her home and declared his love for this girl with cat eyes and long, parted-in-the-middle hair, and told Amanda's mother she was moving in. Amanda's mom surprised her, welcoming the intrusion of this beautiful stranger, perhaps hoping Valentin, her erratic, hyper son, would find a sense of calm in her arms. Her mother was taken in by beauty; like many people, she attached other attributes like kindness or humor to those lucky enough to just have a good face.

Amanda liked Patrice, except when she was particularly slow, even for a downer fiend, staring at cartoons or Bon Jovi music videos for hours on end, not being able to answer a single question asked of her, even the simplest, such as "What's your favorite color, Patrice?" (which Amanda asked only to torture her) or "Do you think the guy from Def Leppard is better off with or without the arm?" But right now Amanda hated her, hated her for taking the baby, knowing she had done it not out of love but out of spite, to get back at Valentin for calling her a name, for hurting what was left of her anesthetized feelings. Patrice must have realized somewhere in the dark fuzz of her brain that Amanda would be worried sick (which is what she felt; Amanda felt ill, physically). But Amanda knew that Patrice was incapable of caring about her feelings. The drugs she had started taking at the age of ten at after-school parties, when most kids were flying home to listen to the Archies or catch the last couple of minutes of *Dark Shadows* if they really wanted a thrill, had robbed her of her chance to become a feeling human being. Patrice was a scavenger, living for moments that would please her and only her, not thinking of the consequences, not thinking of anyone else.

Amanda got herself ready for work, keeping herself steady as she slowed to put on nylons, the same she wore yesterday, the kind that come in the white egg, that seem so extravagant, careful not to rip. Slipped on one of her mother's bigger dresses, noting to dry-clean it before her mother came home (there would be plenty of time, even with Amanda's natural tendency to procrastinate on household matters). Put on her own shoes and thought about a magazine article she had read a couple of weeks ago in *Cosmopolitan*, bought on Patrice's last trek to the grocery store. (Amanda read these mags with the same perverse sensation as someone ogling a car accident.) The article stated one could tell a lot about a person's breeding by their shoes. Amanda looked down at her own. Dark blue leather bought three and a half years ago, bought on sale at a store on Hollywood Boulevard owned by an Iranian man who offered her a free pair for a "date," scratched at the toe, the heel scuffed and lopsided because Amanda walked and stood like a child, on the outside of her feet. Amanda licked her finger and tried to rub dirt from her car off the back of her right shoe.

She would never survive the business. She had dreams of being a writer, a producer, a studio executive, though she had no idea how to get there. She was not cut out for television or film or anything glamorous. She could barely dress herself without bursting into tears, frustrated at the goofiness of her wardrobe, the way it screamed out that she was poor.

Working poor, more specifically, familiar

with discount stores and cereal coupons. On a first-name basis with shame. The McHenrys had never known much luck, and even though she was smart, talented, and in her best moments possessed of a tongue like Dorothy Parker's, Amanda felt she would never hold on to her new job. She was a receptionist at a daytime talk show, answering nine lines with the refrain "*The Danny Markus Show*, thank you for holding" for eight and a half hours straight. Sometimes, when she could get an intern to help her, or a production assistant who didn't think he was above answering a phone (good luck), Amanda could even go to the bathroom. Oh yes, it was a glamour job, and the money it brought in, $250 a week gross, which came down to approximately $189.96, give or take, ensured her good standing in the Fortune 500 list. "James," Amanda would joke, "I simply don't know what to purchase with all my money—should I go for shoes or, say, bread?"

The interview had gone well, her first real interview, the first one that didn't involve a job scraping dishes or dropping food on someone's expensive lap. Joe Artuga, the show's too-hip producer whose oral fixation had given him a hacking cough and a heart that beat like a scared rabbit's, found out that Amanda had been a political science major. And so, for the job of receptionist, he quizzed her for twenty minutes on Central American politics in the 1960s (which Amanda happened to have just finished a class on). Sufficiently impressed with her knowledge of various Chilean coups, and her legs, he hired her.

Amanda had been thrilled. First, she mused how short a time it would be before she was writing sketches for the show—before her talent was discovered and she was swept from the phone lines forever. A week, two weeks? Three weeks, tops. She started taking notes right away, jotting down any funny ideas she had for new characters, slips of dialogue that caught her ear. She was a fresh new talent, a voice for her disenfranchised generation (not counting former frat boys in pressed polo shirts and convertible-driving, alcoholic rich girls). It was only a matter of time before the production team discovered it.

Then she clipped pictures of Sherry Lansing, the first female president of a studio, out of the *L.A. Times*. She watched all her interviews and marveled at her combination of smarts and beauty, and for two days was convinced that hers was the trajectory Amanda herself, receptionist, was on. Three days later, having answered phones for a week, she was convinced she would not only not be in the business, so to speak, but would soon be living in a small town in Kansas or Oregon or Idaho, where she would sell canned peaches or other indigenous fruit to fat and grateful tourists who happened by her tiny yet comfortable ranch off a dirt road twenty miles from civilization, five hundred miles from the nearest McDonald's.

The phones weren't the worst part. Nor was the rudeness of some who called, yelling at her for putting them on hold, threatening her job because they hadn't received their *autographed picture of Danny Markus! Yet!* Nor the children who would call and talk to her, for some reason, about Michael Jackson, who hadn't ever even been on the show. The kids were so lonely and they asked numerous questions about what Michael must be like, and he seemed really nice, and they practiced the moon walk at home, and did she know if he had a girlfriend. (Although that was the saddest part.)

The worst part was reserved for the host of

the show, Danny Markus, a transplanted singing Minnesotan. At first, Amanda had been excited to meet a famous person, even a famous transplanted singing Minnesotan with hair that *did not move ever!* And he seemed excited to meet her as well. But Amanda quickly realized here was one of those men who were excited to meet any ambulatory, not-horribly-disfigured woman who had not yet experienced the seventieth anniversary of her birth. Perhaps the hand that held hers too long after their initial shake gave something away; perhaps it was the way he massaged her neck whenever he passed her station, "loosening up the kinks in her neck," he said, not noticing the kinks in her hands as she rounded them into fists, her knuckles sticking out white and hard and ready. Amanda felt certain she could kick his ass. The dreamy thought of spinning her tight little fist into Danny's handsome, recently reconstructed chin brought her immense satisfaction.

Amanda was thinking all this and more as she made a left turn in her mother's college car, a 1962 baby blue (the kind of blue you don't see on cars anymore, it being too innocent for the times) Ford Falcon, onto the side street that would take her into the television studios on the east side of Hollywood, a neighborhood situated between the poor and the rich, the multilingual and the solely English speaking. The area uncomfortably straddled two worlds, waiting for the horrible inevitable, whatever that was, to happen.

And the inevitable happened to Amanda that morning. She had to brake, a car full of teenagers crossing in front of her, passing through a stop sign like a painter's brush whipping a blank canvas. She was hit from behind, just enough to send her head snapping back, no headrest to cushion the blow, headrests being unheard of in the year of our Lord one thousand nine hundred and sixty-three.

The car behind her took off, though she just about caught a glimpse of the driver's face. A beard. Gray hair. A large old car. Green. Bondo markings. And no insurance. For sure, no insurance. Amanda didn't blame him, really. How could he know she wouldn't sue him for everything he owned, even if all he owned was that old piece of junk? He couldn't have known she was not that kind of person.

Amanda went to the office, neck aching and

stiff as the proverbial board, eyes glassy, knees wobbly, still on time, and set about her day, moving through the hours without her usual humor, without the biting but good-natured snappy patter, without patience for the more-than-occasional long-winded but much needy caller, without hope.

Those she told assumed her somber mood was because of the accident; after all, whiplash would bum anyone out, even a generally cheerful person with a thing for chocolate. But it wasn't the accident, and only Amanda knew this. It was the baby, still missing. When Amanda could, she sneaked a call home. Today alone she had called home seven times. Each with the same answer, but more insistent and more harsh with every passing hour. And more rings, too. The last time she counted nine before Valentin answered. He was getting high.

The day ended in ignominy achingly similar to its beginning; Amanda fixed herself a drink that night, using cheap whiskey from a bottle long forgotten in a kitchen cabinet that hadn't been opened since the last time Amanda's mother had used the liquor in the famous fruitcakes of Amanda's childhood. It was still bitter and cold, the way Amanda remembered it. She drank it straight in a small pink plastic cup, the rim sharpened to an edge after years of use. The bitterness of the whiskey wore off after the first half inch, and all Amanda would remember about whiskey for years after would be the warmth of it, the way it wrapped itself around her body as she sank to the floor of the kitchen, leaning against the cabinet, crying softly as she held Madison's baby jumper against her face and breathed in, the oh-so-sweet smell of his little, innocent body bringing on wracking, primal sobs. Later she made her way into her bedroom, clutching the jumper as though it held her life in its cotton threads. Sleep finally claimed her, and she found peace in her dreams, visited by the man with the strong, helping hands.

Gabe talked to his friend J.D. that same night while they were on their second scheduled ten-minute break, looking out at the night sky, their skin pummeled by the dry heat of Santa Ana. His friend had thick dark skin, unlined though he was much older than Gabe, a shiny face, and a big smile. Gold teeth. Wore his hair in Jheri curls, like a backup trumpet player in a blues band. J.D.'s favorite topic of conversation was sex. How often he got it, who with, who else was getting it, how many times they got it. Really, sex was all he ever thought about, at least all he ever talked about. And Gabe thought of J.D. as the most experienced man he had ever known. J.D. knew everything there was to know about pleasing a woman. Gabe (Honest Abe, as J.D. sometimes called him) felt he had to lie every once in a while. Talk about his weekend as though he hadn't watched TV all day Saturday, worked out in his room, eaten cheese pizza, smoked a joint, then slept in on Sunday and started all over again. (Some days he ventured out. Maybe took a trip with Valentin on the bikes.) So Gabe lied, played up his hand, and J.D. sat there, his forehead pinched together, wondering what Gabe was leaving out. The boy had no gift for storytelling.

But that night, when the talk turned to oral sex, Gabe nearly had a heart attack when he learned that J.D. not only had never gone down on a woman but had no intention of ever doing so. And certainly didn't want his own cherished member swallowed up in some woman's mouth.

J.D. tried that once at the age of fifteen; the faces
the older fat girl, his twenty-year-old cousin, had
made, and the noises—they were enough to scare
the hell out of anybody.

Gabe smiled at J.D., punched him in the
arm—wishing he hadn't (J.D.'s shoulder had been
bugging him; it was the arthritis; Gabe told J.D.
time and time again this was no job for a senior
citizen, which riled the forty-eight-year-old
J.D.)—and kept his words to himself. Because
what he wanted to say would have hurt his old
friend. Because what he wanted to say was that
J.D., king of all that is sex, had never really satisfied a woman in his life.

And Gabe, for all his lack of experience, had.
Each and every time.

Four

It's amazing, Amanda thought, how one drink could lead so easily to two, two to three. How three could lead to the boss's bedroom. To his stuccoed apartment hanging over a carport on a Venice street dotted with weary palm trees. How one minute someone could seem so wrong for her, blearing over her, smiling, iguanalike, through a haze of less-than-superior alcohol; how the next minute all she wanted was his cigarette-choked tongue on her body.

So cut to Amanda, in bed with the sleeping Joe Artuga, not remembering what it was like to screw him and not wanting to remember. All she could see was his face at the bar, cocky, unshaven, seen everything at age thirty-four (though he had seen significantly less than that), looking at her with a mixture of remorse and something else for what they were about to do. What he was about to do to her. She knew he wished, he really did wish, he could feel better about it, feel no guilt over fucking the young receptionist. They were just two people, after all, she could see him thinking—see his thought process, his reasoning, even through the thick shot glass—two people who could ease each other's pain for one night. He was not taking advantage of her. Nobody could accuse him of that. Right?

Amanda had gone to the Formosa Cafe a couple of times in the last week with Joe. First just to be friendly. Hang out with the group after the show. Joe always took a group over, young single people, bonded by bad pay and long hours and adrenaline, every last one, and they'd drink, and they'd drink, and they'd eat bad Chinese food, and they'd drink some more, and inevitably, if any of them had been in a relationship, it would end that night. The Formosa killed a lot of relationships but, in all fairness, birthed even more one-night stands and ménages à trois.

"DiMaggio was the greatest baseball player in all of history" was how Joe Artuga began his seduction. He made this pronouncement to the group, but his eyes were on Amanda. He wanted to see if she had the balls to take up the challenge.

"So, I guess you've never heard of Willie Mays, then?" Amanda asked.

"Willie was great, but Willie didn't have DiMaggio's style," Joe continued.

"I'm sorry, you don't think Willie had style? Where do you think the term 'hustle' came from?" Amanda countered, sufficiently horrified.

"And you've never heard of Joltin' Joe?" Artuga objected.

"Mays. Six hundred and sixty home runs. Two-time MVP."

"DiMaggio. Three-time MVP, fifteen hundred and thirty-seven RBIs."

People were starting to stare, perturbed that their mai-tai-inspired harmony was being befouled by statistics. Few people liked to hear numbers tossed about when they were drunk.

Joe leaned in, nose to nose with his prey.

"The Yankee Clipper had a three twenty-five average."

"Mays has the all-time record for putouts for an outfielder. Even DiMaggio said he had the greatest throwing arm in history." Amanda tripped over the last part; the rum was playing games with her tongue.

Joe smiled. Oh, he liked this girl. "Is that right, Miss Amanda?"

"Yes, Mr. Artuga," Miss Amanda replied, "that's absolutely, positively right."

The funny thing was, Amanda had never watched an entire baseball game in her life. But as luck would have it, she had just finished reading an essay on baseball's greatest in *Sports Illustrated*. During her twenty-minute break she had "borrowed" Joe's own thumbed-over copy from the crowded coffee table in his office; he never missed it.

Even funnier: Joe knew Amanda didn't know squat about baseball. But he so liked her willingness to take a stand.

"Amanda?" Joe asked sweetly. "What's a putout?"

Amanda wrinkled her nose and looked at her mai tai. She was running low.

So. The horrible inevitable happened. Amanda was eventually left alone with Joe. Joe, who was witty and disheveled and raked his hair with his left paw (it could hardly be called a hand, the way he used it) and always had stubble on his face, not because Sonny Crockett decided not to shave but because Joe was genuinely lazy and distracted when it came to such mundane endeavors. And Joe knew. Joe could get away with it. He would always be able to attract the errant fly. The one who needed a ride home. The one who had had too much to drink.

Amanda knew, when Joe looked at her with his sweetly drunk face, lascivious and guilty at the same time, she knew she would give it to him. She didn't even mind that much. She didn't want a new boyfriend. She wanted a warm body. She wanted relief from the grinding pain that had filled her days and had forced sleep from her life. She wanted someone to make her forget that she hadn't seen Madison in two weeks, that the futile, increasingly desperate phone calls to the LAPD and Children's Services were just that—futile. Patrice, Madison's mother, had a right to take her baby wherever and whenever she wanted, period. Amanda wanted someone to make her forget the man she really wanted, the man on that loud motorcycle. The liquor wasn't working well enough. She needed something else.

So when he reached over and kissed her, Amanda didn't think of the impropriety of it. She prayed the pain would disappear into his scruffy wet kisses. She knew it wouldn't even last the night. But all she wanted right now, all she was brave enough to ask for, was twenty minutes of feeling something else besides the unbearable.

Afterward, Amanda spent the entire night sleeping with her eyes open, in a stale wash of smoke and beer, the smells of bachelorhood. As she slowly sobered up into the light of morning, she realized what was barely tolerable in the dark of night should not be seen in the daytime. She left, scurrying like a spooked rabbit, at the crack of dawn. Joe opened one eye and focused on the figure dancing about the bed.

"What are you—are you leaving?" Joe asked, his voice raw with smoke.

Amanda jumped, literally, and screamed. She was hoping she wouldn't wake him—praying, in fact—but she couldn't find her left shoe to save her life. She must have flung it off in the throes of passion, but she couldn't remember having any throes, to be honest.

"My damn—I can't find my shoe."

"It's so early . . . you have to leave?" Joe surprised himself. Where did that needy sound come from?

"Yeah, you know, I work for this tyrant, a real asshole." Amanda was practically under the bed now, her hand grasping at what she hoped was her lost shoe and not something that had crawled under the box spring and died.

"Found it!" she cried, and slipped it on her foot and sped out of there. Joe practically smelled rubber burning as she slammed out the front door.

"You want to get some breakfast?" Joe asked the empty room.

At work that day, Joe behaved alternately too politely, asking if she needed a break from the phones at least twenty times, telling her how pretty she looked (a goddamned lie; Amanda knew what she looked like that day—someone who was getting over a hangover and sex with the wrong person), then too harshly, yelling at her during a staff meeting on an upcoming household and gardening segment for putting too much ice in Mr. Markus's ice tea. Finally, Amanda, fed up with the schizophrenic treatment and buoyed by a wicked, adrenaline-laced mixture of anxiety and grief, charged into his office, sat him down, and told the shocked and befuddled Mr. Artuga the following:

"Let's you and me get something straight. Last night was nothing. It was less than nothing. It was not memorable, it was not unmemorable. It was nothing. Neither of us will ever remember or care to remember exactly what happened. We each had **our reasons**, and hopefully you fulfilled yours, 'cause I sure as hell didn't fulfill mine, but our reasons aren't remotely related to any feelings we have for each other. So let's stop play-acting and tap-dancing and get on with our lives."

She stopped for a breath. Joe tried his best to reply. He wondered where all the endless parade of people were who bugged him twenty-four hours a day for his opinion on Danny's hair, his opinion on Danny's suit, his opinion on Danny's new girlfriend's new chest—where the hell was everybody?

"So we . . . I guess you didn't have a good—"

Before Joe could finish, Amanda surprised herself by opening her big fat mouth again. She assumed she was already out of a job. She was wondering what she would say to her mom, how she would pay her part of the phone bill—too late.

"Don't take this the wrong way, okay?" Lowering the boom. "Frankly, I have a more meaningful physical relationship with my toothbrush." Beat. Then she added, "This won't change anything, right? I mean, you're bigger than that."

By which point Joe's Marlboro cigarette had already dropped right out of his mouth and into his black coffee in the Styrofoam cup with the word BOSS haphazardly stenciled into it in pencil.

And he nodded. Then, realizing the error of his response, shook his head, no. Nothing would change.

From then on, Joe treated Amanda just how she wanted to be treated. Like one of the guys, who never needs a break from the phones to change a tampon. She was not fired. You don't fire a slave; you just make them work harder.

And rather than at the Formosa Cafe, Amanda took to drinking in the privacy of her own home, in the company of her own demons, where she knew her bed would be safely empty.

* * *

Amanda got home, a couple of nights later, just in time to hear her mom's voice on the phone machine. Amanda rushed over, surprised by her sudden anxiousness to talk to her mother ("Could I actually miss her?" she thought), took a deep breath, and answered.

"Honey!" her mom said.

"Hi, Kiki," Amanda replied calmly. Amanda's mother was a very excitable sort, the type to jump into a situation before she noticed there was no water.

"*Hola, mijita!*" her mom said.

"Hello, Kiki," Amanda repeated. Years ago, when Amanda was hitting puberty, her mother had insisted Amanda call her Kiki, her childhood nickname; she also insisted Amanda go clothes shopping with her. Kiki had decided she wanted to dress younger, which meant cramp-inducingly tight Chemin de Fer jeans and spandex halter tops, items that only look good on twelve-year-old girls, nineteen-year-old models (but only if they have a steady heroin habit), and unfortunately for Amanda, Kiki. Kiki had the small bones and tiny waist of an Asian trapeze artist. She was, damn it to hell, adorable. There is no worse trait for the mother of a prepubescent teen.

"Did you notice?" Her mom's voice got breathy in her excitement. "I'm speaking *español!*"

"That's great, Mom—Kiki," Amanda told her, and then gave her, "It sounds like you're doing a great job at it, too."

"Why, *gracias*, chickie." Mom/Kiki coughed. "So, tell me what's all the happenings *en Los Angeles.*" She said "Los Angeles" with an overly correct and very slow Spanish pronunciation. Amanda looked at the clock—one minute into the conversation and already she was annoyed.

Amanda sighed, thinking about the current disasters unfolding: how she was worried about her drug-pusher, drug-ingesting brother, concerned about the semicomatose Patrice, that she stayed awake nights fretting about the baby, her mother's grandchild—not to mention the baby was gone! Yes, she could go on about her lecherous boss, or sleeping, while drunk, with Smoky Joe, her supervisor, or she could even tell Kiki about the bigger-than-life, mysterioso café-au-lait dude on the motorcycle who made her forget all about her mother's favorite, James. "No bad news," she could hear her mother squeaking. "God knows I can't take bad news."

"Everything's great, Ma," Amanda lied.

"How's my grandbaby?"

"Oh, you know, Kiks," Amanda said, her jaw tightening. She thought her face would break. "I think he's perfect."

"Oh, that reminds me, baby," Mom continued. "Johnny baby's on an IV, can you believe it? Montezuma's revenge. Poor thing, he's lost twelve pounds."

"That's too bad." Amanda didn't know what to say. She barely knew who Johnny was. He was some thirtyish car salesman her mother scooted off to Guatemala with on this cheapo tour; Amanda met him once but couldn't pick him out in a lineup.

"Gotta go, baby, this is costing me a fortune!" And with that, Amanda's mom clicked off, leaving Amanda with the bitter taste of having been called "baby" by her mother. She never called her "baby" before she met the car salesman. And now everything was "baby" or "chickie" and Amanda had to force herself to sit down until the wave of anger that made her think of cutting her mother's favorite pink fake fur coat into little, tiny pieces passed.

* * *

GIGI LEVANGIE GRAZER

Later, when Amanda remembered she hadn't eaten all day, she poured raisin bran into a chipped bowl and ate that as if by rote, as if she were trying to remember how to do it, urging the cereal into her stomach so her belly wouldn't be empty when she drank down the cheap bottle of white wine she had brought home from the liquor store on the corner on Sunset.

When the time came, when her bowl was empty, she opened the wine with a flourish reserved for weddings and holidays and births, and took out two glasses, in case Valentin came home. She poured the wine, turned off all the lights, walked upstairs, and sat on the deck in a faded lounge chair filled not so much with polyurethane as with mildew and things that had died, and sipped her wine (making sure the bottle was close by, a hand's grip away).

Her hopes for a relaxing evening, alone with her thoughts, took a turn for the worse. Her noise-filled head tormented her, lurching recklessly and drunkenly from worry about Madison being in mortal danger (or at the very least awakening to strange places and people) to intense anger at her brother, and even more at Patrice, to fear of the future—stemming from the clarity that comes after a few glasses of wine: that one is, indeed, not just unattractive but undeniably Elephant Man material, stupid beyond all . . . well, just plain stupid and, finally, a total, pathetic waste of oxygen.

For a time, Amanda hung on; she pretended it was normal behavior to lie on a pungent cushion on the side of a darkened house drinking alone. Then she pretended it was normal for a girl to think about putting a gun in her mouth. "Ooh," Amanda said out loud, "where'd that come from?" She danced around this thought, reveling in its drama like an angry teenager who'd been grounded for the weekend. Sure, she knew Valentin owned one, kept "safely" in a shoe box at the top of his closet behind a pile of yellowing pillowcases. She even fantasized pulling the trigger and watching her brains splatter the side of the broken house (try selling the place now, Kiki/Mom). If only she could be there to see it.

Amanda closed her eyes. This was normal behavior.

Gabe was riding his Ninja motorcycle on darkened streets on the way to the plant when he thought of stopping by Valentin's house. He hadn't been by in a while, hadn't heard from Valentin, and he had a half hour to kill.

"Bullshit, man!" he yelled over his engine. He knew who he wanted to see, and it wasn't Valentin. It was Amanda.

Gabe shut down his motor as he came up the street, and coasted his bike noiselessly into the driveway. The lights in the house were off. Gabe took his helmet off, breathed in the night air, and got off his bike. Shit, he came all the way over and nobody was even home.

He rang the doorbell. No answer. He looked through the window, pushing the weathered, thirsty foliage aside. Pressed his hands around his face, peering in. Dark. He stood there for a second and thought about leaving a note, hoping she would find it. Then he thought how pussy boy that would be. He'd known Valentin for close to fourteen years, had never written him a note. Val had never so much as seen his signature. Bullshit. He put his helmet back on.

And then the door opened.

"He's not here," Amanda had called out when she heard the bell, very faint, from upstairs; she'd been splashing cool water on her face in a lame attempt to sober up. She figured it was one of Valentin's customers paying a call before hitting the Strip, the clubs, a Mulholland party. Stocking up to get laid. She wasn't particularly frightened—partially because she didn't know enough to be, at that moment, and partially because most of Val's customers were soft-bellied goofy guys whom she could arm-wrestle into submission in two seconds flat. On the other hand, she hadn't heard a car, hadn't heard voices. She put up her fingers, faking a gun in her hands as though she were playing a childhood game with her brother.

Then her heart skipped. It might be Patrice. Patrice never had a key. Well, that wasn't true. Patrice had had many keys and had lost all of them. Amanda and Valentin (suppressing his classic drug-dealer paranoid scenario of waking to find a gun pointed at his head) finally kept a key under a fake rock by the front door that any burglar would instantly recognize as being a fake rock used to hide a key, thanks for making it so easy. But Patrice could never even remember that much, and it used to drive Valentin crazy.

Amanda stood still. If it were Patrice, she wouldn't be able to get in.

The glass slipped from Amanda's hand as she

rushed down the stairs, hoping against hope, and finally knowing exactly what that term meant, because she had never used it in her life until that moment. Please, God, let it be my little baby. Let it be that washed-out drug-addict bitch and that angel masquerading as a small child.

But when she saw the silhouette there was no doubt in her mind who it was. Amanda had spent most of her life taking care of other people; and she felt, instantly, the man at the door was the one who could take care of her. She opened the door, knowing she wouldn't have for anyone else. Knowing the way she looked. Sad, drunk, pasty, pathetic, desperate, Elephant Man woman. And knowing that he wouldn't care. She knew, somehow, he couldn't judge her even if he tried.

As she opened the door to this stranger with the familiar eyes, she realized she still didn't know his name.

Five

James got off the subway at Lexington and Southwall on Boston's east side and watched the girl with the pin-straight blond hair and long wool coat the color of wealth and breeding disappear into the late-night crowd of teenagers on their way to make-out parties and bars with their older sisters' and brothers' fake IDs and drunks and freaks on their way to oblivion in the form of a paper bag or a needle. He was stalking her, this girl. He had noticed her when she first got on the subway car, the way her nose wrinkled almost imperceptibly (to everyone but him) at the sight of the old woman with the soiled orange and blue knit cap and bulbous nose crisscrossed in red and her overstuffed grocery bag, over which hovered a protective arm, hiding her precious cache of old newspaper headlines and orange rinds and yellowed photographs.

"Bitch," he thought to himself. "Fuck you, bitch."

James had been saying these words a lot since he first stepped outside his lousy little sports car and planted his feet on his future. He had made it. He had arrived. The boy who could not speak English ten years ago, who could not ask the teacher with the hook nose and bony fingers and wiry blue hair if he could go to the bathroom, instead relieving himself in his little wood chair with the words "Mrs. Haver Sucks Dicks" carved into it with a penknife and determined hand, the stink rising until finally he was taken out by his ear, the bony fingers poking themselves into his flesh, the nails proving to be equal to the task, breaking the skin until he bled, and the words hissed and low.

"Wetback. Stupid wetback."

How could he tell her his mother was a blue-eyed, half-German beauty queen in his native country in South America, where there were many such beauties; that his tall, dark-haired father had come from a wealthy Old World family, one of the oldest in Caracas; that they had had servants and a driver and ate French food and studied Latin and the men smoked expensive cigars, and his father and his father's father had carried on affairs with maids, young and sweet faced and eager, until one day his father had lost everything, including face, and packed them all up, his older sister and mother and himself, and moved them out here? Out here. To live not in America, not in the land of the free and home of the brave, where cowboys and movie stars hung out on every street corner and drank coffee and smoked filtered cigarettes, but in a place where there were crushing poverty and endless graffiti and screams in the middle of the night, and where his father would sink deeper and deeper into the bottle, the cheap stuff now, an even further slap in the face, the only words he knew in English being "liquor store" and "Fuck you, bitch," which is what he said to everyone and everything that pissed him off.

Despite his long journey, James sounded just like his seriously fucked-up old man. There was nothing else he could say. He was an alien, a Martian, green, with antennae, to everyone but the little chubby girl with the hand that shot up like a rocket at every question, and the dark red hair and freckles, and the smile that was like a sign from God that he would not die alone here in this classroom, that he could go on living, that he existed.

James bit his lip. He would not cry. Even though he was so lonely, even though Conrad, his best friend from high school, with whom he drove out, had joined, inexplicably, a seventy-year-old a cappella group and had found happiness in the arms of a fellow singer, a *guy*, of all things, and had moved out of their shared room. Conrad had declared himself a changed man, assuring James he was not even remotely attracted to him, not to worry, which worried James more than he liked to admit, even though he moved among the masses without talking, without blinking, without being seen. He was invisible once more. Nothing had changed since his first day of sixth grade.

James looked up again and the girl was gone. Maybe he would never get close to a girl like that. Maybe by moving closer to their golden circle he was just torturing himself. He thought about his mother's gray cat with the one good eye, the other lost in a fight. The cat would sit for hours watching his sister's goldfish swim back and forth, back and forth, oblivious, shining, taunting.

He looked through his pockets for change. He would have to take the train back to his stop, which he had passed long ago.

He needed to get to a phone.

In the dank house in Laurel Canyon, Amanda stood, frozen; the man wasn't saying anything. Why didn't he talk? she wondered. She tried to look reproachful. She tried annoyed. She tried impatient, distracted, occupied. He watched her go through her paces, a wealthy Southern gentleman in white linen sizing up a quarter horse, all in the course of ten seconds, which felt to her like a lifetime.

She touched her hair, nervously wound it around her finger. She might have actually tossed it, though she loathed when women sank to tossing their hair, such an obvious signal to the male of the species. And then she opened the door wider, stepped aside, and tried to ignore the warmth moving up between her legs, the butterflies tap-dancing in her stomach. "Get a grip," she admonished herself. "It's not like you've never seen a guy before."

He walked in, still not saying a word. The house was so dark, Gabriel stepped carefully, not wanting to trip. She hadn't said anything to him but he knew something was terribly wrong. Her face had changed, that was the first thing he noticed when the moonlight struck her; her eyes had no light. They were dark, so dark he was almost afraid to come in. Afraid of what he might find. A thought struck him—where was Valentin? Did Valentin bring this change on?

"Valentin's not here," Amanda finally said. What was she supposed to do, stand there drunk and horny and mute?

Gabriel sighed almost audibly. Relief. Amanda looked at him, wary.

"Did you need something from him?" She hoped to God the answer was no, and then, at the same moment, she hoped to God the answer was yes, so she could kick this man out of her house, wallow peacefully in her vat of self-pity, and never see him again.

"Are you okay?" He ignored her question on purpose. Let her insult him a little bit, it was okay. He could tell she'd been drinking, he didn't know how much or for how long. But if he were a betting man, like his father, he'd say the odds were pretty good that she'd been nursing an empty bottle for a while now.

He wasn't answering her question, Amanda noticed. And she was not about to turn on the lights and let him see what she really looked like. Christ, she didn't even want to look at herself.

"Amanda, are you okay?" Gabriel asked again, and this time he used her name. He wanted an answer. Amanda looked at him and started to laugh, and laughed more and did not stop laughing until she started to cry and found herself pressed against this man, sobbing into the leather of his jacket, holding him so close she would not let him go, she was so afraid he would leave and never return. She never wanted him to leave.

"How is it that you could meet a person," Amanda thought, her mind suddenly clear, "not know his name, not know anything about him except this: without him you will fall apart, without him your life is meaningless?"

And then she looked at him, their faces almost one. Her arms ached from gripping his body. And she asked him his name. The answer floored her.

"Gabriel," he said.

Amanda replied, her defenses up, sarcasm at the ready.

"It figures," Amanda said. Her favorite angel had always been Gabriel, the angel of mercy, the angel who grants wishes and hopes to mortals, even the lowliest form of mortal—drunk, moist-faced girls with no future and bad shoes. There was no better name for this man standing in front of her.

Amanda felt ashamed at the sharpness of her words as soon as she had said them. This was not an appropriate moment for her sarcastic tongue. And then she realized. "Valentin's Gabriel," she said. "From school . . ." The familiar eyes had belonged to her brother's boyhood friend, but they were now in the body of a man.

She looked into those eyes again and asked him the question without words.

He bent over her, breathed into her neck, his voice low and clear as he answered what she could not ask.

"I'm not leaving."

And then, as she closed her eyes and confided her torrent of fears about the missing baby,

Gabriel listened and stroked her hair and carried her to her room and lay her down in her bed and took off her shoes and pulled the covers over her and watched her all night, never taking his eyes off her, not even when the phone rang and the answering machine clicked on and a man's voice asked over the static for her to answer, please answer, and he wondered if it was a man that had caused her pain, and he swore to himself that no man would ever cause her pain like that again.

He told his foreman the next day he had had a flat on the freeway and could not call for hours. He was docked two days' pay for not calling, not showing up—rules were rules—and he needed the money, but he didn't care. And J.D. harangued him all night, convinced somehow it was a girl had caused this problem, convinced his little bro was holding back a live one.

Amanda awakened in a good mood the next morning for the first time in weeks. She hardly recognized it, then did not know why; no reason came to her, but when she pieced it together, she realized. He did not have wings, he dressed all in black, his hair was cropped short, his beard slightly rough. But there was no doubt.

"Goddamn," Amanda said to herself, "I got myself a guardian angel."

She was not much of a whistler; tell the truth, was dangerously tone deaf. But that morning as she dressed hurriedly, late as she was, Amanda found herself whistling a love song that last spoke to her in the summer between seventh and eighth grade, and then the realization hit her like a cashmere glove and she stood up suddenly, straight as a ruler. This feeling, this foreign state, was called happiness.

So distracted in her contentment was Amanda as she rushed through the kitchen to grab an apple (knowing there wouldn't be one), she did not notice the phone machine, blinking an omen, seeking to temper her spirits.

And she did not stop to think about what time Valentin had made it home last night, or if he even had.

Then she was stopped cold: the playpen. Still empty. She reached out, touching the wood, remembering Maddie, his little fingers curled around the side. It was not over. Amanda stepped back from it as though it had kicked her. Her nightmare was not yet over.

She stepped out into the dry morning and found herself hoping Gabe would be parked outside, in black, his motorcycle purring, ready to take her away. And she would go. Oh, she would go.

Joe noticed Amanda was in better form this day. He figured it was safe to ask her to grab a snack, safe to take a walk with her to the corner drugstore, owned by the Armenian man who charged him a different price for the same pack of gum every time he came in, depending on his mood. Joe loved this little game, this ritual, sizing up the man's demeanor, choosing a price before he heard it, seeing how close he could get, seeing how good he was. It was the little things in life, his mother always said, and it was at these moments he saw what she meant. All we have are the little things. So when Joe leaned over Amanda's desk and asked her if she'd like to take a walk, he was surprised at his reaction to her simple, noncommittal "Sure. Why not?"

His heart sped up.

Joe gave the job of answering the phones for a few minutes to a squirrelly production assistant who could not have been more pissed about giving up researching what girls were in town for Danny. Joe made a mental note to fire him. For which Joe himself would probably be fired one day. He had eighty-sixed a few too many of Danny's junior pimps, and he had enjoyed it a little too much.

As they crossed the small side street lined with the six eight-year-old Hondas, Datsuns, and Toyotas belonging to crew members and secretaries and production assistants who couldn't get on the lot, filled as it was with Mercedeses, BMWs, and the occasional gold Corvette, Joe was hoping Amanda would ask if the group was heading for Chinese tonight. He didn't want to be the one to ask first. Joe was feeling coy. Joe was trying for the life of him to remember what it felt like to be inside her.

"Thanks for springing me," Amanda said as Joe lit a cigarette, at the same time offering her one. She shook her head.

"I told you I didn't smoke. Don't you remember?" She looked at him sideways, teasing, not caring how he was affected by this, not knowing he felt like shit that he didn't remember, not knowing he couldn't remember knowing. She had never told him.

"Shit. Guess I should have known that."

"What?"

He looked at her. She was a million miles away. Why did he find himself caring so much about her state of mind?

"It's your skin."

Amanda looked at him. Her hand shot up to her cheek, hiding what wasn't there.

"It's too healthy looking."

"Gosh. Sorry. I am working on it." She thought about her drunken state the night before; it seemed like that was another woman. She had changed overnight.

If Joe wondered how much of an asshole he could sound like in his life, he knew at that moment.

"I didn't mean—I meant, you know. You have good skin. Anyway."

Amanda looked at him as they stopped to let an old Plymouth, driven by a tiny, ancient driver, sex indeterminate, pass by at an eight-mile-an-hour clip. Joe was definitely nervous. Stepping off the curb, she had an epiphany that almost caused her to stop in front of a moving pickup truck.

"Shit," she thought to herself, "I'm being fired."

"So, what do you think of Danny's new sketch character, the guy with the turban?" Joe hadn't noticed Amanda had stopped. She caught up with him as the driver honked his horn.

"It's **been** done."

"It hasn't been done that much." He was defensive. After all, it was his idea.

"I'm telling you, it's been done. A million times." She didn't care anymore. She was being fired. Joe was just making small talk before the axe fell on her tense, whiplashed neck.

They walked into the store, its windows covered with cheap, handwritten, misspelled signs. The words assaulted her like bullets: MALT LIQOR, 2.99! CIGARET CARTON $4.99!

"Are you firing me?" she blurted out, practically spitting the words.

Joe was almost inside the store when he turned and Amanda was no longer next to him. He opened the door and looked at her. Angry. She was definitely angry.

"What?"

The sun playing off her hair, making it intense copper, a tarnished, forgotten penny. He wondered why he hadn't noticed the color before, then he realized he had seen her only in artificial light, or in the dark of an old restaurant through boozy eyes, or in the muted grays of his dingy bedroom. He felt ashamed.

"Just tell me. Let's not draw this out, okay?"

She was very young, and very smart, and attractive without being obvious. And he could talk to her. Maybe he should fire her; then she could beg for her job back and he would give it to her and she would be grateful. Joe would like to see Amanda being grateful.

"I'm not firing you. Where'd you get that idea?"

"You're not firing me?"

"No. Do you want me to?"

"No. God, no. I need this job."

"Can I please get my gum now? I've been looking forward to this all morning."

Amanda looked at him, relieved, as he opened the door to the store; her knees slightly buckled as her adrenaline rush subsided. Today would be a good day: she would not be fired. A tarnished brass bell hanging at the top of the doorway heralded their arrival, breaking her thoughts. She realized she couldn't recall ever seeing someone so serious about a pack of gum.

The leather-skinned Armenian man smoking a cheap cigar and reading a weekly paper in his native language at the counter looked up. Amanda thought she saw him smile when he saw Joe head for the candy aisle. She smiled back at him, feeling pretty good about herself at the moment—and then she realized the man was just getting ready to spit a wad of wet, brown chew tobacco into a paper cup, and Amanda turned and headed for the feminine hygiene aisle.

Amanda came home late that night, happy for her job, happy her relationship with Joe was on track, happy she bypassed the liquor store on the corner of Sunset, though she eyed it for considerably longer than it took to make a right turn.

As soon as she put the key in the door, she heard it.

A cough. A baby's cough.

She dropped her purse inside the door and ran to the playpen, to Madison. Flushed and warm, his nose filled with baby snot, but oh, he was beautiful, and Amanda could only think of one other person she had ever held this tight, and she had to remind herself to loosen her grip, for this one was just a baby, only a baby.

She had to get hold of Gabriel. The baby was home. She knew he would want to know.

Madison started crying, and Amanda held him at arm's length and looked at him closely for the first time, and it occurred to her that he had lost weight, and a fury rose in her and she swore on her life that nothing would ever happen to him again, no matter what.

She never even wondered where his parents were, never thought to look for them, never cared. She had her baby back.

She sat down with him at the kitchen table and sang out-of-tune lullabies and held him and did not move until the morning.

Six

Gabriel and J.D. eyed the new C-4, 230-horse-power Corvettes, America's fastest-ever production car, knowing that neither one of them would ever own one. The men of the night shift in their overalls and worn jeans were called into the warehouse by the men in the blue suits and yellow ties to celebrate the first of the new line. The laborers, usually loud, boasting, fat with the pride of simple men, of football games won, of bets forwarded, of nights with heavily mascaraed girls who could say, "The usual," to a bartender and mean it, stood silent.

A slice of light from a lamppost hit the gold two-door through an opened doorway. Gabriel thought for a second that he had been here before, and he knew there was a word for it, but couldn't remember the word before he remembered the feeling this moment reminded him of.

Church.

He hadn't been to church since his early school days, when his mother was still living with his father, before the fights and the tears, before she moved out, before she started living with the ex-marine, a tall handsome black man with the battered hands of a Golden Gloves champ, who would beat Gabriel and beat him until the day Gabriel, age twelve, could not add anymore and knew: he had brain damage, the same as any punch-drunk, over-the-hill fighter. Gabe remembered vividly the day his father came home from the road and picked him up at school and told him he would never leave him again, never ever. He remembered his father's face that night as he watched young Gabe struggling with his homework, the simplest addition and subtraction, and how red his father's eyes were. The next day his father put his saxophone away, deep in the closet, and put on a suit and tie and walked up and down Wilshire Boulevard in Beverly Hills, and found himself a security job.

Gabe and J.D. continued to watch the new Corvettes as if looking for a sign.

"We building those things," is what J.D. said. "We building those things and ain't no way we ever gonna drive 'em."

He stubbed his cigarette out with the heel of his work boot. Stamped it twice.

"Ain't that a shame." J.D. said it without a smile, his stooped figure blocking the light on the gold Corvette as he walked away.

Gabriel stared at that gold one a little bit longer. He looked around the room. They, these rugged forms struck suddenly dumb, had all built this piece of perfection. At this moment, this car, this symbol of the good life, of all they would never attain, belonged to each one of them.

Then he turned and walked out. Each of the men filed out after him. Nobody said a word. But their breathing was strained, Gabriel noticed, and as he looked closer, he saw what their wives and girlfriends and children had never seen.

Tears.

Gabriel had never been to this kind of funeral before.

Gabriel strapped his sweat-stained weight belt around his waist and tried to talk to J.D. between lifts, tried to engage him in light conversation about the Corvette that seemed forced even to his ears, tried to make him feel for a moment something other than bitterness. But J.D. was not hearing any of it. J.D. had spent too long building beautiful things for other people.

So Gabriel lied. Told J.D. what "really" happened the other night to keep Gabriel from the job he had never been so much as two minutes late for.

Gabriel told J.D. he got some. But good. And finally, finally, Gabriel saw gold of a different kind.

J.D. gave him a smile.

"Now you talkin', boy," J.D. said as he rotated his arm, suppressing a wince. "Now you got somethin' of im*po*tance to say to me." Gabriel liked the way J.D. said "im*po*tance," the way he tossed the *r* to the side like an apple core. His dad said it that way, too. "Someday, Gabe, you will be a man of im*po*tance," he used to say to his son.

Gabriel made up a good, long story for their break, juicy and detailed, with exotic phony names (Gabe preferred the name Angelique for this story, in reference to a buxom calendar girl he saw in an ad once) and unusual locations (the shower stall, her backseat, the front lawn). Gabe himself was impressed with his storytelling abilities and thought briefly of sending the story off to *Penthouse* magazine. Shit, it was ten times better than the bullshit they printed. By the time he got through, twenty minutes later, such thoughts were gone; all Gabriel could think about was crawling into that tiny bed with the pink blanket and cracked white frame and having his way with Amanda.

"No more Mr. Nice Guy," J.D. had said to him. "Fuck, yeah," Gabriel thought. "No more Mr. Nice Guy."

Amanda had stolen Gabriel's number out of Valentin's tiny red-leather address book (under *G*) with the Marlboro insignia, which Valentin kept squirreled away, cleverly, under his mattress; Amanda figured he used this lame hiding place in case he was ever busted—most of the numbers belonged to his customers. She had called Gabriel and left a message with an older man named Frank, who she assumed must be his dad, who seemed surprised, then pleased a girl was calling. He said he would be sure to give

Gabe the message, and Amanda knew the man was telling the truth.

When Frank hung up the phone, gingerly, he thought about the last time a girl had called for Gabe. His son had always been so good looking, but he wasn't a con; he wasn't the type of man who would take advantage of a girl. Gabe had had a relationship a few years back with an Asian girl, a nice, petite girl with a sweet smile who seemed to really like his son. Her family, though, was a different matter. They weren't about to see their daughter married off to the son of a black man. And when she left, when she stopped returning phone calls, when the answering machine emptied out to nothing, Frank looked into his son's newly jaded eyes and knew he would have a hard time ever letting himself love again. Frank recognized that look—it was the same one he saw in his shaving mirror every morning since Gabe's mother walked out, years ago.

His son was born with a soft heart, just like his old man.

* * *

The wind was strong in L.A. and Amanda sat on the slow-rotting deck with the baby, pointing out in the clear sky the constellations so intense they seemed cut out of midnight blue construction paper with sharp scissors. She talked up the Big Dipper and the Little Dipper and Orion in her most assured high-school-astronomy voice, and Madison looked where she was pointing, and Amanda would swear on a bowl of fresh buttered popcorn he understood every word. A burst of warm air made Madison squint and laugh as it tickled his nose, and Amanda laughed with him, and somehow, ensconced in their little world, they were able to ignore the slamming doors and the viciously thrown words downstairs and a million miles away.

"I know you're fucking him, bitch! I know you're fucking him!"

That would be Valentin.

"You're high!"

Patrice.

"Don't you lie to me!"

"I hate you!" Patrice replied in her usual calm manner.

A cabinet banged shut, open, shut. Valentin looking for cereal.

"That's *it!* I'm not giving you any more!"

"You're an *asshole!*"

Stomping feet across the wood floor. Another door slammed.

Amanda held Madison's drowsy body against hers and measured her breaths against his and wondered when the fires would come. Every year, whipped by these winds, a tony part of the desert city would go up in flames and the news anchors would struggle to suppress their glee at having an event to name. She wondered what it would be this year: FLAMES '86; L.A. BURNS: 1986; INFERNO OF '86. She thought briefly of going into the news, so impressed was she at her burgeoning talent for insipid headlines.

She laughed to herself, stood to put the baby to bed, and wished she could have shared this moment with Gabriel, believing he'd find it as perfect as she. Then she wondered why he hadn't called her back and for a horrible moment she let herself believe she was mistaken about him.

So she was mistaken, she thought, drifting down the stairs. She'd been mistaken about men before. That didn't mean she wouldn't enjoy a good romp in the hay with the guy. Even if he turned out to be the Marquis de Sade . . .

Especially if he turned out to be the Marquis de Sade. "Amanda," she said to herself, "are you aware you've lost your mind?"

Gabriel got off his shift at 2 A.M. and rode east on the dead stretch of Hollywood freeway at speeds that would land him in a holding cell in County, making time with gang bangers and dopers, if the police could catch him. Tonight he was not going to be stopped.

As he sped down the off-ramp outside the Hollywood Bowl, Gabriel realized he hadn't said good-bye to J.D.

Amanda awakened with a start sometime in the middle of the night and her heart quickened, thinking it was the baby, thinking that Patrice had gotten up and taken him away, the closing of the front door waking her as it shut forever behind them.

But it was not that. It was an engine, cut in midpurr, sliding up the driveway.

Amanda jumped out of bed and wiped the sleep from her eyes and ran her tongue along her teeth and thanked God her mother was still in Guatemala with her sick car salesman. For even though Kiki could not bother herself with Valentin's random sex life (he was a boy, after all), she was not above poking her pert nose into Amanda's sad little escapades, especially as Kiki was fond of James, who had a knack for buttering up Amanda's mom—"What's that scent you're wearing, Mrs. McHenry? It's driving me crazy!" or, "Is that a new dress? Red is definitely your color, you know that?" he would tell Kiki, causing her to blush and stammer while Amanda rolled her eyes and coughed. Where he came up with this shit, God only knew.

Amanda ran silently to the front door on unsteady legs and opened it, and there he was, and there were no words as he took her in his arms and pressed his mouth to hers and picked her up as though she weighed nothing, and Amanda could not breathe but found strength to speak. What was it about this man that she could not get from James? It was as though Jimmy had all the right pieces to the puzzle, had memorized all the combinations, had worked on her from the beginning as though she were a test, calculating what she needed and when, how much manipulation would keep her on the straight and narrow, when to withdraw love, and when to give—all the while, Amanda felt, thinking of how best to serve himself, to service James's "big picture." Amanda had come to realize that deep inside James's love for her was something cold.

With this man, Gabriel, there was chemistry—something Amanda had read about (granted, in the less than completely scientific pages of *Cosmopolitan*) but never took seriously, for it had never happened to her. She didn't know how far the chemistry would take them, how long his scent would carry her, but she didn't care, because there was something beyond chemistry. She felt, at her core, that this man was good.

"What took you so long?" she demanded.

"I get off at two, baby," he purred.

Oh, his voice was raspy. Amanda wanted to hear that voice order her around, demand breakfast in bed, a foot rub, a blow job—whatever.

"Hope I'm not too late," he said, knowing he wasn't.

"You remember where my room is?" Amanda was breathing in the staccato rhythms of a four-minute miler. She wondered if he could hear her heart beating, so loud it was. Gabriel smiled, his full lips curling around his strong white teeth. Oh, he remembered. It had never left his mind.

He lowered her into her fourth-grade bed and stared at her intently, his eyes green and gold through eyelids lowered to half-mast, and Amanda's body shook and she heard herself whimper as though the deed had already taken place. For a terrifying moment, Amanda thought she had actually peed herself.

She did not make any other sounds, her fist lodged tight inside her mouth to keep her from screaming.

She did not want to wake the baby.

They slept until dawn. In spoons. Amanda awakened with his arms wrapped around her as though warding off evil spirits. She had just opened her eyes to the first light when a banging at the front door made Amanda draw in her breath sharply, choking on fear.

Gabriel, whose hands had been intertwined with hers, put his finger to his lips and slipped out of her tiny bed and into his jeans.

The front door was pounded again. Gabriel tipped his hand, palm down, gesturing for

Amanda to be calm. He winked and was out the door, closing it softly behind him as though she were still asleep.

Gabriel passed Valentin and Patrice's bedroom, the door closed, and continued to the front door. He could see the old lumber vibrating under the beating it was taking.

And Gabriel knew then that these weren't friends of Valentin.

"Police! Open up!"

Gabriel closed his eyes with the world's fastest prayer and opened the door before they broke it off its creaky hinges with their clubs. He had seen what the LAPD could do to a wood door. He had seen what the LAPD could do to a black man at a routine traffic stop, much less a black man slamming a drug dealer's clean white sister.

His hands were up and he was on his knees before the door completed its arc.

It all happened too quickly.

"Police! Hands up!" His hands were up. The boys in blue were too keyed up to notice.

"On your knees!" Gabriel was on his knees.

"Get on your knees!" They weren't seeing him. Gabriel could smell the adrenaline.

"Hands in the air!" His hands remained in the

air. He was hoping they would take this into account before they shot him.

The pounding came fast and furious and Gabriel's head hit the ground sideways, a billy club at his neck, cutting off his air. He fought to stay conscious and he remembered his cousin, an athlete on a basketball scholarship, who had been found hanging in a cell in Cook County, the belt wrapped around his neck by sheriff's deputies after using a choke hold to "calm the boy."

Gabriel twisted his head and tried to talk, but he could not, and all he could see was a dozen black Florsheims scurrying across the floor and dust balls gathering in a neglected corner.

And for some reason, Gabriel looked at those dust balls and thought of Amanda, and while the policeman leaned into his back with his knee, Gabriel was thinking that this girl needed him more than anyone had ever needed him before.

And he smiled.

"What're you smiling about?"

Damn, his knees were sharp. Gabriel couldn't see him, but thought for sure it was a skinny white guy who he had probably smacked around in high school in his ROTC uniform, all proud of himself.

"Nothing, Officer," Gabriel said.

"What're you on?" the man asked him. Gabriel had no time to respond.

"What are you on, *creep?*" He wasn't asking this time.

"Nothing, sir." Gabriel had learned in high school after being pulled over for looking like someone who robbed a 7-Eleven (the perpetrator had skin like ink, five eight on his tippy toes) to call these guys "sir" and not vomit at the same time.

"Then what the fuck you smiling at, *boy?*"

Gabriel smiled again. A small, satisfied smile just enough to show his pearly whites. Hell, he just couldn't help himself. "Sir . . ." Gabriel almost laughed. "I'm in love, sir."

The man cracked him with his club and the last thing Gabriel heard before passing out was Amanda's scream.

Amanda had barely slipped into Gabriel's work shirt before the scared-looking policeman with the baby face put his gun in her face.

"Freeze!"

She froze. Her shirt opened, revealing her

white skin and his face flickered downward, and she knew what he was thinking.

"Can I . . . ?" She was asking if she could button her shirt. She was quite obviously unarmed. He nodded quickly, his face flushing bright red, and she thought he must smell sex on her to be that flustered.

She buttoned slowly.

Two policemen kicked open Valentin's bedroom door.

Amanda lunged quickly toward them, past the freckled officer. "Madison!" The officer held her back. Amanda looked at him, flushed, eyes wild.

"There's a baby in there!"

"Get your hands up!" The baby-faced officer was yelling at her now, their intimate moment forgotten. Others were already upstairs by the sounds of their heels on the parched wood floors.

"But there's a baby—" Amanda didn't recognize her voice, pleading.

"Just be quiet." He motioned for her to step in front of him. "Put your hands up. Please." She did so, even wrapping them around her head like she had seen on television, and she thought even though she was hyperventilating, she was handling this moment pretty well, considering, and she also thought this was because she had watched far too many episodes of *Starsky and Hutch* as a child.

Amanda heard Valentin's groans. The skinny bastard had slept through the whole episode. Amanda shouldn't have been surprised. Valentin had lived in California his entire life but had yet to feel an earthquake; he slept like a drunken infant through each and every one, whether they came at early morning or midafternoon, or ten o'clock at night, for that matter. Amanda hadn't slept for more than three hours at a time since she was in high school. Until last night.

"Get your hands off of me!" The high-pitched screech could only mean Valentin's stranger half had been rudely awakened as well. *"Pigs! Fucking pigs!"* Amanda hoped Madison would not remember this scene.

Amanda looked at the young police officer and studied his freckles and thought about the stars she had shown to Madison just last night, a night that was now worlds away.

She was about to tell him she was sorry for Patrice's shouted insults, but then she saw Gabriel, crouched like a child sleeping on its stomach, his head turned away from her, and then she saw the cop lift his billy club, which seemed so incongruous a term at that moment, so agreeable, and then she heard herself scream.

James sat alone in the overhip, overpriced coffee shop in Harvard Square teeming with college students and all he could think about was why Amanda had not called him yet. He turned it over again and again in his head as he stared through the clear glass and the swirling pattern of coffee and cream. He poured a little more cream in. He didn't like the taste, but he liked to see the result.

He had lost weight. The old camel-hair coat with the torn, stained lining he had bought from a thrift shop on Melrose was not holding up well under the Eastern winter. Neither was he.

He was supposed to meet a girl here, a nice Jewish girl from a New Jersey suburb—he forgot which, there seemed to be so many—with smooth olive skin and short, dark, shiny hair and a pediatrician father and psychologist mother who found him, he knew, exotic and challenging. All he could think of was Amanda.

He had met the girl with the upper-middle-class bearings and the private school education a couple of weeks ago, but he hadn't much noticed her until he was sure the blonds would continue not noticing him. She sat next to him in Constitutional Law 101, the class taught by the famous legal author with the steel-wool hair and a penchant for listening only to himself and screwing idealistic freshmen. Her last name started with a *D*, that's all he could remember, for *D* came after *C*, the first letter of his last name, in the alphabet.

One crisp brown morning, James had faltered badly on a question shot at him from the podium about civil contracts in the year 1654, and the girl had whispered the answer to him as she dropped her newly sharpened pencil. And then, after class, in the warmth of her room, furnished with frilly things she had told him were Laura Ashley (a name he memorized, knowing he would run into it again in this land of opportunity), she had given him chamomile tea sweetened with honey and listened to him in silence as he prattled on about Amanda and his loneliness and his anger, and had nodded empathetically. And though she made him feel vaguely like something squirming under a microscope, he had fucked her and it hadn't been half bad.

Though she hardly moved, her skin was soft and her breath was sweet and so it was fine. For now.

He looked at the picture window and through the red and green lettering saw her as she jog-walked toward the coffee shop, late and anxious and neither attractive nor unattractive, and he realized that this was a woman who knew her place in a man's life, any man; she would be the one to listen to him. He felt a twinge of guilt and as she came in the door, he gave her his best smile.

And then he thought he was glad she had one of those telephone calling cards. He knew she'd let him use it.

Amanda awakened to the sharp odor of smelling salts and the sight of Gabriel, partially blocked by the skinny cop with the trigger hand, leaning against the wall next to the front door, a bandage to his face, holding it up to stop the bleeding, and Valentin and Patrice, in handcuffs, sitting back-to-back as officers milled about as though in after-party motion. Amanda was relieved Gabriel was sitting up, but was equally mad at herself for fainting. What a wuss.

She looked up as a female officer, hornet's nest hair in a tight bun, walked by holding her nephew. Amanda called out to stop her.

"Madison!" The freckle-faced officer looked over at her. The female officer was walking out the door. Amanda was trembling—where was she going?

"Madison!"

"Hey, that's my kid!" Valentin was now joining in. Patrice looked up in slow motion, her expression groggy. "Go back to sleep," Amanda thought.

The freckle-faced cop looked from Amanda to the female officer and stood up and walked outside, where Amanda could see the witch was bouncing the baby in her arms. Amanda was riven with jealousy, of all things. Who was this bitch to bounce *my* baby?

She looked at Gabriel, who looked back at her, cocked his eyebrow, as if asking if she were okay.

"You're bleeding . . ." ("Oh, good, Amanda," she thought to herself. "As if he doesn't know.") He gave her a small shrug as if to say he'd had worse. She wondered if it was true.

Then he pursed his lips together in a kiss and Amanda had to look away, because with all the chaos, the living nightmare swirling around them, she suddenly wanted to fuck him again. Her breathing sharpened. She badly wanted to rub herself between her legs, rub herself against the old piano bench like she did when she was five or six, but thought the police could very well take this the wrong way.

The phone rang. Thank God, thought Amanda. She wanted to get her mind off her crotch. She suddenly knew what it felt to be a fifteen-year-old boy. Out of control. She had never felt this sensation before, not even when Jimmy had given her her first sex-oriented orgasm (the first official one having occurred at the age of twelve, on a particularly fondly remembered sunrise bicycle ride). Sure, she had been grateful, but even then she had felt like a patient on an operating table—Jimmy the surgeon crowing afterward that the operation had been a huge success. The patient would live, after all.

The skinny cop walked over to the kitchen, glaring at Amanda as he passed her and answered the phone.

Then she got angry. "Can he do that?" she asked no one in particular. The young cop, her baby-faced supervisor, was still outside with hornet's nest and Madison. Valentin leaned his head toward her.

"Shitheads can do anything they fuckin' want."

"That's great, Val. That's just great. I think it's good to make them more mad," Amanda said through sorely gritted teeth.

"Fuck you."

"Fuck me? Am I the one who invited them here? I don't think so."

"You two shut the fuck up." An officer Amanda couldn't see jumped in with his two cents.

"How long do we have to stay like this, sir?"

"I said shut up."

And for one minute, everyone did.

The skinny cop came back into the foyer. Okay, it wasn't really a foyer, but Amanda liked the word. He was snickering. Amanda had never seen anyone snicker before, but she could say with confidence she was seeing it at that moment.

"You Amanda?" He was smiling over her, a mean, cock-of-the-walk grin.

"Yes?" She wasn't sure she wanted to be Amanda at that moment. Maybe he had the wrong Amanda.

He laughed, his hand shooting up to his face

as if catching the contents of his mirth. "That was, ah . . . James . . ." The man could hardly get the words out. "He wanted me to tell you he missed you."

He laughed again. Amanda's face burned red. She did not look at Gabriel, but she could feel his eyes on her. She looked in the cop's eyes and said nothing. He stopped laughing and looked for a distraction in the form of his fellow officers. "What we got?" he demanded to know. This was the guy in charge.

Amanda studied the threading on Gabriel's blue work shirt and chewed on her lower lip. When she looked up again, Gabriel was looking outside.

"You fucking my sister?" Valentin wanted to know. He was staring straight at Gabriel, and the question shocked Amanda, given the circumstances. Shouldn't he be more concerned about the implications of the cuffs cutting into his bony wrists? Amanda knew Valentin and Gabriel had been friends for a long time, recently (and thankfully) reacquainted, but why would her drughead brother be so concerned? He never cared that much about Amanda's nocturnal life before.

"Let's not get into that, man." Gabriel's tone

was stern but understanding. A parent talking to a child.

"Oh, man. You're fucking my sister." The officers were starting to look over. Amanda dragged her nail on the termite-sampled floor, hoping to dig a hole large enough to crawl into.

"It's not your business, my friend." Amanda could hear Gabriel's voice tighten, and suddenly she knew it went beyond what Valentin was saying. It was how he was saying it. Gabriel was not "fucking" her. Gabriel had true feelings for her and was clearly insulted by the vulgar nature of her brother's diatribe. Gabriel clearly had feelings for Amanda.

Tears formed in her eyes. The most romantic moment of her life was being spent in handcuffs in the company of L.A.'s finest.

"Oh, God, my sister." Amanda looked up and Valentin was looking at her. His eyes were moist. "My God," Amanda thought, "my brother's feelings are hurt because I slept with his friend." Did Valentin need Gabriel to be his friend more than she needed him to be her lover?

"Val," Amanda said tentatively.

"Fuck you," Valentin replied, with no hesitation.

An officer came out holding Patrice's purse. He handed it to the skinny Hess look-alike and whispered in his ear. Hess smiled—could crack a mirror with that smile, Amanda thought. "This yours?" He was looking at her. Amanda was horrified at the thought of what was in the purse, and that this guy could think she could own a purse like that, rancid with the smell of pot and heavy cologne and cigarettes. God knows what teeming things lived in that purse. Hess looked at Patrice, snoring softly, her tiny mouth partly open. "Well, well, well," he said before she was rudely awakened for the second time that day by another member of the vice squad and taken away in a black-and-white, siren off.

Valentin was also taken, although they really had nothing on him. Even his gun was, smartly, registered. But they knew about him, these cops, and they'd been watching him for some time, and they weren't about to let him go that easily.

Gabriel went, too. They weren't going to let a large black man go after arresting two white suspects in the same house. He seemed resigned to it, and as he left, he looked at Amanda with what can only be described as a look of love, although, again, she was not sure, never quite having seen that look so boldly before.

The young cop with the familiar freckles came toward Amanda and helped her up. Amanda wondered what she would say to Joe when she used her one phone call to call work. She wondered if he would even come to the telephone; she should have been at the show an hour ago. She stopped wondering when the young cop took the handcuffs off her.

"I'm not being arrested?" ("Stupid question," she thought. "Stupid, stupid, stupid.") "I mean, not that I want to be."

Hornet's nest came back inside with Madison, who was playing with the badge pinned to her ample chest. She looked at Amanda questioningly, then handed him off to freckles; she didn't want to be responsible for whatever terrible things Amanda, obviously a heroin addict, would do to the child. Hornet's nest walked out without looking back, and freckles handed Madison, looking for another badge, to Amanda. The other cops had cleared out after making a mess out of what was already a mess.

Amanda, gripping Madison, looked at the young cop and her mind flashed on *Happy Days*, and as she stood there, in a fog, it occurred to her she had definitely watched too much television; she should be thinking about more pressing matters—her job, which she would now, for sure, lose; her new lover, who was now going to prison, or at least jail; how to fix the front door and the damage left behind by the cops, with $12 in her checking account . . .

She thought about who to call first.

And then she thought, in her most eloquent fashion, "Damn-fuck-piss-shit. What the hell am I going to say to Jimmy?"

Seven

Joe Artuga woke up and rolled over, looked at the girl next to him, and thought, "Oh, shit."

He had been thinking that a lot lately. He sat back against the wicker headboard he bought at a secondhand store ten years ago, when wicker was cool, and thought of the night before and tried to piece it together as he always did, and then he lit a cigarette. He looked at the girl again. Did he work with her? Was she a waitress? He lifted her left arm, which was blocking part of her face. Blond hair. That was a good start. He didn't know a lot of blonds. But he fucked a lot of blonds. He bent his head to the side to study her face more. She was hard but young, mid-twenties. She was pretty, even under all the makeup, but not smart and not interesting and not funny.

Joe could tell this much from the shape of her nose: a shade too delicate, a shade too perky. There was no dignity in the silhouette. He had a theory about women's noses, that the shape, whether hooked and bitter or wide and forgiving, had a lot to do with character, and he had never been wrong. Men's noses he couldn't give a shit about, except when they had been fixed by some Beverly Hills doctor, and these men, usually actors, Joe Artuga just felt like spitting on. He sat back again on the headboard and smoked and scared himself when he suddenly thought of Amanda and wondered what she would think of him, sitting naked in his bed right now. He knew what she would say; he was learning the rhythm of her speech. "Joe," she'd say, "this does not appear to be your finest hour."

He grabbed the sheet and peered underneath, a sudden thieving gesture. A snapshot had cleared in his head, and he wanted it confirmed: she was an actress; she had been on the show . . . He looked at the two machine-tanned globes point- ing determinedly at the ceiling. The eight-year-old in him had an urge to poke them; he had forgot- ten what they felt like and he knew he wouldn't be in their company again anytime soon.

She stirred. The globes remained resolute. He wondered how fast he could make it out of the apartment. He hoped it was fast enough to not have to talk. He hated having to lie all the time.

Minutes later, as Joe, dressed in rumpled khakis and randomly buttoned, striped cotton shirt (his last clean one), started his Alfa Romeo Spider convertible with shaky hands and pulled out of the carport, he thought to himself, "I'm too old for this. I am too fucking old for this."

He adjusted his mirror and caught a glimpse of his face in the unforgiving morning sun and realized that he needed someone. He had proven he was not able to take care of himself. He was pale; he hadn't eaten regular meals in fifteen years. His stubble was showing gray. There were creases on his face where he slept, and lines where he stayed awake too late. He knew he needed to drink more than he wanted to drink. Who the fuck was he kidding?

He stopped at the light on Fifth and Main and did not realize the light had changed twice until cars behind him were honking in angry alliance. Jerking awake, he sped off, thinking he had been blasted by a street cleaner, not realizing until he wiped his face with the back of his hand that he, Joe Artuga, had been crying like a baby.

James dropped the phone into the receiver and sat back with a thud. He had just told an L.A. cop, of all people, that he missed his girlfriend. He selected a contracts law book from the cluttered tabletop, weighed it in his hand, making sure it was his heaviest one, and began beating his head against it just enough to knock the embarrassment away. "Stupid, stupid, stupid," James said out loud, echoing with each whack. He stopped a moment later. The shame subsided. He felt better now. He got up to make more coffee.

He opened the kitchen cabinet, populated with mismatched, stolen coffee cups, and selected one from Denny's. He poured beans from a jelly jar into a grinder (a gift to himself in his second week of law school, courtesy of an oversized backpack and a lonely housewares aisle at the local Sears). Stealing the grinder from under the nose of the dismissive clerk made James smile, which recurred every time he used the thing. James had been stealing since his third day in America, when the jeans his mother bought from a thrift shop got him beat up: they were girls' jeans. The horror was compounded by the fact he had liked the way they fit, had worn them proudly to his sixth-grade class. He later found out what his aggressor was wearing, and after school made a beeline for the army-navy store on Western. The stolen Levi's 501s bridged a culture gap not even English could conquer.

His mother questioned him when he brought home a new soccer ball for his brother, a pink satiny blouse for his mother he had seen her admire in the Sears window; she questioned him when he turned up with a new blender; his father chased him around the Formica kitchen table, whipping the air with his belt. But when he brought home the Zenith color television set with fourteen channels, no one asked questions. And no one chased him with a flying belt.

Why not steal, he thought, when his own life had been stolen from him?

James drank his coffee and settled on what to do about Amanda. The cop he had spoken to was an asshole, a game player. He knew the cops didn't have anything on her; she had never done drugs, not really. They had smoked a few joints on midnight trips to the desert, that was about it.

She was in trouble, the house had probably been under surveillance, but he knew she wouldn't be going to jail.

Strangely enough, James felt comfort in this crisis, because it occurred to him he alone could save Amanda. He hadn't been thinking of coming home for Thanksgiving, he really couldn't afford it. But he thought of this new girl, that she would lend him the money, she would do anything for him, and all of a sudden he felt happy, more happy than he had been since he drove out to Boston. He would surprise Amanda, go home for the holidays. Suddenly he was very grateful to Valentin, because Valentin the drug dealer had placed a need there that wasn't there before. Valentin had given James a chance to corner Amanda. She hadn't written him since October, and she hadn't returned his last phone call, and James was going to find out why.

Because, though he liked to steal, James didn't like to be stolen from.

James unwrapped the last letter he received from Amanda, folded up so many times (so he could carry it in his wallet) that the paper was falling apart, the ink fading in the folds. He read it again, for what could be the hundredth time. He felt great solace in the words of the girl who knew him when, and would know him always.

She had written about the travails of her work, the tragedies of her home life, but in a light, entertaining way. James knew she didn't want to bother him with being too heavy— Amanda complained constantly, but it was barely noticeable, for her complaints were covered in a fine veil of humor.

He read the last words she wrote, just above her name. "Love always," she wrote. "Love always," James repeated the words to himself. Because in those words lay a secret. In her first letters, Amanda had finished off by writing, "I love you." In this subtlest of changes everything James needed to know could be found.

Amanda paced the kitchen floor holding the baby, trying to collect her thoughts. She didn't know where to start—should she call Gabriel's father, should she try to contact her mother, should she track down Patrice's family? She didn't figure they could hold Gabriel; she prayed he didn't have anything on him. She started shaking her head. No, they couldn't have anything on him. The thought of being here alone, without him, would be too cruel.

Amanda called Gabriel's father first. He answered in the tone of someone who was halfway out the door, but couldn't mask his natural gentleness.

"Mr. . . . Williams?" Amanda had forgotten Gabriel's last name. She was losing her mind.

"Yes?"

Amanda wanted to hang up. She didn't want to be the one to break this man's heart, even a little bit.

"This is Amanda . . ." No response. "I'm a friend of Gabriel's."

"Yes. Oh, okay . . . yes."

"Uh, sir. I don't know how to tell you this." She hesitated.

"'S'ere something wrong with Gabriel?"

"No . . . um . . . Mr. Williams, your son, the police just picked him up."

The phone was silent.

"He wasn't doing anything, sir. I'm afraid it's my brother."

"Where they got him?"

Amanda blinked. Where do they have them?

"The Hollywood station." It must be the Hollywood station.

"All right, then." He was about to hang up. Amanda wished he would yell. She wished he would accuse her of something, blame her for this mess. She couldn't tell him about Gabe's head, about the nightstick.

"Mr. Williams?" Amanda's voice cracked.

"Yes?"

"I'm sorry. I'm really sorry." She started to sob. There was a moment.

" 'S okay, young lady. 'S okay . . ."

Amanda hung up the phone and kissed the top of her nephew's head and let her lips linger on the soft down of his hair, and tried to crawl into the moment and stay there.

But she had to call the Hollywood station. And she had to call James.

An officer told her they hadn't even arrived yet, and when they did arrive, it would be a couple of hours before she could even contact them, or they contact her. He wasn't rude, but he wasn't nice, either. Just tired.

Amanda rolled the phone over in her hand and looked at the kitchen clock. It was still shy of eight-thirty, but if she really hustled, she could make it to the office by nine. That is, if she didn't have a baby. Madison was asleep on her chest. She knew no one who could baby-sit. She would not be going to the office today.

She dialed the office. The phone rang nineteen times. Not a good sign. Joe answered. Really not a good sign.

"You're late."

And not a good start. Amanda held Madison closer. She did not want to lose this job—sure, it was shitty, but it was a start, a stepping-stone to something better. If she couldn't even hold down an entry-level job answering phones, well, who would hire her from here? Besides, there was still a stubborn, flickering hope that Amanda would come up with an idea for the show so brilliant, so dazzling, Danny Creepy Hands would immediately hire her at $2,500 a week (starting) as their new ear-to-the-ground, finger-on-the-pulse sketch writer.

Amanda sank back to her reality and saw her future flash in front of her eyes. It looked empty.

"I have a problem."

"I know. You're late."

"I . . . I can't come in."

"That's not an answer."

"I can't. I have a—"

"Look." Staccato. "I'm working here. Whatever it is, solve it and get your ass in here ASAP." He hung up; the dial tone drilled a hole in her head.

Amanda decided to call James from work and got ready as fast as anyone holding a sleeping baby could and hiked it down to the station, Madison still curled up in her arms. Joe took one look at her as he was scurrying across the hallway, from coffee to cigarettes, and lost his mind.

"What is that?"

"I tried to tell you—"

"Get in here." He gestured toward his office. "Get in here!" Amanda hurried in and sat down. Madison started to waken. He was grumpy. Amanda wondered if God had it in for her.

Joe's face was red. His cigarette spilled ashes on the disaster he called his desk. He gestured toward Madison as though the kid was a pee stain on an Oriental rug.

"What's the meaning of this?"

"I can still answer phones."

"Bullshit."

"I am so sorry about this. It's just for one day." First lie of the morning. Amanda didn't know how long it would be.

"Amanda." Joe strode around his desk, and sat back on it, almost landing on his ass as he slid off the side. The baby chose this moment to start crying. Joe recovered his bearings and cleared his throat.

"Amanda . . ." Now Madison was wailing. Amanda bounced him on her knee, rubbed his back. He promptly spit up, drops of digested milk hitting her mother's silk blouse. She pretended not to notice.

"You can't bring a . . . a . . . a kid in here!" Joe shifted. The baby was crying louder. Faces gathered in the doorway.

"I know, I know. You're right."

"I could fire you for this!" If Madison could have gotten any louder, he did. Joe wasn't sure Amanda even heard him, as she was now staring at the baby, reading his face.

"Oh boy." Amanda put her nose in Madison's diapers, then pulled it away quickly, as though she'd been smacked in the face. Joe closed his eyes.

"Joe, can we talk about this later?"

Joe's eyes were still closed and his cigarette burned to the quick as Amanda ran down the hallway, Madison in one hand, a twenty-pound diaper bag in the other. The phones were ringing off the hook.

"Parker!" Joe screamed for the new PA with the blond cowlick and chiseled jaw and Harvard MBA and threw his empty pack of Marlboros against the wall. He needed more cigarettes. And he wanted Mr. Harvard to get them.

"Parker!"

Amanda sat at the reception desk and mothering types of both genders in the production offices took turns holding Madison, playing with him, bouncing him on their knees, and throwing him in the air, until seven-thirty at night, when even the nutcases, settling down to their Swanson frozen dinners or taco combos, weren't calling anymore. Joe looked at her for the first time since that morning as she passed his doorway, the diaper bag dragging on the floor behind her, the baby asleep on her sagging shoulder. Walking down the hall, Amanda watched the door leading to the outside as if it were her only means of escape. She did not look in his office; Joe knew it was on purpose.

"Amanda."

Amanda stopped, backed up. She had almost made it.

"Yes, Joe?" She tried to sound subservient. But inside, she was screaming at him not to mess with her.

"Tomorrow?" he said. Pause. "No baby."

"Right." Amanda was glad there was a tomorrow.

"Absolutely."

Joe waved her off. She gave him a nod good-bye and was halfway out the door when she heard him grunt to himself: "Cute kid."

Amanda walked to her car and wondered who, if anyone, would be at home. The police would still not give out information, though she had called every hour on the hour, each time talking to a different officer in command. She also called Gabriel's father half a dozen times, each time hanging up on the machine with the stilted message. She was too shy to leave her name, too ashamed. She knew Valentin would be able to bail himself out, and maybe Patrice, depending on the charges. But she could not bear the thought of Gabriel being in jail because he was at the wrong place (her house) at the wrong time (early morning).

As she drove home, she realized she had never called James back; she wished she had another place to go.

Joe sat in his office until it was dark, chewing ferociously on an old stick of peppermint gum he had found in his drawer from the last time he quit smoking, two, three years ago. Here he was, a guy famous for firing people for the tiniest infraction—a FedEx package arriving an hour late, a cup of weak coffee on a bad day, answering the phones after four rings, not three—and this chick walks in *late*, with a *baby* of all things, and turns the place upside down, and what does he do?

Nothing. What was happening to him?

He shook his head, ran his fingers through his hair again, assessed his rakish figure in a coffee spoon. The memory of last night's follies with the girl with the gilded chest had evaporated from his bachelor's mind sufficiently enough. Joe draped his suede jacket over his shoulder and cornered a couple of the postproduction boys with pale skin and underdeveloped chests and an outsider's sense of fun into sharing mai tais and warm beer and greasy short ribs with him at the Formosa. Who knew? Maybe he'd get lucky again.

Gabe's dad wouldn't look at him on the way home. And he didn't say a word. But as they pulled into their driveway in front of the ashen house, just as Gabe was opening his door, his father spoke, low and sober.

"I never told you what to do, have I?" Gabe looked at his father, smaller now than normal, in his old sport coat, cleaned so many times it had a kind of shine to it, and the hat. The hat reminded him of old pictures of Sammy Davis Jr. His father was staring through the windshield, seeing nothing.

Gabe looked ahead, his hand on the door handle. He squeezed it. "No."

"I'm telling you this. Stay away from this, son." Gabe's father looked at him, and in his eyes was something Gabe had never seen there before: fear.

"Stay away from this."

The words echoed in Gabe's mind as he showered. They echoed in his mind as he dressed, as he took a tug on a leftover roach, as he passed his father's bedroom, where the television set threw shadows on the wall. And as he got on his bike and sped toward the hills, where he knew Amanda would be waiting.

Amanda opened the door, put her fingers to her lips. Valentin had posted bail, was already asleep in his room. The house was dark again. Amanda had moved the baby's pen to her room.

Gabriel took Amanda's hand in his and put her fingers in his mouth and licked her palm slowly, and they did not make it into her room before their clothes were off; they did not make it inside the house before he had come inside her with a force that scared him because it took all of his strength, before he had ground the words "I love you" into her neck, her head stretched back against the pavement, eyes clenched shut against the night sky.

They did not notice Valentin as he crouched inside the foyer, absorbing the silhouette of two bodies huddled against the rays of the street lamp, his green eyes squinting, then widening in understanding, then narrowing in rage. His nails scratched tiny specks of blood from the palm of his hand even as Gabriel covered

Amanda's mouth gently with his own to muffle her cries.

Valentin stood up slowly, noiselessly as the bodies then lay still, their breath in the chilly night air the only sign of life.

He loped, faltering, to his room, arms outstretched to keep him from falling, dizzy, anger bitter in his mouth. He had forgotten the glass of water he had risen for. His mouth was dry; he couldn't speak to save his life, but he dropped to his bed and tried to bleed the pictures from his brain, and when the pictures would not fade, he pummeled his body with his thin hand until he no longer felt desire, and then he went back to sleep. He would deal with this in the morning.

Amanda lay on Gabriel's chest and brushed the small patch of curly hair nestled between his rounded muscles with her fingertips and tried to think of a time when she felt more alive. She really tried, because she thought it was sad that fucking on her front steps was the highlight of her short life.

He was staring at the sky, as they were still on the front steps, cold concrete at their backs.

Amanda rolled on top of him and put her face in his, demanding attention.

"I love you."

"I know."

"No. I really love you."

"I know, girl."

"Oh. I see. You know." Amanda smiled. "How do you know I'm not just some incredibly needy chick?"

Gabriel's lips curled up slightly at the sides. He put a large hand on the left side of her chest and held it there, and looked straight into her eyes and through to her very soul. And Amanda held his gaze but had to remind herself to keep breathing.

"I know. I know what's in there."

Amanda curled up on top of her man, and there she lay like a newborn until they were wakened by Gabriel's inner time clock, and prickly cries of a baby boy.

James lay on his back on the dark-haired girl's downy bed, awakened by a burning sensation in his gut. His hand clenched his stomach, careful not to wake the girl who was sleeping soundly beside him. He knew what the sensation meant.

He was angry. Amanda was fucking someone else; he knew it. He had woken up in a veil of sweat, suddenly sure in the knowledge. Amanda had found someone else.

One time, James had been this angry. So angry. James bit his lip. He did not like to think about this.

It was in high school. James was bad; he had the place wired. Not only did he have the top grades in his class, he was an athlete, the center on the championship varsity basketball team.

His AP history teacher, a guy with a beard and a conscience from the sixties, found out he was stealing from the Student Council coffers. James was the treasurer. James, the thief with the impeccable credentials, kept the books. So what if he took a little? Big deal. Twenty here, ten there. His best friend, white boy Conrad, was doing it as well. Maybe they had taken, at most, five, five-fifty. They had been good at covering their tracks. For a long time.

The guy wouldn't let it sit. He wouldn't let go. He wanted the school to press charges. He wanted the school to drop James as a valedictorian candidate; he wanted the basketball team to drop him. James had no choice. His mother, the ex–beauty queen who was now cleaning rich white people's hilltop houses, would die if she found out. The dishonor would kill her.

James did what he had to do. He was up against a wall, anyone could see that.

James tracked the teacher for two weeks. Found out from the chubby office administrator with the cute, big ass where he lived, followed him when he ate dinner at a cheap Chinese restaurant with his mousy wife every Tuesday and Saturday (of course these two had no children; why would they sleep together?), where he jogged in his red high school shorts and knee-high sweat socks every other morning before dawn.

And one morning, he just ran him over.

The teacher had turned to cross the street at a lonely residential stretch. Few people were up at this hour. James saw his eyes, saw the stunned look of recognition and the flash of disbelief before the car spun him around with a vengeance and his head hit the pavement.

No one saw it.

The school held a memorial service, and James skipped basketball practice and went to pay his respects, dressed in a suit he had lifted the day after the horrible accident from

JCPenney. Walking past the mousy wife, her face red and puffy and even more unattractive, he was shocked to see, in her arms, a tiny baby.

Throughout his young life, James had managed to hide the depth of his anger from those closest to him: Amanda, his mother, even, sometimes, himself. He had a gift, a knack for convincing himself that his punitive actions were not his fault—that if only people would treat him right, with due respect, he wouldn't have to punish them. He took great strides to hide his dark side—he covered his tracks whenever he stole or broke or, even, just this once, was forced to kill. Sometimes he slipped up; Amanda had seen him put his fist through his windshield once after a stupid argument, then seemed to notice every little crack in the glass afterward.

But the people who loved him would never understand; they didn't live in the place James did. He had to protect them.

He tried not to get so angry anymore. Sometimes it was hard. He hoped he was wrong about Amanda.

Eight

Danny Markus, Minnesota's immovable-coiffed, bonded-toothed, sociopathic late-night response to Johnny Carson, was in a good mood. It was going to be a long night.

When Danny was in a good mood, it meant one thing. Anyone on the production team who preferred to keep their job would be working well past the dinner hour, well past aperitifs, well past tucking the little ones into bed. Danny needed stroking and false camaraderie from the very people he'd fail to recognize if he ran over them in his 1950s starlet-lipstick red Ferrari Testarossa.

Amanda wanted to keep her job. Thus, tonight's gaieties posed several wretched yet compelling quandaries. Number one, Amanda had a baby. Number two, she could not take the baby to work. Which meant she could not take Madison with her to Danny's house. Number three, she could not leave Madison at home, alone with his father. Valentin was acting strangely; yes, okay, Amanda knew Valentin was a strange number to begin with, but the rub was, now he was quiet. Quiet was something different altogether. Val, ever since he was a child, would move through a room with the subtlety of a train wreck; women would fall at his long, lissome feet; men would gather like flies at a dog park; even very small children, their vocabulary limited to grunts and squeaks, would follow this bold, agile figure with the mop of dark hair with their new eyes. Amanda, his little sister, was content just to be in the same room as her brother, the star. "Quiet" was not an adjective one used to describe Valentin.

That morning, when Amanda shook him to ask about leaving the baby with the older woman next door, the one with the painted face and unlisted phone number, he did not yell at her for waking him up. He just looked at her, through eyes puffy from fatigue (Valentin's long, nocturnal work hours were harsh on the human body, and as yet there was no dealers' union to report to), and gave her the slightest nod. Amanda could no longer read her brother's eyes.

She thought about a game they used to play in childhood. Amanda would sit across from her brother, real close, almost face-to-face. "C'mon, squirt. Guess what I'm thinking." He'd laugh. And she would stare into his eyes for the longest time, until she was almost lost. And then she would see it. "You're thinking about marshmallows," she'd say, or, "You're thinking about playing with Scruff," his favorite dog, a pug with a bad case of asthma.

Whatever Amanda guessed, she was always right. Valentin would act amazed at her mindreading abilities, her sixth sense. It was only later that Amanda realized he was just playing along. He was just being kind.

And now Amanda looked into her brother's eyes and saw they were vacant, no longer asking or telling anything. Without his usual judgments. But also without warmth. It's not that he shrank from her touch. No caustic remarks sprang from his barbed tongue. In his silence, Amanda could feel his thoughts careening through his mind, bumping against one another, confusing his already chemically challenged brain. He did not want to speak them yet, these thoughts. But Amanda was quite sure, when he was ready, she would bear the brunt of what he had to say. He was measuring her, and himself. He was taking stock. Amanda had the horrible suspicion that once he said what was on his mind, what was the root of this silence, their life together would be over.

Amanda closed his door behind her, then pressed her ear against it. It was eerie, standing there, listening to her brother's labored, unsure breathing. She was so used to doing the same with his infant son.

Patrice was not coming home. She was going to do time. Her bail had not been set, but her first court hearing was next week. There had been two grams of coke in her purse. Amanda knew Patrice had other sources. Some "producer" she fucked who pumped her up with drugs and promises of big money, posing for vagina magazines. Probably her other dealer-lover, a ponytailed, strapping blond who had been a national skateboard champion and who was known for his sexual forays into the dark side. He was young, in his late twenties, and he liked kinky sex with both boys and girls, as long as they were young as well, and lost. Preferably runaways. Rumor had it a male prostitute barely out of his baby-fat years died during a Memorial Day weekend session. After several days of sleeplessness and ingesting fistfuls of multicolored pharmaceuticals, the boy hanged himself (ironically employing a third-level Boy Scout knot) with a pair of very expensive French nylons that belonged to Mr. Ponytail. It was supposedly a joke gone awry. Mr. Ponytail was quite upset, understandably. The black nylons could only be found on the rue de Flaubert during the fall season, at more than eighty francs a pop, not counting shipping and handling.

Amanda remembered how Patrice defended Mr. Ponytail to Valentin. Valentin replied by shoving her against the kitchen sink and calling her a slut; Patrice then grabbed a dull kitchen knife that could not be trusted to cut a banana and threatened his vitals with it. An average Saturday night. And yet, Valentin was missing her.

Amanda made arrangements with Mrs. Selby, her next-door neighbor who had once baby-sat for Amanda herself, to baby-sit Madison all day, and into the night, if need be. She had even taken her lunch hour, an unheard-of concept in television production, to drive across Hollywood and back, twenty-six minutes there, thirty-four minutes back (fender bender on Franklin), to check on the baby because she trusted her eyes better than her ears. Mrs. Selby was losing her hearing, though she stubbornly refused to wear a hearing aid; Mrs. Selby, a pin-curled starlet under contract with Harry Warner himself in the forties, had rigorously withstood the perils of the passing years. Or so she thought. Her eyesight was not much better than her hearing, and unfortunately, starlets also did not wear eyeglasses.

And so Mrs. Sheldon Selby seldom answered the phone, but could hear the doorbell thanks to her miniature wirehaired dachshund, Harry Jr., whom she had named after her mentor—and, Amanda thought, incidentally, one and only love. Harry Jr. worshiped Mrs. Selby, having slept with her for the full fifteen years of his life (five more than Mr. Selby himself, who lasted only until Mrs. Selby kicked him out of her chest-high four-poster bed, laden with down pillows and short, wiry hairs). She was sick to death, the old woman had said, of the demands he made on her time and her body.

Now Mr. Selby conveniently lived at the Motion Picture and Television Home in the hot, smoggy Valley. He seemed to be a very quiet, docile man when Amanda met him as a child. She remembered him being frail and jumpy. As an adult she understood why.

Amanda got to spend exactly three minutes with Madison on her lunch break. She checked on Valentin, too. She had left him a note to tell him again where she had taken Madison, hoping he would leave the baby be. With all her quirks, Amanda trusted Mrs. Selby, having been baby-sat by her when the earth was new and videotapes were unheard of and VJs were, mercifully, not yet born. Besides, she'd left Madison fat and happy in a playpen, filled with new toys, bottles, his small, fat hand stuffed with processed cheese. She'd even left a couple of her favorite books in there—*Charlie and the Chocolate Factory* and an old paperback of Truman Capote's *In Cold Blood*, perfect reading material for a tyke who would not be able to read for years to come.

Amanda knew Mrs. Selby would not leave Madison's side; she loved babies, though she had never borne any herself. The old woman had not wanted the figure of her youth ruined, and so she was left to help raise other people's children.

Amanda left Mrs. Selby's house and walked to her car, breathing a sigh of temporary relief. Emphasis on "temporary." As her key went into the door of her pathetic, rusting hulk, Amanda witnessed a trio of Valentin's customers tumbling over one another out of an avocado green Rolls-Royce with a beige, cigarette-burn-modified leather interior. Amanda caught the initials *BIA* on the side door panel. These people were not shy. The driver was good looking in a swarthy, untrustworthy, movie-pirate kind of way. He was short, though, a problem his over-sized purple lizard cowboy boots only accented. Amanda wondered briefly if there were such things as purple lizards. The girls, however, were another story. One blond, one brunette, each with hair inching toward the sky as if in a race, their bosoms abnormally rounded and large and severe, placed on their chests as if in military fashion. They wore matching shiny spandex jumpsuits (in different colors, however, to mark their individual spirits). The blond wore blue, probably the color of her eyes, unless those too were phony. Colored contacts were the newest trend. Her eyes were hidden, though, from the sun and cash-strapped suitors with oversized white reflective-lensed sunglasses. The brunette wore a red jumpsuit, and Amanda noticed she was showing more cleavage than the blond, the zipper playing footsie with her navel.

She forgot where she was for a second until she saw the door to her house open, and Valentin standing in his boxer shorts, skinny legs bared to the world. Valentin had lost his sense of vanity. He hated his knees. Amanda knew this as a child and made fun of them—"Girly legs! Girly legs!"—until Valentin sat on her ten-year-old chest and ground those very knees into her collarbone, causing excruciating pain.

Valentin was making a sale, a big sale. Everyone knew the Iranian crowd had a lot of money and the young ones spent a lot of their cash on drugs. "What the fuck is my stupid, bony-kneed brother doing?" Amanda wondered aloud.

She ran across the street and into her house. Valentin was sitting, his body bent over the kitchen table. Wriggling in his lap, giggling nervously, sat the blond chick. Valentin, intent on his work, paid no attention to her. The Iranian dude's head was on the table, and Amanda, as she came closer, saw he was busily snorting up a line. His head came up, his cockeyed mustache flecked with powder. He noticed Amanda and smiled broadly and would have probably stood up had he not had the heavier of the two girls on his lap. Amanda wondered if there was a sudden lack of chairs in her house.

"Hallo!"

Valentin turned, his head first, his eyes after. He never took them off his stash.

"Hallo!" The man repeated again, still grinning from ear to ear. This man had the face of someone with too few responsibilities and a miserable future. So far, neither Valentin nor the girls had said anything. Valentin's eyes were back on the table as soon as they had flicked onto her. The girls just stared at her, having already assessed that this stranger posed no sexual threat. Amanda smiled back at the man. He was a fool, but a kind fool.

"Val, can I talk to you?" Amanda managed to say without displaying all of her disgust.

"G'head."

"It's . . . it's sort of private."

"I'm working."

Amanda stood closer to Valentin, behind him. He did not look up, but she could see his shoulders tighten.

"Do you think this is wise?" She struggled to remain calm. She kept her hands tightly at her side, working against her instinct to strangle him in front of three strangers.

"Vallee? Is zere a problem?"

The girls giggled at this and looked at each other.

"Let me try it, Bijan!"

"Can I try it?"

"Girls, girls. You try later. In my room."

This sent their lacquered mouths into full pout. Bijan batted his eyes at them.

"I give you a little now. Valleee?"

Valentin was almost finished packing the coke into tiny plastic bags that looked like something Barbie would pack a low-fat tuna sandwich in for a picnic with Ken. Valentin scowled but drew a slim line for the blond. Then the brunette. "So true," Amanda thought. People never looked so unappealing as when they stuck something up their noses.

Bijan suddenly clapped twice, a move Amanda had only seen done once before, by Yul Brynner, and for Christ's sake, that was art. The girls giggled and looked at each other and wiped their noses and licked their lips and Bijan grabbed his bag and rose, placing a rolled-up wad of bills in Valentin's grasping hand before he left, one arm around each supervixen.

Valentin packed up his paraphernalia and passed Amanda, and did not look at her as he slammed shut his bedroom door. Amanda followed, yelling, the closed door giving her courage an open door would kill. She was afraid of Valentin. It was as though the rational part of his mind was slipping away—her brother wasn't stupid; he must know that it was only a matter of time before he got caught, put in jail to do real time, or before someone got hurt, or worse. Amanda was chilled to think Valentin had a death wish.

"You can't do this, Val!"

Valentin turned on his stereo, turned up the bass.

"I know you can hear me! Your girlfriend's in jail! You can't do this anymore!" She tried again.

"Valentin!"

The only reply came from Iron Maiden, the lead singer scream-singing something about Satan and true love. Valentin was probably losing himself in a box of Lucky Charms, Patrice's last purchase.

Amanda had to get back to work.

She drove toward the station as though her piece-of-shit Ford Falcon were a Porsche Carrera and the dingy streets of east Hollywood were a racetrack in Monaco; she knew she was pushing her luck. She tossed off her priorities in her head as she rounded a grimy street corner onto even grimier Vermont Avenue. "Let's see," she thought. "There's baby; that's one through twenty. There's job; that should be near the top . . ." Despite herself, Amanda still coveted a bright future to bury her tarnished past and, incidentally, wanted to buy groceries from time to time.

And then Gabriel's copper skin and almond eyes popped into her brain, and here, suddenly, was her new priority. This surprised her, although it probably shouldn't have—after all, she was in love with Gabriel. He was her boyfriend now. Amanda got giddy for a second. Her *boyfriend*—how incredibly corny.

Three priorities. Something was going to have to give, and she sorely didn't want it to be her central nervous system. Suddenly she remembered something, a last priority, which felt more and more like an obligation: James was that something.

Amanda arrived back at the office and moved toward her desk quietly, avoiding eye contact and sharp furniture corners, quickly thanked the new intern with the short skirt and snotty attitude, and stuck the phone in her ear. Moments later, she felt the hands with the short, stubby fingers kneading her diamond-hard shoulders and realized that Danny was in a good mood, and that's when she felt like crying.

Run-D.M.C. lay down booming tracks on his box as Gabriel lifted a barbell, 105 pounds of weight at either side. He was lying on his back on an incline bench his father bought him years ago, when his body had potential. The black, fake leather was frayed at the edges now, and the metal was rusted where the dog with the cropped ears and tail peed on it as a puppy. Gabriel had wiped the thing clean more times than he cared to remember, but still the animal had made its mark. Gabriel had never disciplined his dog, though. Had never raised a voice to it, never swatted it with a newspaper or an open or closed hand. As a result, the dog loved everything and everyone who came near it, always expecting what he had been raised with: kind words, a belly rub with a firm hand, a piece of chicken tossed from his hungry owner's plate. Gabriel's father said he was too soft with the dog. Gabriel thought he was probably right. Now he couldn't get the damn thing to do anything but lick his face and wag his tailless ass when he came in the door at four-thirty in the morning. He could count the number of times the dog had barked on one hand.

Run finished off their raw "It's Like That" as Gabriel gave the bar a shove, pushing it up in four counts, lowering it in six, holding it to his chest, then up again and into the rack that held it above his face, the face with the purple gash across the forehead, beads of sweat lingering around the wound; a crowd gathering around a burning house. Gabriel slid from underneath the bar and sat up and stared at the phone.

He had pulled it in here from across the hall, so as not to miss the call. He was becoming a goddamned girl. Did she forget she was supposed to call him? Maybe last night was a dream. Gabriel checked his crotch to make sure he still had a dick, then lay back with a resounding thud and proceeded to bench-press 210 fucking pounds twelve times in a row without stopping until he was sure he was having a heart attack. The girl had gotten the best of the big man, Gabriel thought. "She got me," he said to the wagging dog, happy for a brief round of attention.

Gabriel had started thinking about the future. Sometimes it presented itself in the form of an unread book, of which there were many in his life. He hadn't been much of a reader since the sixth grade. There was a time before then, a short time bright as the flash of a camera, when Gabe sat in a crowded classroom filled with hyperactive, mismatched kids and cleared his scratchy throat and read the first paragraph of *The Indian in the Cupboard*. His teacher, with the cat eyeglasses and the pillowy body stuffed into her flower print dress, thanked him with her cheery, lilting voice and told him he, Gabriel Williams, was a very, very good reader. Gabe's young chest swelled with pride, but he held back his toothy smile, protective of his already-tough rep.

Gabe had run home from school to tell his mother the news, and was met with an empty vodka bottle and a note telling his father she had left him. For good this time. Young Gabe had been a witness to her comings and goings in the last two years; he was aware that she was not as focused, as sharp as she had been; he was aware of her increasing interest in alcohol, her decreasing interest in the young son she had loved so well.

He was accustomed to his father telling him not to worry, that his mother was visiting a sick aunt or that she had taken a week off, suddenly, for a vacation. But Gabe had heard their harsh words, flung at each other in the night without a thought of their love, his mother's voice increasingly slurred.

She had never left a note.

Gabe looked at his mother's letter and memorized the words in an instant. "Frankie," she wrote in her nervous hand; Gabe remembered the crooked letters, the way they careened off the side of the page, illustrating the swiftness of her decision. "Frankie, I can't take this sort of life anymore. I am tired, so tired. Please take care of my baby. Please tell him not to hate his mama."

If there was more, and Gabe was sure there was, he couldn't recall. By the time he read the first lines, he was through with the letter, through with his mother, through with the female species in general.

He had tried to hide the note from his dad. He tore up the letter and threw it in the wastebasket, and said nothing when his father came home to an empty bed and his only son.

But now, in secret, Gabriel had picked up a book from his father's musty room, where the old man had them stacked in rows of ten and twenty, each row dustier than the next. He could tell which stack was newest by running his finger along the side like a piano player running down the keys of an unused instrument. Gabriel looked quickly through the titles; he didn't feel right going through the old man's things. He found one, a hardcover biography of a great horn player named Miles Davis, tucked it under his massive arm, and stole down the hallway into his own bedroom, locking the door behind him.

He had selected this book for three reasons.

One, he could see Miles Davis was a black man (looked like a crow, though, Gabriel thought, with his sharp nose and hooded eyes; he didn't look like no brother Gabe had ever seen), and two, he wanted to know what important thing this black man had done to warrant a whole goddamned, heavy-assed book. Three, the man played the horn.

Gabriel's father had been a saxophonist of some note in 1950s Chicago; Gabriel had even read his name on the liner notes on a yellowing stack of albums his mother said she would give him one day. His father hardly ever spoke of those times, and when he did, his sentences were short and without color. When Gabe would ask him, "Pops, tell me a story about the circuit—I know you gotta have a story," his father would say, "It's all just dust to me now, Gabe. My old stories are just that—old."

Gabriel was hungry, suddenly, to know more; this could be, Gabriel believed, like reading his father's unwritten diary; it could be like living his father's unrealized dreams.

Amanda felt Danny's spearmint-scented breath on her neck. "We're having a brainstorming

meeting tonight. Like your input, Mandy."
Amanda wondered who Mandy was. Nobody had
ever called her Mandy in her life, not even when
Barry Manilow sang the song of the same name
that caused seventh-graders in the throes of
exhausting, all-consuming puppy love to swoon
in sympathy with the singer; not even then.

"I'd like your input, Mandy," he repeated himself. This was significant. Had the cement-
headed Danny actually noticed the sly witticisms
she tossed out at the staff as she handed them
their precious pink "While You Were Out"
notes—her tasty little bons mots . . . ? "Oh wake
up!" Amanda practically screamed at herself.
"You'll be the sap taking coffee orders and cleaning up the writers' snot-and-cocaine-filled tissues
afterward!"

"Gee, thanks, Danny. I'll be there." Amanda
smiled up sweetly at him, a grand view of his
nostrils and his shiny, pill-like, nefariously white
teeth violating her eye line.

"Bring your thoughts, Mandy!"

"I will!"

Four long hours later, Amanda was sitting in
Danny's California ranch-style living room with
four other staff members—the intern with the

short skirt and, as Amanda could have guessed without a gun to her head, white Rabbit convertible; Danny's pimp and otherwise production assistant, the nervous, hirsute Bergin; two middle-aged writers who should have been at home with their wives and children and dogs and cheap corduroy-covered overstuffed chairs, but instead were here, too frightened to turn Danny down. Besides, maybe they could get into the intern's skirt as well.

"Not likely," Amanda thought to herself.

Joe Artuga looked at her. "You say something?" Amanda cringed and shook her head. She hadn't meant to say anything out loud. What if she became one of those little old ladies, bent over their shopping carts like life-sized question marks, babbling their memories and their anger out loud as they crossed busy streets without caring to look up? "Hmm," Amanda thought, "now there's something to look forward to."

Amanda half smiled. "I don't think I said something."

"How can you be high? We haven't smoked this puppy yet." That was Bergin. He was rolling a fat joint in a contraption Amanda hadn't seen since fifth grade (things being so upside down in

L.A., Amanda smoked a joint long before trying a cigarette). Bergin was a strange and foul combination of anxiety and arrogance. Amanda had seen him more than once rush out of Danny's corner office, giant beads of sweat rolling down the side of his face, wiped away with a shaking hand as he ran past her to his cubbyhole, where he'd cry quietly into the coffee cup his mother had sent him as part of a congratulations gift basket for becoming a producer on Danny's show. But Amanda had also seen him driving Danny's second car, a black turbo Porsche Carrera with tan interior and a six-thousand-dollar stereo, careening past her down side streets, wearing Danny's three-hundred-dollar sunglasses and a mean grin. All he was doing was driving to the Valley to get the car washed and gassed up, but they meant a lot to him, those sad little pilgrimages. "Pathetic" didn't begin to describe it.

Danny strode meaningfully into the living room; Amanda thought he should be comfortable in his black cashmere robe and slippers and carefully mussed hair. But from the bent look on his face, he wasn't. He had just finished what seemed like one of his more successful outings—the live audience had enjoyed his skits. They laughed at his jokes. They endured a song that was old when it was written. But still he was not happy.

"Bergin."

"Yes, Danny?" Bergin replied, his voice twitching.

"Isn't that ready yet?"

Amanda noticed Joe had picked up a *McCall's* magazine and was seemingly immersed in it. Bergin handed Danny the joint and lit it for him, willing his hand, the one that wanted to throw the match into his talk-show-host face, steady. Danny puffed for a second, then took in more, and finally smiled.

"That . . . is good shit." He said it as if someone had a clamp on his chest, gripping his breath. Amanda smiled to herself, thinking how ridiculous these words sounded coming from a guy who used the same hair spray as Pat Boone.

Danny handed the joint to the intern. Amanda dropped her inner smile. She tried not to hold the girl's material possessions—her car, her clothes, her daddy's credit cards—against her, but she was losing the battle. Watching the girl take the joint between her shell pink lips, Amanda wanted to strangle her. The girl puffed once and started to cough. Danny slapped her on the back. The girl tried desperately to stop coughing, all the while thanking Danny for his heroic measures. The writers were busy wasting away the joint, watching this spectacle and ruing their own cowardly lives, and then it was Joe's turn, but he, without looking up from an article on planting spring bulbs early, just handed it to Amanda. Amanda hesitated, then put it to her mouth. Enter, stage left, Danny's wife. Amanda reminded herself of her favorite law, "Just when you think things can't get worse, they do."

Tracy Markus was not beautiful. She was, in a land of faux celebrity, however, very talented, and vivacious, and genuinely nice. But definitely not beautiful. Her blond hair was the right color; her eyes, blue, were also correct, though a shade gray. Her height was good, her weight was fine. But her bones were big, and her jawline a bit too strong, too masculine. She was attractive—the most appealing girl, perhaps, in a small Minnesota town, but merely one of the masses in Los Angeles. (Alas, oversized bone structure is the one thing that even the best Beverly Hills plastic surgeon couldn't tackle.)

She was carrying a tray of coffee cups and a

silver coffeepot, her arms straining under the weight but her smile resolute. Amanda quickly put the joint out, licking her fingers and applying them to the burning end. It hurt, but it was a fine trick she learned between geometry and home ec class in junior high.

"Would anyone like some coffee?"

Danny looked up at his actress/singer/soap opera star/housewife. Amanda recognized his slack, eyes-glazed-over expression; he was not high—it was the one he used on guests who bored him. Amanda then noticed the intern. Her posture had changed, her legs were drawn inward. She would not look up. Amanda realized the girl could not meet Tracy's eyes.

"Oh," Amanda thought, truly to herself this time, "they've already slept together." Amanda looked at Joe, who was also taking in the unsaid information. He hopped up, greeting Danny's better half.

"Just what I need, Trace."

"Great." Her reply was light, but it could not cover her deep gratitude.

"I'm dying for some coffee." Amanda popped up and took a cup from the tray. Tracy poured the coffee, her hands trembling the slightest bit.

Amanda noticed the tiny red lines crisscrossing the sides of her eyes. She noticed Tracy had recently powdered her nose, saw the puffiness under her eyes. Tracy looked up at her and smiled. Amanda wanted to cry.

"Amanda. I answer the phones."

"Tracy."

"Thank you."

Amanda took her coffee and sat back down on the couch and pretended to drink, though it was too weak, while the writers conferred with Danny and Bergin on that night's performance. The intern sat frozen in her seat, unable to look at anything except the Italian leather shoes that graced her small-boned feet. Joe sat back with his coffee, watching them. Tracy had already walked out of the room as quietly as she had come.

Amanda wondered how often Tracy Markus cried. Out of the corner of her eye, she saw Danny slip a comforting hand on the intern's knee.

Nine

Amanda was thinking about luck. Here she was, being eaten by an eight-thousand-dollar, over-stuffed, excruciatingly uncomfortable peach and green Southwestern sofa (something one would never find in the Southwest) in the playroom of a home a smidge south of $2 million in a rarefied area of the L.A. basin known as the Palisades. The Pacific Palisades, where soft ocean breezes mingled with the smell of new Mercedeses and suntan oil and brand-new tennis balls, where the wealthy built gates of wood and brick and steel reaching for the gods to keep out the riffraff, who then worked in their homes and raised their children.

The people who lived in this house, the Markuses—Danny, Tracy, and their two tow-

headed, overweight, sullen, and generally un-
pleasant children, Christian, twelve, and Bailey,
ten—were very, very lucky. When Amanda went
to the bathroom (sorry, powder room) an hour
into their jam session, tired of discussing skits
and character franchises and the benefits of
inviting lissome, ambisexual, androgynous rock
stars on the show, she sat on a padded pastel
pink toilet; it made a hissing sound when she sat
down, and so she did this several times. The toilet paper was peach in tone, plush, and quilted,
each square a Barbie doll's comforter. The walls
were covered in a shiny ivory fabric. Amanda
touched them, drawn to them like an heiress to
love—she could not help it—and found the walls
were padded as well. Amanda laughed as she
poked at them, taking her time. She was in no
hurry to get back to the meeting. Amanda loved
to write, to come up with ideas, to make people
laugh. But she was not good stating her ideas in
front of others. She could put paper in a typewriter and tap a witty missive about the misuse
of the coffee creamer in the office kitchen. The
staff looked forward to her sarcastic memos
about parking spaces (IS YOUR NAME DANNY
MARKUS? THEN YOU CAN PARK IN DANNY MARKUS'S

SPOT. THANK YOU), empty cartons of milk, and the suspicious and perpetual lack of paper towels. There was also a memo Amanda had sent off about the Mesozoic-era toaster that no one dared use, afraid as they were of the petrified crumbs hiding in its depths. It turned out that this was the one that had caught Danny's eye, that had brought about her first serious invitation into these late-night brainstorming sessions—in which she would be a small step above an indentured servant. An idea of Amanda's had already been used in the show, though she was not sure he was aware of its origins. It was a skit about a retirement home for bitter comedians. Amanda didn't have to walk far for material.

Her joke had, as they say, brought down the house. Amanda's name was on the small plastic placard with adhesive on the back that was stuck on her chair: *Amanda McHenry, Receptionist*. It was nowhere near the end credits of *The Danny Marcus Show* under "writer" or even "production assistant." Amanda was too excited and flattered to care. All she knew was that Danny had said her words on national television. It was enough to push her to keep writing. Credit, Amanda thought, would come later.

Amanda splashed cold water on her face from the gold-plated faucet in the pink and white marbled sink. She checked her teeth in the mirror. After a few minutes of this, Amanda realized she was a little high, if only from second-hand fumes. She enjoyed the feeling. She wanted to leave. She wanted to get out of here and find Gabriel. If she was going to find him, she needed more coffee. Coffee was imperative. And she needed to make a couple of phone calls. She hadn't checked on Madison, safely ensconced in the nutty Selby household, in several hours.

In the hopes of finding a private line and caffeine, Amanda hurried into the kitchen. Tracy must have gone to bed. The tray of coffee cups sat unwanted on the counter next to the coffeemaker with the Belgian name. Amanda had never seen a coffeemaker so technical—it looked like a pacemaker attachment. As she dialed Mrs. S. on the wall phone, she stared at that coffeemaker for a moment, deciphering the buttons. Did she want her coffee for one or two people, or four? Did she prefer it strong, medium, or weak, perhaps for a sensitive stomach or a late night? Did she want to wake up to a freshly made brew? Amanda wondered if it doubled as an oddly shaped vibrator. She thought of Gabriel, working tonight. He was her kind of oddly shaped vibrator, thank you very much.

Mrs. S. was not answering. Amanda could have guessed that much. She hung up the phone. Should she call Gabriel? Have him meet her? She closed her eyes and pictured his face, and felt her stomach drop. How could she need to see him this much?

Amanda heard a noise behind her and turned too suddenly. She chastened herself silently. She had made herself look guilty. Yes, it was Danny. Amanda smiled, then got mad at herself for smiling. "Dope," she said to herself, "if you smile, you won't be taken seriously."

"That's one hell of a coffeemaker," she said. "Does it do laundry?"

"Better than you would think."

Danny opened the refrigerator. Amanda glanced to the side, surreptitiously. There was no one else behind him.

"You hungry?"

"Ah, no." Actually, she was well into starving mode. And looking at a rich person's refrigerator, full of foreign-sounding food in tiny jars that belonged in dollhouse iceboxes, did not help. Suddenly she wanted to throw Danny aside like so much dirt and shove her face into a jar of anchovy paste, down a bottle of raspberry-fennel vinegar in a thirty-dollar bottle. "Thank you, marijuana," she thought ruefully. Amanda often thought she'd be one of the few fat junkies if she really got into drugs. Everything seemed to amplify her appetite. Drugs, alcohol, depression, a warm sunrise, a soft pillow, a cat, turtles, a harsh word aimed at the fleshy part of her thighs, a compliment aimed at the same spot. Everything.

"Have fun tonight?"

"Sure." Beat. "I find these sessions really"—*find the right word; avoid sarcasm at all costs*—"valuable." Well, she did find them valuable, in that she had fun after the meetings, not during—when she was alone, in her pajamas, with her notepad. And Doritos. Amanda saw Doritos in Danny's open refrigerator. In a refrigerator. Was this something new?

"Amanda. You have so much potential." Danny turned toward her. He had just pulled out a plate full of something that looked close enough to fried chicken that Amanda would actually kill to get to it. Danny was in danger, grave danger, and he didn't even know it. Amanda snapped out of her bloodthirsty reverie. The man had just told her something. Something incredible. A compliment.

"Thank you. It means a lot to me to hear you say that." Amanda's heart lifted. It felt, for this single moment, that everything was going to be fine, just fine.

"If only . . ."

"Yes?" Amanda's heart skipped a beat, and she suddenly knew what the term meant. She knew what Danny was going to say, knew why he chose this moment to be alone in the kitchen with her, instead of on a hard, ridiculously expensive, not to mention ugly, couch with the pretentious yet hacky writing team, the willowy, wealthy, pouty intern. He was going to finally say the three words she had been waiting for him to say: "You are a writer." Okay, four words. And then he would say, "We happen to have a spot open on our team for a young female writer," or, "If only I had known earlier, you could have saved my ass in those skits I did last season."

"If only you would open up more."

Amanda looked at Danny and hoped he could

not see her deflate. She felt like Alice, as though she was getting smaller and smaller, her body shrinking along with her hopes. Her back was against the restaurant-quality stove, a copper awning hanging above her head. Danny was leaning up against the huge chopping block that ate up half the huge, aggressively white kitchen, a chopping block that was used primarily as a spot to dump take-out pizza and oil-free, taste-less Chinese food. The heavy-looking oak knife holder caught Amanda's eye momentarily, and a vision danced in front of her head as her eyes flickered back to Danny. Amanda was almost surprised he did not have one of those heavy-duty steel German knives hanging out of his chest, bursting in crimson, his face a grotesque mask of shock and sadness and fear. Alas, it was not to be. Amanda could see Danny's teeth, large, white, bonded, expensive. He was smiling. Amanda was not.

"I see."

"You think about it."

It was one of the few moments in her life when Amanda could not find the words to suit the situation. If only she had had a pad, a sharp-ened pencil, the smell of lead still fresh; or a typewriter with those ink cartridges that ran out so quickly (the same cartridges that were impossible to put in without getting ink all over those brand-new white jeans). Maybe she could have found the right, tart reply, the pithy retort. After picking her jaw up off the ground. Danny came right out and said it. She would go places, but only if she slept her way up the rungs of the ladder of success. (What if the ladder was metal, not wood? Wouldn't it be cold on her back? Wouldn't it feel like a graying doctor's stethoscope or, worse, like that metal thing the nice gynecologist with the soothing voice and diploma rams into your vagina, at the same time asking how your mother is, has her condition cleared up—a condition that until this moment had been a merciful mystery to Amanda? What if the ladder was wood? Wouldn't there be splinters?)

"Thanks for the tip." Amanda turned away from Danny and headed back into the living room, as stiff and creaky as the Tin Woodman. She needed to see Gabriel. She needed a big, strong shoulder to cry on.

* * *

Amanda drove home on an empty freeway as fast as a twenty-five-year-old car with a bone-dry oil pan could take her. At least the intent was there.

Mrs. Selby opened the door in a silk night-gown and robe and marabou slippers after a good ten minutes of Amanda listening to the barks, whines, and scrapes of her ten-pound dog. She narrowed her eyes, struggling to focus on the sniffling girl on her doorstep. She had not been awake.

"Mrs. Selby, it's Amanda." Amanda tried to keep the panic from her voice. She knew Mrs. Selby didn't like to wear her bifocals.

"I know who it is, child." Mrs. Selby coughed. She smoked her last cigarette three years ago, after the doctors took out a piece of lung and several lymph nodes. But her voice still crackled like a fledgling female impersonator's.

"I just came by to pick up—"

"Your brother came and got 'im."

"My brother?" Oh, shit.

"Sure." Mrs. Selby looked at Amanda. "That's okay, isn't it? Val's always been such an awful nice boy."

"Awful, yes," Amanda thought. "Nice, not even close."

"He's a gem." Amanda smiled at Mrs. Selby. "Sorry for waking you, Mrs. Selby."

"I was awake. I'm always awake."

Amanda smiled at her, this old woman in a Miss August 1962 ensemble with the small, mean, overindulged dog. She didn't want Mrs. Selby to worry. That was Amanda's job. The pay sucked, but she was getting very good at it.

Of course, Valentin was nowhere to be found; he was not in his darkened, smoke-filled cave; he was not facedown in a bowl of Fruity Pebbles. He was not bundled up in his closet, a clean, pin-point-neat gunshot wound between his luscious bedroom eyes, which was precisely where Amanda feared she would find him one day. Amanda went through the house on her half-hearted mission, but she knew her brother was making his customer runs. His business was, after all, mostly night shift: black-tie parties in Beverly Hills and the hills of Bel Air, the yellow and red Ferraris, white Bentleys, late-model BMWs crowding the large, open, palm-tree-shaded streets; the younger, hipper, rock 'n' roll boîtes of the recording industry set, Hollywood hills cobblestone driveways filled with black Porsches, silver Porsches, white Porsches, but most of all, black Porsches, convertibles all. On occasion, the night would take him to the outskirts of L.A.: a condominium complex in the Marina filled with anxious, middle-aged dentists and doctors, all recently divorced, and young stewardesses looking for a white knight and some good blow; a surfer party in Manhattan Beach where everyone glowed with the power of youth and a giddy lack of ambition; a party in Baldwin Hills, identical in every way (from the houses to the cars to the shrubbery to the tile on the kitchen floor) to the Beverly Hills parties, except that everyone here was black. And the music was better. Valentin would sometimes save the Baldwin Hills parties for the last of his run, because they were, in his opinion, the most fun, the least bullshit. Just a bunch of people having a good time.

Amanda wondered why Valentin would have brought the baby with him—why he would have bothered. After all, a baby on any job is a nuisance—but a baby on a drug run is just plain bad for business! And then she thought, briefly, maybe his father missed him. And she hoped that there was still enough of Valentin left to experience that feeling.

Amanda sat, suddenly familiar with the phrase "bone tired," in one of the four kitchen chairs that shifted with every subtle move, on account of one leg being shorter than the rest. The chairs had been this way for twelve years. Very little changed in this house, except the colors, but only because they were slowly disappearing. The colors of the walls, the floors, the furniture, the framed poster "paintings," the baskets that held various dying houseplants (even the ones impossible to kill were committing suicide), the serape rugs from Pier 1, everything was fading. Only Madison's furnishings, his playpen, his favorite blanket, his pajamas, play toys, and books, with their bright, happy colors, their yellows and reds and blues and greens— only Madison's presence proved that not everything in this house was fading away. Not everything was doomed.

Amanda dialed Gabriel's work number, written in neat, careful lettering on a matchbook cover. She ran her fingers over the number; even the way he wrote was sweet. She dialed on the kitchen phone, though the receiver had a heavy, lingering smell, like the breath of a hard-core, four-pack-a-day smoker. (So Valentin was smoking cigarettes again, after insisting it was unhealthy to smoke, even as he sniffed mounds of high-grade Colombian into his nostrils.) A man answered, short, gruff, in a hurry.

"Is Gabriel Williams there?" Amanda's voice went on automatic high. A damsel in distress.

"He's on the floor." There was going to be no debate.

"Can I leave a message?"

Beat. "Hold on." The voice was gruff, but not without heart. Amanda waited, heard papers being shuffled, mutterings about lost or stolen pencils. Finally he got back on the phone.

"Go 'head."

"Tell him Amanda called. Tell him to call me tonight. If he can." She added that last part; she didn't want to sound too desperate. She knew she wasn't going to sleep, though, until Valentin came home. With Madison.

"'Kay." Pause. "He'll get it on break."

"Thank you."

"Yeah." The man hung up. Amanda sat in the rickety chair and gathered her thoughts. She could try to track Valentin down. He had a beeper, but Amanda had used it only once, when Patrice was going into labor late on a work night. She couldn't remember the number.

Amanda got up, knocking the chair over, and went into Valentin's room. Maybe there was a bill, an address book, something with the number. She hated herself for becoming so disorganized in the last couple of years, even with all the crap she had to deal with. She hated this house for the same reason. Papers and bullshit moved in and never left. The important stuff could never be found.

She turned on the light on Valentin's desk, the same one he had in junior high and high school. Etchings and pen marks had been there since Amanda was a little girl. Though his room was a mess, Valentin's desk was the pristine replica of an anal-retentive fourth-grader's. Envelopes were in one file, notepaper in another. Tax records (dating back several years, when Valentin had a clerical job that required withholding and social security taxes—he had worked, of all things, in a lawyer's office; the lawyer was a big fat man who looked at Valentin like a son, until Valentin crashed his new Jaguar) were in yet another neatly recorded file. His old high school diploma was in another drawer, framed. Amanda wondered at this. She had never had her high school diploma framed; but then, she had graduated from college. She held it for a few seconds, then put it back, suddenly deeply saddened.

Her hand happened upon a manila envelope, stuffed with what felt like letters, and Amanda, behaving like the thief in the night she was, peered inside. The envelope held old letters from older girlfriends, and photographs. Amanda looked through them. The girls were very young and very pretty, the picture of glowing California health. The boys were cute, long hair, white teeth. There was one of Gabriel with Valentin, the both of them in swim trunks, their arms around each other, holding illicit beers. On the back, someone had written: "Kickin' back. '77." Valentin was looking up at Gabriel, his smile wide, his shoulders filled out. Amanda had forgotten Valentin's smile, laid across his beautiful face, free of agenda. But there was something else in the picture. Amanda looked closer.

Valentin loved Gabriel.

As she looked at the adoring expression on her brother's teenage face, she realized they had once been very close—even closer than she imagined.

Amanda sat there, soaking in a memory she had long since forgotten. She was eight or nine, Valentin was a couple of years older. She was in the backseat of her mom's old Chrysler, playing puppets with her socks slipped over her hands, while her mother ran into the drugstore to pick up a prescription.

Driving back, up a busy, steep street, Amanda saw her black-haired brother, Valentin, and Gabriel, his hair wild in a 'fro, careening down the hill on skateboards in the opposite direction, in and out of cars. Amanda's mouth opened wide, and before her mother spied her adrenaline-junkie brother and his partner in crime, Amanda screamed. Her mother whipped her head around to look at her, just as Valentin passed them. "My God, what is it?" Amanda just looked at her mother, placid faced. "I dropped my sock."

As Amanda's mother glared at the road, Amanda looked back at the disappearing figures, so brave and mythic to an eight-year-old, and smiled. She had saved her brother and his friend.

Suddenly, Amanda realized the level of Valentin's anger toward Gabriel the day he was arrested made sense. Amanda, by sleeping with Gabriel, by loving him, was taking something Valentin loved. Amanda was seized with a need to hug Val, a move she hadn't dared in years, not even after the birth of his son. Valentin, with his sharp tongue, his wary eye, the boniness under his sallow skin, had gotten progressively less huggable over the years.

The phone rang, an alarm reminding Amanda that she was looking for clues to Valentin's whereabouts. An emergency room filled with screaming children flew into her head as she ran into the kitchen, tripping over the chair she had knocked over. What if something had happened to Madison? Anything could happen—Valentin was high all the time now, driving his car like a maniac, a murderer dancing in front of the cops, aching to get caught. . . . She was saying hello before she picked up the phone.

"Amanda."

It was him. Amanda had to remind herself to breathe. Why oh why was she so fucking crippled?

"Amanda?"

"Gabriel." She felt his arms around her. Everything was going to be all right.

"I'll be there in an hour." Again, a statement. Amanda's knees buckled. A bead of sweat rolled gently, silently, down the back of her leg, behind her knee.

"Amanda."

"Mmm." She hadn't replied. She was wondering how she would be able to wait that long. A whole hour. Who needed sleep? She closed her eyes for a moment. He was coming.

"Is everything okay?" Amanda's eyes snapped open.

"Val. His beeper number. Do you have it?"

"What's wrong?"

"Nothing. It's just . . . He has the baby."

Amanda understood Gabriel's silence to mean he did not like this news, which made Amanda worry more.

"I have it at home. I'll get it there first. Then I'll come by."

"Don't do that. That's too much—"

There was a sound in the distance. A horn blowing. A signal. Amanda was reminded of turn-of-the-century black-and-white photographs with sweaty men and tired women and children with deadened eyes standing before giant metal life-stealing machines. The horn meant Gabriel had to get back to work.

"I'll pick it up first."

"Thank you, Gabriel."

"Go to sleep. I'll wake you."

Amanda smiled. She was going to tell him she loved him, that everything in her tired soul cried out for him to be the one to take care of her. He hung up before she could say the words. She closed her eyes, suddenly weary and needy of her old, familiar bed and her faithful, faded blanket.

Gabe hung up the phone. A furrow formed between his brows, and he wiped the sweat from his forehead. He turned away, and there was J.D. smiling at him, the gold in his mouth beacons of goodwill.

"That her?" J.D.'s "her" sounded like "huh." Gabriel knew what he was getting at.

"I ain't tellin' you, my man." Gabe slipped past him and onto the floor. The five-minute horn had sounded. This conversation would take longer than that.

J.D. laughed and laughed. "Oh yeah, you is, son. You's tellin' old J.D. everything!"

Gabriel moved toward the line, stopped and tightened his weight belt. J.D. was next to him in a flash. The man could move when he wanted to.

"Whatchoo want from me, old man?"

"Jus' your money and your life." Men around them hooted.

"And your bitch!" someone hollered. Gabriel looked up from his belt, his mouth tight, his breath deep and hard. J.D. put a father's hand on his shoulder.

"Don't."

Gabriel looked at J.D.

"You got it bad, huh, boy?"

Gabriel sucked air in; the smell of burning metal filled his chest. He felt like crying.

"You got a picture?" J.D. said it soft. Gabriel couldn't look at him. He nodded. He dove into his back pocket and picked out his wallet, thin, navy waterproof. Dirty from his working hands. Gingerly he opened it, and with his fingernails pinched a small photograph and showed it to J.D. The men around them raised an eyebrow or sniffed louder than normal, but pretended not to notice. J.D. looked at the photograph. It was Amanda's high school picture, from her senior year. It had been cut out of a yearbook. J.D. stared at it for a moment, then handed it back to Gabriel. Gabriel watched as he went to his station next to him. Gabriel shrugged and stood before the great machines that would be sending engines his way. He spat at the floor, pissed.

"Boy."

"What."

"Remember when I said I'd never eat that female part?"

"Yeah." Here comes an engine. Gabriel took a breath and guided it on a chain-link cable from the rail above his head into a chassis, careful not to lose a finger as he dropped the engine down into the frame.

"I was wrong."

Gabriel looked at J.D., his smiling-ass face filled with gold bullion.

"I was wrong."

Gabriel turned back to the line and to another engine, coming fast. He smiled and shook his head.

*   *   *

Valentin had made out that night. Made out. Pretty soon he'd be able to retire from this game. At a hilltop party filled with job-eyed centerfolds and jowly hacks, he had cornered this one dude, a middle-aged regular with long gray hair to match his long gray beard; the dude looked like Jesus if he had gotten old and fat and taken too many drugs. Valentin told the guy he was thinking of getting out of the business. He was sick of the hours. He didn't want to go to prison. And honestly, he wasn't thinking right anymore. He was losing his temper too quickly. The other day, a lawyer-looking asshole in a black BMW cut him off in traffic, and at the first hint of a red light, Valentin got out of his car, got his baseball bat, his old Little League Louisville Slugger with the slash marks on the neck—twenty-five slashes for twenty-five home runs, that's the truth—out of the trunk, and strode calmly over to the BMW and proceeded to *smash every single window in*, not to mention the driver's side rearview mirror. He then walked calmly back to his car, got in, tossed the bat in the backseat, and drove off. And turned on the FM station that played fifties jazz tunes, and after thirty seconds of Miles Davis, forgot about the whole thing. His mind was scattered. He had lost too much weight as well. He looked like fucking shit, that's the truth.

The dude listened to him, this fucking comic-book wise man sitting at the top of a cliff; the cliff just happened to be under one of those stilt houses these dudes loved so much, way, way up in the hills. Valentin could never live in one of those places. They got great views, for sure; you could see everything, from downtown to Catalina to exotic places like San Clemente, where that cheat president lived, Tricky Dick. So the dude listened, then asked Valentin what it was he wanted to do.

That was just it. Valentin didn't have an answer. He knew he wanted to get out, go legit. He even, in his most honest moments, fantasized about what he'd look like in a suit. But he didn't have any skills, had less schooling. What the fuck was he supposed to do, become one of those boys on Santa Monica Boulevard, sucking old men's dicks for fifty a pop? He was probably too old for that, even; most of those boys looked fifteen and had soft, corn-fed skin. He didn't know, he didn't know. Valentin was struck dumb, suddenly overcome by the hopelessness of his situation. He was going to be one of those wrinkled, pitted fifty-year-old guys (if he lived that long), sucking down watered-down whiskey in a cheap bar, selling shoes or delivering mail or driving a motherfucking bus. He, Valentin, was never going to be someone important. Drug dealing was the end of the line for him.

Valentin sometimes wondered, when his mind was clear, how he had ended up like this. Like such a loser. He had been a good student up until junior high, up until the time when an older kid, a boy he looked up to, took him up to his mom's apartment on Hobart and taught him how to use a bong. For most kids this wouldn't be enough to push them over the edge, but Valentin the overachiever rode the wave from bongs to quaaludes quickly, listening to Led Zeppelin and old Doors for hours and hours every single day. At the age of twelve, Valentin was gaining a reputation as a stoner.

There was a time when Valentin would look back at his elementary school pictures his mother kept in a cardboard box, and he would study the dark-haired boy with the toothy grin, his head cocked to the side in a pleasing manner. And he would say to his younger self, "What happened to you, kid—what the hell happened?"

He seldom looked at those pictures anymore.

The bearded dude was on the verge of getting bummed out; Valentin could see this. So he changed the subject, asked the dude if he'd like to sample some killer sinsemilla he had gotten his hands on over the weekend. The dude lit up like a Christmas tree. Old Jesus loved coke, but he loved pot better; he preferred a mellow high.

Valentin left the house on the cliff with a burden buried in his thin chest, a deep, arresting anger at discovering what he always knew . . . he was nothing. A small-time drug dealer. He knew, as though it were carved into his forehead backwards, something he could read every morning through bloodshot eyes: he would end up dead or in jail long before his thirtieth birthday. Madison had garbage for a father—just like Valentin had.

Jail made him think of Patrice. Patrice's mother, who lived in Vegas with a blackjack dealer, had told her she would pay her bail if she would come live with her. But her mother would not take Patrice and the baby, which was okay with Patrice. Valentin found out about this after he had gone downtown to Sybil Brand to visit her. As much as he wanted to smack Patrice for being so stupid all the time, that's as much as he wanted to kiss her. He was missing her long, lean form, her skinny ass in his bed, even if he could not really get it up anymore, at least for the time being. Valentin found this amusing: drugs made him horny and unable to fuck at the exact same time. It defined the term "irony" for Valentin.

It was only five minutes later, as he was cruising Sunset toward Laurel Canyon, sucking cocaine from a glass pipe and avoiding pedestrians, that he realized he had left his son at the party, in the company of a young woman in a red dress who reminded him of Patrice, except that she was Spanish and had giant tits, and who had traded ten minutes of baby-sitting for two lines of the best coke in Los Angeles. Valentin looked at his steel Rolex, one of the few gifts he had given himself. The ten minutes had become forty-five. Valentin hit the steering wheel with his open hand and cursed his luck. Now he owed the bitch.

He turned the car around in the middle of Sunset Strip; smoke came off the wheels.

Ten

Gabriel cut his motor as he turned onto the cracked cement driveway in front of his house, the house he and his father rented from a Korean couple who had been in the States for three years. Three years, and they owned a home. Two homes, for crissakes, plus three liquor stores in South Central. Frank Williams had been in this country sixty years, ain't never owned a home, never would. Gabriel thought he wouldn't either, until he had a dream a couple of nights ago that had taken hold of his mind and his heart. Like one of the Miles Davis tunes his father listened to that he could hear over and over in his mind long after the record was back in its yellowed plastic jacket, this one would not let go of him.

First, there was the tone. So bright, like a

flash from an old camera. Gabriel was sitting on a padded lounge chair in someone's backyard, one of those big backyards with a lush green, newly cut lawn and a pool the rich blue-green of a turquoise stone. The sun was large and red and hot; it felt like he was in the San Fernando Valley somewhere, but in one of the nicer neighborhoods, like Sherman Oaks or Encino, where the white residents drove Mercedeses and BMWs and voted and sent their kids to private schools and read newspapers, and not just the sports section. And there were children, three of them, two little girls and a boy, their skin the color of coffee ice cream, his favorite, dancing in the pool, laughing, splashing water in one another's faces. Gabe remembered looking at them, their delicious skin, and wanting to eat them, to kiss their faces and their toes and arms until they would push him away, laughing, to jump back into the pool. Next to him was his wife. Her eyes were closed, but she smiled at the voices that belonged to her children. In the dream, Gabriel petted his wife's dark red hair, and then Amanda's smile was on him, and her eyes were open, and Gabe's chest swelled with pride.

When Gabe awoke, the contrast of his lifeless

bedroom, with its dull green walls the color of jails and hospitals, the joyless air, crushed him; it was the closest he had come to tears since his mother had left him, her long skirt flying up in a warm current as she ran to the car of her latest boyfriend. A familiar pain rose in him like a great wave, tightening his chest, squeezing the air from his lungs.

But then Gabe thought maybe it was a sign. Maybe God was trying to tell him that he could make something of his life.

Gabe made a pact with himself. He was going to put his sorry-ass mind to work. He had read almost a whole book in the last month and it didn't kill him; he even enjoyed it. Secretly, the morning his dream awoke him, he sent for a schedule of classes from the local junior college. The dream had shown him the difference, and he wanted it. Badly. Gabe would change his life; and when he did, he would get Amanda to marry him.

Gabriel turned his key noiselessly in the door and opened it slowly. His father was in his usual spot, in front of his old TV set shooting black-and-white images out onto this sleeping old man in the overstuffed, fake leather La-Z-Boy Gabriel had bought for him with his first week's pay from the plant. The dog with the spiked collar was at the old man's feet, curled up like a sleeping child; he didn't even bother looking up. Gabriel stopped for a moment and stared at his father and was overwhelmed with a feeling of affection toward the old man; he felt like taking his bald, black cue-ball head in his hands and kissing the top of it, but he knew his father would wake up and swipe at him. Gabe smiled and touched his father's arm gently, and felt for the first time in his life that he would be able to take care of the old man someday.

Gabe ran upstairs on the balls of his feet, three stairs at a time. He ran into his room and opened his dresser drawer and looked for the number he had written on a piece of paper a year or two ago. He found it, finally, in the pocket of a pair of black jeans he hadn't worn in a while, and he reminded himself to wash them so he could wear them again. Before he walked out, he dialed the beeper number and pressed in Amanda's number, so that Valentin would call there. And then he was out the door, down the stairs, and gone.

*   *   *

Frank Williams awakened to the sound of a motorcycle taking off, and called out to his son.

"Gabe? 'Zat you?" The dog with the spiked collar looked up at him dolefully to tell him Gabe had left already to see the redheaded white girl, but he didn't have the heart. He went back to sleep.

"Time is it?" The old man asked the dog. Frank looked bleary eyed and sixty at the television set and cursed the day he bought it. He hadn't gotten a good night's sleep since he bought the damned thing. Never practiced his horn anymore, neither. He'd get rid of the TV tomorrow, he would. There were a thousand secondhand shops within a mile of the house. He'd take care of it first thing.

He got up and leaned back into his hands to rub the small of his back, tired from hauling the gut around that hadn't left him since his forty-second year, no matter that he cut out ribs more than two, three times a month. No matter that he secretly did fifty sit-ups ever morning, even before he took a piss.

His father, a man who had worked on the Atlantic Railroad serving folks food with a smile and a kind word, in fourteen-hour shifts, had a favorite saying, "bone tired." "Bone tired," Frank heard his father's deep rumble of a voice, as he ambled slowly out the front door, the dog with the spiked collar dutifully on his heels. It was time for their nightly walk.

Amanda was asleep in bed when her door opened. She could not see; the room was dark, and her eyes unfocused.

"Gabe?" She wondered how he got in here. She didn't remember opening the door. She sat up in bed; she shivered as the covers dropped.

"How did you—?" The question went unanswered as a mouth covered her own; for a moment, Amanda thought Gabriel had smoked at work; this mouth tasted not sweet, not warm, but bitter and cold and chapped. And then she knew.

"*Get away!*" she screamed, but her brother kissed her again, harder. She pummeled him with her arms, flailing wildly, until finally she remembered the school yard training Valentin himself had imposed on her, and she grabbed her brother, her only sibling, by his inglorious little nuts and squeezed until he released her from his bony grip and sank to his knees in a wheezing, trembling heap.

Amanda stood and ran to the door and flipped on the lights with shaking hands.

"What the hell is wrong with you?" She could barely breathe, but somehow she could scream. Amanda marveled at the strength of her lungs, and suddenly was filled not with fear but with pride. The only way Valentin could beat her right now was with a weapon. Her mind, alert as a Russian chess champion's, was already three moves ahead of this lump. She thought about his gun, the one hidden in the closet. She'd have to get rid of it.

"Valentin! It's *me! Amanda!"* There was no reply. "Are you *crazy?*"

Valentin's eyes were unrecognizable when he looked up. Amanda stopped breathing for a second. She did not know this person. The person here, with his dirty, musty-smelling, loose-fitting jeans and dingy tank top and deep lines running from the corners of his mouth to his nose, and the gray-green of his skin, this person was a stranger. Where was that boy in the photograph? And, oh God, where was that boy's son?

"Madison. Where's Madison, Val?"

The thing looked at her and laughed. Amanda let out a muffled cry and ran out of her bedroom and down the hall, careening blindly into Valentin's bedroom.

The bassinet was empty. Amanda's eyes filled with angry tears, and her chest ached and she wanted to die, but instead, by rote, she ran outside to check Valentin's car.

Parked on top of the curb, the keys still in it. As was the baby. Amanda peered at him through the window. He was asleep. The kid was asleep.

Amanda opened the door and took him out of his baby seat, and murmured lullabies to him as she sat on the curb in her thin nightgown and waited for Gabriel. For a moment she marveled that the baby had actually been in his car seat, for crying out loud. Then she wished she had a cigarette and then remembered she did not smoke.

This she needed to correct.

The baby pursed his lips in his sleep and furrowed his brow and Amanda took it back. She would not have the luxury of an early death; she had another life to take care of.

When Gabriel rolled up ten minutes later, Amanda was still stationed on the curb, ready to flee at any sudden movement from her home.

The purr of Gabriel's Ninja engine was the most comforting sound Amanda had ever heard; she could fall asleep to that purr. When he got off his bike and came to her, his arms open and his eyes shining like a man who had come home, a man in love, Amanda melted into his chest and knew that, at least for that night, it would be all right.

James told his professors there was a family emergency, and that he would be gone less than a week. He knew he was on shaky terms with his illustrious professors anyway, but he did not care. He had to get home; he liked the sweet girl with the good family, but he was sick of feeling like a science experiment, a cool way to rebel or show off to Connecticut sorority sisters. He got on a no-frills, red-eye flight, bought with a stranger's credit card, thank you very much, joined by a dozen or so illegal aliens, placed there by people who sold them to low-wage jobs in L.A.; old people on fixed incomes visiting their sons, daughters, grandchildren one last time before the inevitable; several students (who had the terrified, exhilarated expressions of someone who had dropped out of school with no future in sight); and faceless types, pasty white, lower middle class, lumpy—these had no characteristics that defined them, not even their sex, save for their Celtics T-shirts and Nike shoes.

James sat between a Greek Orthodox priest (he gathered from the man's black robe, giant baroque cross; plus, conveniently, he was perusing a Greek newspaper), who smelled as though keeping an eye over your followers were a physical endeavor—the man reeked—and a large woman in a flowery print dress with glasses and stiff, hair-sprayed hair, who sighed and shook her massive head every five minutes for the whole of six hours. Every five minutes. James wondered what could make a person so sad, but he was afraid to ask her, fearing she would tell him. Besides, he could look no further than his own life. He was a failure. He hated law school—he hated the ambitious, loquacious, smug professors who drank French Bordeaux and smoked their students' pot and could tell one Brie from the next; he hated his fellow students: coddled fat boys and ruthless rich girls who had never suffered a day in their lives. And if they had, they were the quota students everyone knew about: those who got in not because of great grades but their ancestral names, or the color of their skin, or the number of vowels in their name. He hated himself. Because as much as he hated this world, he hated more that he did not fit in. He was an outcast even amongst the outcasts. Sickening.

James smiled joylessly and sank back into his seat while the lady next to him sighed again. Wouldn't Amanda be surprised? He laughed and the fat lady looked at him and James ordered another scotch from the harried stewardess with the red lipstick and chunky ankles. He loved those little bottles.

As the stewardess found change, James turned to the fat lady. "Would you like to hear a story?" he said. She looked at him and said nothing. He thought he heard her sigh again, and he took this as a yes.

"What do you think about a guy who gives up everything to go back home to a girl who's been cheating on him?"

The woman's eyes got huge. She shrugged her massive shoulders. Her sleeves rustled.

"You know, I'm not from here. I'm not from this country." James was proud of this fact.

The lady nodded. James could see the light turn on in her eyes, eyes that on another, slender woman would have been considered beautiful.

"I'm an immigrant. I learned the language. I had no money. And you know what—I'm going to Harvard Law School."

"Why, that's wonderful." She smiled as she said this in her surprisingly high, soft voice.

"I hate it. I hate everything about it."

"You do?"

"Did you go to school?" James had to know. He felt he related to people who didn't go to college better than those who did.

The woman shook her head no. "Just high school. I'm a beautician."

"I'll bet you're good."

"Why, thank you," the fat lady gushed, her cheeks turning crimson. James realized she might think he was trying to pick up on her.

"I feel like shit," James said. And suddenly, without warning, he started to cry.

The fat lady put one hamlike arm around his skinny shoulders and held him while he sniffled like a baby. And for the rest of the flight, for the six hours to come, James cried and confessed his fears to the fat lady with the stuccoed hair. And when he finally deplaned, James felt like a new man.

Eleven

Joe could not sleep. Four A.M. and here he was, eyes wide open again. What was the phrase? No rest for the weary? No rest for the wicked? Joe cursed his college education; he had spent too much time at the University of Chicago fucking and drinking and smoking and not enough time going to classes. He got up and walked around his bed, careful not to stumble over the towering high heels that were casually tossed off in earlier hours. He could not even bear to look at this one as he lurched into his hallway toward the kitchen. He knew what she looked like. He knew who she didn't look like.

Joe opened the refrigerator and immediately regretted the move. If he could have found his voice, he would have screamed into the bright fluorescent light that hit him in the face like a big-knuckled punch. He regained composure only after crouching to his knees on the cold linoleum, and reached in toward the lone beer cans that shared space with mustard and batteries for that Nikon camera he never used anymore. The cool of the beer can soothed him—for some reason, he was burning up—and he placed the can to his forehead, to the hair matted in sweaty clumps.

He did not feel good. His throat had a scratch in it he could not shake. He had cut himself shaving a week ago, and his skin had not healed. His tongue was coated white, and his face had lost the rosiness of his youth. And now, more nights than not, he woke up in a coat of sweat.

Joe Artuga was sick. It was over two months to New Year's, but Joe knew he had resolutions to make, and he made them on the cold of the linoleum in the darkness of a city in the early morning hours. He would quit drinking, he would quit smoking, he would exercise, and he would stop fucking every whore in sight (knowing full well that's exactly what he himself was) and find himself a nice girl.

Joe coughed and smiled at this, his eyes crinkling in the corners the way women liked. He had found many nice girls. College girls in Birkenstocks with hair under their arms and fire in their rhetoric who would melt faster than an ice cream cone in August; upper-class girls, the daughters of dentists and doctors, in ice-skating skirts; girls in crisp cheerleading uniforms and white cotton underwear. So many nice girls. And he had screwed each and every one of them over, the same way he had the girls with no character, no morals—the girls he felt more comfortable with and, at the same time, completely repulsed by. And somehow Joe Artuga, because he was a rogue, so charming and puppy-doggish with his unkempt hair, so quick with a joke, was able to remain on friendly terms with the very women he fucked over. For this he was first surprised, then grateful, then self-loathing. He was an asshole who lived in the skin of a best friend.

He thought of Amanda—their playful, unself-conscious banter, the funny way she strode into a room, like a five-year-old boy feeling his oats for the first time, the way she refused, politely but firmly, to take the shit he so effortlessly doled out to his staff, the way a lock of her hair flipped up stubbornly on her left cheek, never to be tamed. Even her ingenuous dream to be a writer, worn so glaringly on her sleeve and in her increasingly bold and funny little memos that circulated throughout the office, appealed to Joe. In this girl was Joe's last shot at a sane life.

It had been years since Joe Artuga had courted a girl. The last time he could remember was sixth grade, when he sent a smudged Valentine to the blond girl with the puffy pink lips like a movie star who sat in front of him, whose presence caused him to stammer his multiplication tables, whose freshly laundered smell made him woozy during spelling bees. The smudged Valentine did not work. And so he gave up such things. But now, sitting on his kitchen floor in the dark, he felt ready. He, Joe Artuga, would set out to win over Amanda. For deep in his dark, undisciplined heart, he felt that she, the only human being he felt he knew, was the one who could save him.

Joe thought about the blond girl with the puffy lips and cold heart, and took brief, mean pleasure in the fact she was probably fat with children and a semiliterate husband named Jake who managed the local Wal-Mart. "Who's laughing now?" Joe thought, and he chuckled as he leaned back on his refrigerator at four-thirty in the morning with the cold beer can still pressed to his head.

"Living well is the best revenge," he thought as he avoided his face in the hallway mirror and tried to recall the name of the girl snoring in his bed.

Amanda and Gabriel made love quietly and slowly as the baby slept, innocently, in his crib at the foot of her bed. Amanda did not want to tell Gabriel what happened with Valentin because she was not sure herself. She knew Valentin had been doing more coke. She could hear it in his constant sniffling, the way he spoke through his sinuses, like some Saturday morning cartoon character ("Uh, what's up, Doc?"). She did not want to think about the tarnished pipes, the burning plastic smell, the empty cartons of tinfoil. She closed her eyes against the slow death of her brother.

Gabriel, the comfort of his whole body on her, ran his hands through her hair and massaged her head with the tips of his fingers and brought his lips to her cheek and then to her ear, his breath steady as the movement of his body, and he whispered in her ear in a voice low and fine. "I love you, Amanda," he breathed. "I will take care of you always. I am the one."

Amanda started to cry. "No one's ever taken care of me before," she said, softly.

"I know," Gabriel replied. "But this is me, Gabriel, talking, and you have to understand one thing. I never lie."

"Promise?" she asked.

"Oh, you know I don't need to promise," Gabe said. "I'm yours. And this," he put his hand on her chest, "is mine."

"My heart," she said.

"Your heart," Gabe replied. "I'm keeping it."

Amanda looked into his eyes and wondered what she had done right in her life to hear this man's poetry. Gabe was so straightforward, so true—she had seen this type of man in black-and-white Gary Cooper movies, but in real life? Ha! With the men she knew, from James to Val to Joe to her absent father, even, there were agendas and frustrations, and anger. A lot of anger. With Gabe there were no eggshells to walk around, no secrets to keep hidden under sharpened, defensive words. Gabe did not have the benefit of a university education—but he had wisdom that could not be taught.

Amanda fell asleep, comforted by her lover's arms and the knowledge that earlier she had tiptoed past Valentin, a neophyte cat burglar, as he lay passed out on his floor, and removed Valentin's gun from his closet. He would have to kill her to get it back.

Amanda opened her eyes to a loud series of noises coming from the garage, and it took seconds before she recognized the rush of skateboards back and forth on the concrete. Valentin's customers. Against the bright light of the sunrise, it took Amanda several more seconds to acclimate. The baby was not in his crib, and Gabriel was not in her bed. She listened. There were no shouts, no baby crying. The drama of the night before had faded into a new day. Amanda placed her feet on the floor and took a deep breath and thanked God it wasn't Monday. A new scent hit her as she searched the air. Cooking. Someone was cooking . . . pancakes? Amanda figured it must be coming from next door, or across the street. She tied her old robe around her waist with a mismatched belt from a later version Patrice had taken and went in search of whatever would find her. At the very least, she looked forward to kicking some young skateboard ass off her property.

Amanda slid into the hallway and realized the

smells of home were not coming from next door. She forgot about her screaming bladder when she peeked inside the kitchen.

Gabriel held Madison in one large brown arm as though he were a small toy, while the other arm expertly flipped cinnamon-colored pancakes on a long-forgotten grill. Amanda wanted to cry. Gabriel turned his head toward Madison. Amanda ducked back into the hallway and listened.

"You see that? That's perfect. That's the color you want." Madison gurgled and laughed.

"Oh. You think you can do that, huh?" Madison laughed again. "Takes many years, my boy. Many years."

Amanda said not a word but turned toward the bathroom. She wanted to brush her hair, to get herself right for the picture she had just seen. There are few things, Amanda thought, as beautiful as a big man cooking. There is nothing more beautiful than a big man cooking while holding a cooing baby.

She reached for the door, which opened from inside. Valentin stood there, wearing the same tank top, the same jeans he had worn from last night. Probably the night before as well. His eyes were red slits trapped in swollen tissue; his posture was stooped, his back curved like an old man laden with the past, defeated. He looked past her toward the kitchen. Amanda could decipher no memory of last night from his bloodshot eyes.

"Who's here?" Valentin's voice was a laceration on the morning. His eyes clearly weren't adapting to the hour as well. Amanda wondered if bats had the same problem.

"Gabriel. He's cooking breakfast." ("Please don't fuck with him, please don't fuck with him," Amanda was thinking.) Valentin adjusted his eyes again, narrowing them further. He didn't say anything.

"I think you have company." Amanda changed channels. "I heard skateboards."

"Huh." Valentin walked back into his bedroom with the small, tentative steps of a hospital patient and shut the door behind him. Amanda breathed a sigh of relief and went into the bathroom and immediately recognized the discouraging presence of vomit and bile. At least he had flushed.

Amanda's face was like a ten-year-old's, her eyes clear and shining, the old robe wrapped around

her like a good friend. Gabe had never seen anyone so beautiful. He shifted Madison from one
arm to the other.

"Mmm. You're gorgeous."

Amanda, on her toes to kiss his cheek,
stopped midair and looked at him. Looked for
the joke inside the words. It was seven-thirty in
the morning. She knew what she looked like.

"What?" Gabe looked at her. And she realized
he was serious. He thought she was beautiful.
Not just cute or (as a college buddy had told her,
thinking he was being complimentary) a seven,
maybe even a seven and a half, if she had lost
five, six pounds. Gabe Williams thought she was
beautiful. And so did Madison. That was enough
for any woman.

"Are they ready yet?" Amanda smiled as she
peered around Gabe's burly body.

"Oh, no. You take a seat. I'll be with you in a
sec." Gabe pretended to be gruff.

"You want me to help?"

"Do I look like I need help?" Gabe joked. "You
are looking at a master in the kitchen, baby."

"I thought I was just looking at a master in
the bedroom."

"And you know that." He blushed when he

said it, shattering whatever was left of the shell around Amanda's heart. Her hand rose to her swelling chest and stayed there.

They ate pancakes and drank orange juice Gabe had squeezed from "borrowed" oranges from the overburdened neighboring tree and ignored Valentin, who pointedly ignored Gabe as he dragged his old man body into the garage to sell his wares to a couple of skateboarders Amanda swore were no older than twelve or thirteen. Amanda shifted in her seat to get up to tell them to scoot, to tell them she was going to call the cops and they shouldn't be doing drugs, and what kind of drugs are they doing anyway, and where are their parents, but Gabe placed his hand on her thigh as if to quiet her, and she looked at him and settled down. When Valentin came back inside, silent but for his glare at the exotically domestic scene, Gabe quietly got up from the table, asked Amanda if she and the baby needed anything, and when she said no, excused himself and followed Valentin's path into his room. Amanda looked after him, and then sat back with her cup of coffee and tried to read Mrs. S.'s newspaper, and Madison tried to rip it up with sticky hands.

Gabe sat down at the edge of Valentin's bed. "You fallin' apart, man."

Valentin said nothing. He shifted his body slightly away from Gabe, burrowing into the corner of his bed, covering his face with its unwashed, faded sheet. Gabe looked at his big hands and sighed. He knew about trying to save people. He knew about hiding bottles; he knew about flushing pills, pills the color of fire engines or sunflowers or the bluest ocean. He knew the sting of a slapped hand across a boy's face as a thank-you. Thank you for trying to save me. *Whap!*

"You need help, Valentino." Gabe hadn't called him that in a while. His nickname in high school, when he couldn't keep it in his pants 'cause the girls wouldn't let him. "Valenti-no!" He could still hear the girls cry out across the quad. Gabe used to shake his head in awe mixed with a quiet judgment. He wasn't a pussy, he just never wanted to get it on with that many women. Val used to joke him about being a fag, but Gabe just insisted he believed in being "precious with his seed." Maybe Val hadn't learned anything from growing up in a broken home, but Gabriel had.

"I think your mama's calling you." Val smiled

the cockeyed grin of a drunk. "Isn't she your mama?"

Gabe sat silent as Valentin's smile widened into a malicious grin, his expression saying, "Go ahead. Hit me."

"Now, why do you be doing that?" Gabe asked him. "Why you going there, huh, boy?"

"Why're you fucking my sister?"

"Val."

"What?" Surly, like a dirt-faced kid.

"C'mon. You want to talk—talk."

"Wha-at?" Now bratty, like a spoiled girl.

"Okay. Here it is." Oh, he was going to catch shit for this. "I love your sister. I love Amanda."

"Bullshit."

"Ain't bullshit. It's the truth." Gabe waited a second. He didn't want to wait too long, didn't want to slide back now. "Someday, I'm gonna marry her."

Valentin looked at him, stunned. And then his face broke up into a hundred tiny parts as if in slow motion, and a sound came up from his throat and he laughed. And he didn't stop laughing. Gabe waited him out. He rubbed his hands together, waiting for the wheezing to subside.

"You done?"

"You shittin' me!"

"I'm not." Gabe's own voice surprised him. He sounded like an adult. "I'm going back to school. I'm going to graduate. I'm going to marry your sister."

"Can I be the best man?" Valentin was laughing again. Gabe stood and walked to the door in the slow, even step of a man fighting his rage. "Okay, man, you can laugh. But you laughing by yourself." He put his hand on the doorknob, his fingers tightened.

"Listen up, Val."

But Valentin wasn't finished. He squeaked out a couple of more giggles and wiped his nose with the back of his hand. Gabe noticed his nails were too long.

"No more dealing here. You got a son. You got a good sister taking care of him." Beat. "You take it somewhere else." Gabe gave him a look that said he meant business and when Gabe gave that look, men twice Valentin's size stepped aside gracefully. Gabe cracked open the door.

"Remember when we were kids? Remember how you'd protect me when I fucked up?" Val sounded almost mournful. "When I . . . I picked on that Mexican dude, and his big brothers came after me, and here comes Gabe Williams, man, and he kicked the shit out of every one of 'em." Val lifted his bony fists into a boxer's stance.

Gabe looked at Valentin, and brutal sadness came over him. Val's face flashed before his eyes—the one without lines, the one with the quick, easy smile. The sweet, young face.

"I remember."

"Good. Good," he replied, distracted. "You were my best friend, man. We were blood brothers."

"Elbow to elbow," Gabe said. He thought about the skateboard injuries, the scraped-up, banged-up knees and joints, and how they rubbed their bloody badges of honor together and vowed that no one would break their bond, ever.

"Gabe."

"What's that?" Gabe looked up at Valentin, whose eyes were wide open for the first time that morning. Gabe had not been scared of anyone for many years. But those eyes, Valentin's eyes, belonged to someone who no longer had anything to lose.

"You a loser, boy. Just like me. You ain't marrying nobody."

Gabe's knuckles turned white against his skin as he opened the door and reminded himself that there was a baby in the house. No slamming doors.

Twelve

James tapped his fingers against the steering wheel of the cheap import he had rented with the girl with the brown hair's money and waited for the throbbing in his chest to subside.

He had been sitting in this tiny car, his body all cramped up, ever since he saw the large light-skinned black guy exit the house an hour ago to gather oranges (and the next-door neighbor's newspaper) in his full arms and return to Amanda's house and close the door behind him. The sight of the man had turned him into stone and James was not sure why. As much momentum as James had worked up to drop classes for a week inches away from midterms and hop on a dank, crowded plane in the dead of night and rent a lousy tin can with his last twenty bucks and drive up this street to the side of Amanda's house, all that momentum had come to a crashing halt at the sight of this one man. James had met the immovable object in the shape of a petty thief gathering items for what James could only guess to be a romantic breakfast. No man in his right mind would make orange juice for himself. And this guy, with his bulk (and, Christ, James knew that had to be his bike and his helmet)—this guy wouldn't be stealing a paper for himself to read. And so James sat and panted like a thirsty dog and his heart pounded so that he could not hear the birds of Laurel Canyon above the hammering in his chest. Amanda was fucking this guy. James knew it. He also knew he had seen this guy before, and it didn't take his facile mind long before he put his finger on it: This guy was standing in Amanda's kitchen, the day James left. James physically shuddered, his teeth chattered as his mind raced over the fact that Amanda could have been fucking Mr. Big even before he left town.

James pondered what move to make next. He was dead-ass tired, and as he looked at his face in the rearview mirror, he recognized the disfigured soul staring back at him, wild eyed. He had seen that face in his father when he beat him and his little brother in the night, and he had seen that face on himself after he left his teacher's crumpled body in the middle of a quiet suburban street.

He should go back to school. He should go back to school now.

Amanda watched Gabe closely as he walked back into the kitchen and started cleaning the dishes. She noticed a slight tremble in his hands, the tightness around his mouth that wasn't there but five minutes ago. Amanda jumped up, leaving the baby in his high chair to bang spoons at will.

"Let me do those."

"Nah. I got 'em."

"But you made breakfast. Let me do something." She pushed him with her body, moving him over. "Move it." She looked at him, trying to make eye contact as he rolled up his sleeves and dipped his hands into the sink, into the warm, sudsy water.

"I got it."

She turned his face toward her with her cold,

dry hands and his eyes finally met hers, a reluctant child.

"What happened?"

"Nothing."

"What did he say to you?" Amanda was scared. Had Valentin told him about last night? Had Valentin told him a lie, that she attacked her brother, rather than the other way around?

"I love you." Amanda blurted it out, and immediately felt her face go scarlet.

Gabe lifted his arms out of the soapy water and reached around Amanda's waist and kissed her, burrowing into her lips until she was sure she'd die of suffocation or extreme happiness or both. And then he let her go and went back to the dishes.

"Okay, then," Amanda said. She tidied her hair and walked like a cheap drunk out of the kitchen and toward her nephew, who was busy discovering the pleasures of ripping thin paper napkins into shreds.

Gabe put the newspaper neatly back together, as though it had never been violated, and handed it to Mrs. Selby, who was much charmed by the handsome, strong, chivalrous young man with the teeth that reminded her of a movie star she dated once in the forties, whose name she could never remember but whose hands she remembered all too vividly.

Amanda and Gabe sat in Mrs. Selby's living room and talked for a few minutes about the weather and talk shows, and how the movies have suffered mightily since the second war, and Amanda was impressed with Gabe's patience with the old woman, who so obviously flirted with him, touching his arm whenever she had the chance, giggling like a Catholic schoolgirl. Amanda was afraid she would reach over and touch the tiny curls of his hair; she could see it was only a matter of minutes before the old woman asked. Amanda nudged Gabriel's knee to signal they should leave, and Gabe took her hand in his and squeezed it gently. He was giving Mrs. Selby her time.

They left Madison with Mrs. Selby and were on the bike, Amanda holding on to Gabe's waist, her head swimming in a borrowed helmet, which he lovingly tightened, almost choking off her air supply ("You gotta wear it tight"), before Amanda noticed the rental car parked just beyond her house; she thought it was strange that the car careened toward them as they were leaving, and then jerked away from them, as though the driver had changed his mind about hitting them at the last second. Gabe just shrugged; a lot of people in cars seemed to have it in for bikers.

They hit the road. This perfectly crisp fall morning would be spent on the edges of the coastline, in search of memories they could rely on in the future. Amanda just knew, as she tightened her grip around Gabe's waist, that this would be a day she'd long remember.

"I love this!" Amanda screamed into the wind, not knowing or caring whether anyone heard her.

"It's only starting, little girl!" Gabriel yelled back. "We got everything ahead of us!"

Amanda hugged Gabriel's back and closed her eyes, and embraced the belief that she would never be lonely again.

James sat and smoked a cigarette and pushed at his fries at the hamburger stand on Sunset and watched the Saturday-morning hookers and was grateful, finally, that he had straightened the car out at the last second. Even though his suspicions were confirmed, even though he was blind with jealousy, he was finding it easy to smile. He always liked a challenge. And he knew he would win this one. James, Harvard Law School student and streetwise killer, would win Amanda back. This was just a fling, this half-breed black man. He didn't stand a chance against the love of her life.

A honey-skinned Latina, loaded with her older sister's ID, platinum blond hair spun into a haystack, and pink hot pants gripping a healthy pair of thighs, eyed James's fries and his clean-shaven presence and smiled invitingly. James smiled back and held up the rest of his fries; he was feeling generous.

"Me gustaria tener mas dinero, mamacita," he said to her as she took the fries. She looked at him in surprise. A white boy who could speak the melodical Spanish of rich men. She beat her eyes at him, humbled, and walked away, tugging at her shorts. She had a nice pair of legs and a big honey-colored ass. "I wish I had more money, little mama," he said to himself.

Santa Barbara was pure bliss. The two spent much of the day gulping hamburgers and chocolate malts at a beachside cafe, and watching seagulls dance with surfers in the murky waters of the Pacific. Gabe, who had surfed in his teenage years, even bought Amanda a wet suit and convinced her to follow him into the water. They borrowed a longboard covered in tribal designs off an older guy who was happy to trade his stick for some of Gabe's homegrown.

Gabe, wearing a pair of old trunks, grasped Amanda's small hand and led her into the cool water. It took a moment for Amanda to catch her breath—even though she was a California girl, she had never learned to trust herself in the ocean. Repeated episodes of being rolled by waves, gulping seawater and sand as she scraped along in the undertow, had scared, almost literally, the shit out of her as a child.

Moments later, however, she found herself on top of the surfboard, paddling like a desperate puppy, lying underneath Gabe. His long, strong arms propelled them through the choppy water as though the Pacific were a backyard pool. Amanda relaxed after a moment, hypnotized by the rhythm of his stroke.

When they landed on the other side of the break, they sat up together on the board and looked out at the shore, and Amanda's heart stopped for a second; she had never done anything this brave before. Gabe wrapped his arms around her and they lounged there, bobbing in the water, watching and waiting, their breaths as one.

They stood vigil for the wave that would take them in. Their wave. Gabe waited and waited, his patience lulling Amanda into a deep sense of security.

And then it came.

"Up," Gabe said calmly, and before she knew it, Amanda was standing, feet splayed, arms in airplane position, and dammit, this girl was riding.

"*Ahhh!*" She screamed louder than she had ever before, her scream serenading the two lovers all the way into shore.

They ran in and collapsed on the sand in a fit of laughter.

"What was that scream about?" Gabe asked. He had never heard a pitch quite like that, not even from an animal. "And how come you haven't done that in bed yet?"

She looked at him, her eyes dancing.

"I think I just had an exorcism," Amanda said.

"No kidding. You want to go again?" he asked. But Amanda shook her head and wriggled into his shoulder.

"Why mess with perfection, huh?" Gabe said. He knew what she was thinking. He wiped the sand from her forehead and he kissed her and the hours passed for everyone else but them.

Gabe rode Amanda to his house; his father's car was not in the driveway, and Gabe gave a silent thank-you for this. One thing at a time. He opened the door to his home, and the dog with the spiked collar greeted him, his great ass whipping back and forth in a happy fury. The dog liked Amanda as well, judging by the way he planted his paws on her chest to get a better shot at her face with his tongue. Amanda squealed, delighted that this fierce-looking creature was so sweet; at the same time, she knew Gabe would never own a killer.

"Get down!" Gabe ordered the spiked-collared dog, who would not listen, delighted by the sounds coming from this new person's throat.

"Down, you evil dog! Down!" Amanda laughed again as the dog jumped in the air, happy for the attention. Gabe took him by the collar and sat him down with his other hand.

"He's sweet."

"He's stupid."

"No, he's not. He's sweet. Like you."

"Now you're going soft on me." Gabe rolled his eyes.

"Okay. He's sweeter than you are. But other than that, he's just like you. Large, dark, and handsome."

"I don't have a spiked collar."

"It's on my list."

"Oh, really." Gabe smiled. "And what else is on that list of yours?" He got closer to her. She could feel the warmth of his breath.

"That list is top-secret, classified information," she replied unsteadily. Gabe was now, slowly, backing her up against a wall. Amanda reached behind her, automatically, and touched the curled-up edges of old wallpaper. "No one, not even the federal government, knows what's on that list," she continued.

"Oh, I know ways I can get that list out of you." Gabe's voice was lowered and smoky, and Amanda almost stopped breathing.

"So you think," Amanda replied. By now, the shakiness in her voice was giving everything away.

"Baby, anything I don't know about you will be revealed to me," Gabe said.

"What if," Amanda said, and now she was serious, "what if you don't like what you find?"

Gabe lifted his head from the side of her neck, where he had found one of the items on her "list," and stared at her, straight in the eye. She turned away.

"Look at me," he said. "Look at this man."

Amanda looked at Gabe.

"This man loves every piece of you, even the parts you don't like," he told her. "And by the way," he added, "for the record, this is not a man who scares easily."

And with that, Gabe took Amanda's hand and they walked up the stairs and into his bedroom, and the dog with the spiked collar sat outside the door with all the patience his dog mind could muster and wondered what all the commotion was about. And when he would be fed.

Twenty minutes later, Frank, the old master, came by the door and greeted the dog and was about to knock when he, too, heard the noises, and the dog saw his gentle eyes widen, and then the old man went back as he came, quietly down the stairs, whistling a silent tune. The dog looked at the closed door again, gave a final whine, and went down the stairs in search of food and company.

Joe Artuga sat with his hand on the phone for half an hour before he finally dialed. When he could not figure out what he was so afraid of, he had nothing to do but punch in the numbers. A brusque voice greeted him, a voice he recognized as his own when nights were too long and the morning came too soon.

"Yeah."

"Ah . . ." Joe wanted to hang up. Fucking wimp. He spent one second belittling himself before he asked for Amanda.

"Hello?" The voice grew more impatient.

"Is, ah, Amanda there?" What was he so nervous about? He was her *boss*, for crying out loud. "This is her . . . This is Joe Artuga."

"So."

"So . . . I work with her." He was on the spot with whoever this asshole was. He didn't like it. "I'm her boss." Pause. Now Joe felt like an asshole. "Employer." Pause. "We work together?"

"She ain't here." The guy's voice had gotten

soft, scratchy. He was fading. Joe wondered if this was the brother. She mentioned she had a brother. She forgot to mention he was a fucking weasel dick.

"Can I leave a message?"

"I don't have a pen."

"Can you remember a name?"

"What is it."

"Joe. Joe Artuga."

"Joe. Gotta go. I'm expecting a phone call."

"Just tell her. Okay?"

The guy had hung up already; the dial tone blasted Joe's ear; he didn't remember it ever being quite that loud and humiliating.

Joe knew the brother would never give her the message; he'd just have to swing by himself to give it to her. Joe knew her boyfriend was in law school somewhere, out of town, and this being Saturday night, she might want something to do. And it was Joe's goal to show Amanda a good time.

An hour after they had buried themselves in Gabe's room under his burnt orange velvet covers and the strains of Marvin Gaye, Luther Vandross, and Peabo Bryson, Amanda and Gabriel emerged and tiptoed naked down the creaky wooden hall and into the shared upstairs bathroom. Amanda had resisted, deathly afraid of running into Gabe's father, but Gabe would not listen.

"Follow me," he ordered. "Come on, now." And he pulled her as she dragged her heels across the floorboards.

"No!" she said, in a loud whisper, louder than her normal voice. "No, no, no, no, no!"

She slipped out of his grip and tried to run back into the bedroom, but he came after her, laughing.

"Girl, you get your butt down here or you are in for some punishment." He could hardly get the words out, he was laughing so hard.

Finally he just spun her over his shoulder, and Amanda covered her eyes and prayed that no one would be a sorry witness to the sight of her big white ass draped over Gabe's statuelike body.

Gabriel ran warm water in the oversized sink that was old twenty years ago as Amanda stood, shivering at the way her body had been spent; though she was numb, she was not in the least bit cold. Gabe wished he could have run a

bath, but the yellowed porcelain of the tub was
cracked and worn, and would not hold water.
He unwrapped a new bar of soap and placed it
beside the sink and then turned to Amanda,
who continued to stare at him; she did not com-
prehend his intentions until he lifted her with
two large hands encompassing her waist and
placed her gently into the sink, in which she fit
like a baby bird in its nest, a child in her
mother's arms. She looked up at Gabe and
could not speak except with her damp, shining
eyes as he wrapped one arm around her still-
shivering shoulders, quieting them, and with
the other bathed her body gently with the soapy
water, his fingers running over her, reminding
her of the magical afternoon she had spent in
the backyard of her grandmother's old house in
the Wilshire district, her eight-year-old body
pummeled gently by rain as she lay on her back
in the grass, her eyes closed but her mouth
open and laughing and her heart open even
wider. Looking back, Amanda did not know for
the longest time who that little girl was or what
had possessed her to dive into the grass in a
rainstorm, soaking her brand-new patent
leather Mary Janes and catching a cold that

veered precariously into pneumonia, keeping her home for two weeks.

Amanda wrapped her arms around Gabriel's neck and swore her heart to him forever. The little girl with the ruined Mary Janes was back.

Gabriel brushed Amanda's hair and hummed a tune he recognized after several passes as being an old Southern lullaby his mother once sang to him. This stopped him cold for a moment, this sudden connection to his MIA mother, and Amanda turned and looked into his eyes with the playfulness of someone whose problems were far, far away. "Done?"

Gabriel smiled at her; she looked all of about five years old, freshly scrubbed, cheeks flushed, only not from a warm bath with a foam toy but from an afternoon of great regret-free, loving sex.

"Shit." He had been counting. "How many was that?"

"You're the hairdresser, monsieur."

"Okay, then. We start all over." Gabriel started counting as he brushed her hair. "One . . . two . . . three . . ." At one hundred, Gabriel started over at one again, and Amanda suspected he would brush her hair all night if she let him. And she would let him.

"Let me do you."

"Uh-uh."

"C'mon. I want to comb your hair."

"Oh no." Gabriel got up, shaking his hands. "No one touches these curls but me." He pointed at his head, his jaw jutting forward.

"Oh yeah?" Amanda grabbed a comb from an open cabinet and jumped at him, holding it like a switchblade, tossing it back and forth in her hands. *West Side Story* with hair accessories.

As she jabbed at him with the comb, Gabe stepped sideways and grabbed her by the waist and flipped her over his shoulder backwards; she beat his back with her hands and kicked and screamed and laughed, and her towel slipped from her body, giving Gabriel ample space to dole out punishment in the form of spankings.

Whack! They sounded worse then they were, an open hand against moist flesh. *Whack!* Amanda screamed louder and pummeled him with her fist as he taunted her: "What was that? You see something back there? 'S there a mosquito back there?"

"I'm going to kill you!" Amanda screamed. Gabriel responded by taking her ass in one hand and gnawing on it hungrily.

"Gabriel!" She was choking on her own laughter as he opened the door to the bathroom. Carrying her on one shoulder like a sack, a rifle, he ran-hopped down the hallway, a naked caveman, threw open his bedroom door, and hurled his prey onto the mattress, which swung back and forth in waves. And then he leapt, an Olympic high diver going for gold, and Amanda saw her life flash before her eyes as this huge body sailed over hers, finally landing next to her, the bed a sea of exuberant motion.

They did not notice the open door or the dog with the spiked collar who watched them, confused and worried at the sounds the humans were making. The dog wondered, as deeply as a pet-store-purchased inbred could, why his master wanted to hurt the other human so bad. He wondered if he should growl at his master to get him to stop, but then thought better of it and curled up into a ball and slept the unfettered sleep of dogs, sociopaths, and babies.

*   *   *

When she woke with a start, Amanda grasped for the phone and dialed Mrs. Selby's number, even as Gabriel rolled over and reached for her, wrapping himself around her as the phone rang and rang. "I have to go," she said. "I've got to pick Maddie up."

Gabriel sprang out of bed and almost tripped over the dog with the spiked collar, but was dressed and ready to go before Amanda was. He took this shit seriously, this baby shit. Yes, he wanted her to stay; yes, he wanted more than anything for her to spend the night. But this baby was hers—more than Val's, more than Patrice's. And who was he, the son of a mother who ran, not to respect that?

"I'll meet you outside." Gabe was out the door as Amanda buttoned her blouse and searched for her purse. She was so relieved at what he did not do: He did not grimace, not even a furrow. He did not whine. He did not ask for a little more sleep or more time with her. ("Don't you love me?" James might have said.) Nothing. He respected that Amanda had a responsibility, and a big one at that. She looked at her reflection in his smoky mirror. "This is not a man you find every day," she told herself. Her reflection nodded its agreement, and somehow Amanda found the purse that had gotten up on all fours and walked away from the top of the scratched wood dresser she put it on several hours ago.

James had never liked Valentin, even when Valentin had some semblance of charm. The two had never gotten along; James was too straight for Valentin, too book smart, too ambitious to get inside a world Valentin would never have entrée to. James wanted to be better than Valentin, and Valentin knew this. But James had never tripped over the real reason Valentin set his sights on James so regularly, tormenting him by standing too close when James got milk out of the refrigerator, hissing curses at him as he walked by, taunting him with references to "illegals," "beaners," "wetbacks," then falling all over himself to correct his faux pas. "Oh, sorry, James, I forgot. You're . . . Hispanic, right?"

Asshole. James would respond by using insulting multisyllabic words that he knew Valentin didn't understand. "Valentin, I forgot. You're . . . a caprophagous catamite, right?"

Valentin's face would slacken, his eyes narrow. All he could respond with was a typical "Fuck you, beans" and a huff. James was happy at these times for the hours he spent as a child flipping through the school library dictionary he had made off with in elementary school. Calling Valentin a shit-eating boy kept by a pederast warmed his soul.

But it never came to blows. Amanda loved her brother; saw his flaws but was firmly attached to his good side—the generous, fun-loving, risk-taking boy she had grown up with. But now he was beyond saving; James saw that as he opened the door to 1963 Diego Drive. The guy was a fucking skeleton, his skin almost translucent, his cheeks sunken into the gray face of an old man. And it was only in this moment, looking into the decaying face of his former tormentor, whom he hadn't thought about in six months, that he saw why Valentin hated him. James had taken Amanda from him; Valentin was jealous of James's relationship with his sister. Obvious. Yet up to this point, a mystery. James started laughing at his own stupidity as Valentin stood there, his cigarette shaking in his hand, his expression going from surprise to something bordering on pleasure to confusion to irritation.

"What the fuck's your problem?"

"Sorry." James pulled himself together. "Can I come in, Val?"

"Your girlfriend's not here, man." Valentin sank into the voice of the tormentor one more time.

James was not going to bite. "I'll wait."

Valentin smiled at this. "Your funeral, beans."

They shared one beer and then another and by the time the headlight of the motorcycle splashed across their faces from outside, they were old friends. Valentin even offered James a free line or two, but James declined. His marathoner's heart was beating at a steady forty-eight per minute even as he heard the purr of the motorcycle outside the picture window; he did not want to change that. Valentin looked at him and smiled wide, his gums receding, his teeth yellowing. "She's home." Strange, in that moment James felt sorry for Valentin. More sorry for Valentin, even, than for himself.

Amanda saw the rental car outside her house and knew. It was the same one from this morning, the one that had almost run them over. She hadn't seen the driver, but she knew, in her heart, who had considered hurting them.

Jimmy was home.

Gabe got off the bike and lent Amanda his hand. He could tell something was wrong. He figured Amanda was worried that the old lady hadn't answered her phone. But Gabe wasn't concerned; he knew the baby would be all right. That old girl loved that kid.

Gabe trailed Amanda to Mrs. Selby's front door, his head and body filled with love as he watched her boyish walk, her head bouncing up and down with each step. She could take on the world. He wondered when would be the right time to ask her if she could see marrying him.

Amanda rang the doorbell. She hadn't looked at Gabriel yet, but as they waited, shivering, listening to the tiny, mean dog yapping away, Amanda turned quickly to Gabe and blurted out his worst fear: "James is here." Gabe looked at her.

"What?"

"Jimmy. He's here. That's his car." Gabe looked to where Amanda pointed. A rental car.

"How do you know?"

Amanda shook her head. "I just do. I just do."

Mrs. Selby finally opened the door, and smiled at Amanda and beamed at Gabriel, behind whose polite smile was a dream that had just ended.

The walk to her house, next door, was the longest they had taken in their lives. Amanda held one of Maddie's hands as Gabriel held him in his arms. Maddie babbled on and on, occasionally saying the small, mean dog's name, and Amanda and Gabriel stared straight ahead. Walking the plank.

When they finally arrived at the front door, James was standing there in the dark, the light above the front door having burned out weeks earlier.

"Amanda."

Amanda jumped. She thought about James's temper.

"James. What are you doing here?"

"School break. I wanted to come see you."

Gabe held the baby, silently watching, looking for a sign. James looked at him abruptly. "We met, right?"

"Right."

"You're Valentin's friend."

"This is Gabriel, James." Amanda tried to tell

James a world in that sentence. "This is Gabriel, the man I love, James," is what she hoped he heard.

If he did, he didn't care. "Good meeting you." He turned to Amanda. "I think we should talk." There was a finality in his voice that had to be addressed.

Amanda froze, retreating into the familiar position she took with James during their conflicts; he would talk and talk and talk and she would listen, until whatever argument she possessed, whatever point she wanted to make, whatever lucid claim she could hazard would be rendered lifeless.

Her face locked in a portrait of torment. She longed to run, to leave her whole life behind as she and Gabe and the baby disappeared.

Gabriel looked at Amanda, who stood there, paralyzed; he already knew his place. Back door, back of the bus, back, back, back. She turned and stared at his chest but could not meet his eyes, and he knew, as sure as he knew anything. He realized he still had Madison in his arms, and with all the strength left in his body he handed the baby over to her, feeling her arm against his, her breath on his skin.

He was on his motorcycle and down the street doing ninety before the tears came streaming down his face, fogging up his helmet. He did not care. He did not want to see. He did not want to hear as Amanda called out his name in a voice that said it was over.

Thirteen

Joe Artuga first stopped off at the liquor store at the corner on Sunset to pick up a carton of orange juice and a packet of multivitamins for men. He had been feeling pretty low and he knew that cigarettes somehow depleted your vitamin stores, so he thought these would give him some of that energy he had when he was in college. "Christ, is thirty-two that old?" he thought as he threw his wares on the counter in front of the polite swarthy-looking man with a name tag with more vowels on it than Joe thought were in the alphabet. Joe turned when he felt the large deep-set brown eyes of a well-known television actor hoping to turn movie star eyeing him with a vigor that should have been reserved for his tall blond movie-star wife. Joe turned back to the clerk. "Throw a couple of Marlboros on there, will ya?"

Joe walked out of the liquor store, the brown eyes still on his back, and chuckled as he washed down the vitamins with the orange juice. He felt better already. At least he wasn't living a lie.

He drove up one hill and down the next, downshifting jerkily on narrow, winding streets that ended in words like "Trail" or "Way" or "Terrace." He checked and double-checked the address in his head against the faded numbers on every curb. Either no one had repainted the numbers in years or Joe's eyes weren't so great anymore after dark.

After driving for an hour, he still could not find the house on Diego Drive. His *Thomas Guide* was years old and tattered from overuse, and even if it weren't, page thirty-four was missing, the page on which the elusive Diego existed. Page thirty-four had been missing for several years; many people lived on page thirty-four. It was a midrange page; the people on it, from the hills just above Sunset to the ethnic pockets on the east side, were neither rich nor poor, though both could be found; they were not just black or white or brown; they were all these things. Page thirty-four represented the Los Angeles Joe fell in love with twelve years ago, and page thirty-four was no more. Joe gave up and found a street that was heading, mercifully, down. Turning onto the road, slick with mud, his eyes were blinded by a single headlight, plowing into the darkness with a vengeance. A teenager, Joe thought, on a motorcycle joyride.

"Fuck!" Joe cursed as he slammed on his brakes, the back end of his convertible slipping into a half spin in the muddy bank of road, suddenly more out of control than its driver. Joe waited a moment, caught his breath. "Fuck you. Thank you, God. Fuck you," he choked.

To die alone in the hills above Los Angeles because some ass-wipe teenager got in a fight with his mother or his drug dealer or his girlfriend—that would be just Joe's luck.

He turned on his left blinker as if he were fifteen again and just learning to drive, and gingerly made his way down the hill. He landed finally, by the grace of God, on his favorite street in the world, Sunset Boulevard.

The lights of Sunset soothed him; the people on Sunset, the girls in their tight, shiny outfits and stiletto heels, the boys with their long, feathered hair, their slender bodies straining against their faded blue jeans, these sights gave Joe a warm, secure feeling. He was not one of them: He drove a late-model Italian convertible. He had money. He was young enough to be hip, old enough to be interesting. He was in the prime of his life. What the fuck was he doing driving around winding, narrow roads searching for a girl he had already fucked? All he had to do was tool down Sunset at the right hour of the night, and the town belonged to him. The girls, the boys, if he were so inclined, the drugs, the lights, the dancing, the laughter. He had made it in a town that fought every step.

He pulled into the swamped driveway of Carlos 'n Charlie's, a Strip restaurant and nightclub popular with grandiose people with fancy cars and no discernible income (no legal income, anyhow). The funk singer Rick James, his gold-tinted cornrows hanging over his head like a Jamaican Easter bonnet, revolved precariously out of his metallic purple Rolls, the door held open for him not by a red-coated valet but by one of his numerous white-blond, Lycra-impaired girl-friends. Joe recognized the fervent look in the blond's eye and her clenched smile as she helped

James out of his car. There was no anger in the way she put her arm around the singer's shoulder, the way she hung on to him as they walked up the stairs into El Privado, the private bar upstairs (which was not so private if you held out a hundred for the bouncer). Her teeth were clenched, her eyes on fire from doing too much coke. Joe hoped there were more like her upstairs. These girls were beautiful, and the rules were simple: Don't try to engage them in intelligent conversation; they're like puppies or small children, they bore easily. Don't come on to them; let them come on to you. If you spend enough at the bar, they'll find you (lots of drinks = money = coke). Don't be nice to them. These girls don't like nice men (nice men = losers). The colder you are, the less you notice their perfect hair, their sultry eyes, their slim-to-nothing bodies with pumped-up breasts, the higher the chance of getting them in your bed that night. This was a lesson Joe learned early on in Los Angeles. For two whole years, Joe couldn't get a date with any girl in L.A.—the pretty ones thought they were too good for the nice Midwestern boy working his way up in the television jungle; the ugly ones didn't trust his

interest in them. He didn't blame them—
he couldn't trust it himself, not for more than
one or two weeks.

Finally, his mentor, a fifty-year-old producer
with a drawer full of cheap coke and four marriage licenses to his name, sat Joe down and gave
him the run of the land. "You're too nice," the guy
told him between puffs on the old-fashioned
Salems in the green and white package, the kind
Joe's mother smoked in the fifties. "You'll never
get anywhere. Not with chicks, not with television, not with selling shoes. Get mean, get tough,
grow a set of big, old, hairy, steel-plated balls, or
get the fuck back home, cheesehead."

That night, Joe had gone out, treated a girl like
shit for the first time, and fucked her brains out.
Waited ten minutes, then left and never called. He
wondered what happened to that girl. He always
meant to thank her. She had changed his life.

Joe pulled forward in the black convertible.
He loved to see the admiring looks on the valets'
faces as he pulled in. "Hey," the looks said, "this
guy's made it. He's figured it out." It was at these
moments that Joe loved his life. He looked at a
group of college-age girls, USC students by the
cut and color of their hair (pin straight, shoulder

length, Clairol blond #10) and the make and color of their car (Rabbit Cabriolet, white). He guessed they belonged to one of three sororities that he often hired interns from: Tri-Delt, Delta Gamma, Kappa Kappa Gamma. God had graced him by not allowing him to find Amanda. What did he need with love anyway? What he really needed was a new set of interns for the station. He felt his head; his fever was no more. The vitamins were working.

Gabriel took three stairs at a time and was in his room before the front door had closed behind him. This was going to be the hardest of the nights ahead of him. The first night. His chest ached and his mouth was dry, and he was glad for the cheap malt liquor he had bought from the store on Venice, the one the black folks went to. He had bought six of the sixty-four-ounce bottles. He hadn't had a drink in a while, and he had forgotten how much it took to make pain of the emotional sort go away. He figured three would do it. Three for tonight. Three for tomorrow night.

He took his father's Charlie Parker record

from its jacket, blew the dust off that had settled in the last week, and put it on his turntable. He popped open a Schlitz malt liquor bottle and sat watching the record go round and round, until he could no longer see it through his tears.

Amanda watched James. She did not dare move. She held the sleeping child against her chest and watched as James talked. She could not hear what he was saying, but his lips were moving, and he was looking at her, not five feet away. He paused for a moment; he had been talking long and fast.

"What are you doing here?" she found herself asking. "What are you doing here?" She was repeating herself. She hadn't heard one word he said.

"I just told you. Aren't you listening to me?" Amanda looked at her hands, clasped around her nephew. James was back, and he wanted answers. "You have nothing to say?"

Amanda was aware of Valentin, still in the house somewhere, listening.

"Come on, Amanda, this is me talking." James shifted. "Your Jimmy. You and me, we grew up together—we'll always know each other." Beat. "And we will always love each other. Nothing you've done can change that."

Amanda looked up at him. Her face told him her answer. She hardly had to shake her head. "Jimmy . . ."

"Okay, here's the thing," James said. "You fooled around, you feel guilty . . ." He looked at her. "Oh, God. Tell me you didn't blow him," he thought to himself.

"I don't want to discuss this with you or anybody," Amanda said. "And besides, you're the one who left."

"You don't want to talk about this with your best friend? I'm the person who knows you, Amanda. I know everything about you."

"Maybe you don't, Jimmy," Amanda said, defiant. "Maybe there's a small part of me which is a complete mystery to you."

"I don't believe that," he said confidently, "and neither do you."

"Oh fuck me," Amanda said and sat down in a heap. She checked Madison, who was still sleeping. "See that," she added, disgusted with herself. "You made me swear in front of the baby."

"I'm sure he'll live," James said. And then he

thought, "Damn that baby, anyway. She should be holding me, not him."

"Why did you just look at him like that?" Amanda demanded.

"Look at who like what?" James felt like kicking himself—she could read his mind. The bitch was psychic.

"You're jealous of everything—you're even jealous of a little tiny baby."

"Now you're really getting crazy on me," James said in his most believable wail. "I love babies." He reached out and tried to touch Madison, but Amanda's maternal glare stopped him.

"Didn't we have an agreement? Didn't we say it would be too hard to have a long-distance relationship?" she said. And then Amanda added, after thinking a moment, "Wait a minute—I'm not the one who said those words, you freakin' asshole lawyer. *You* are."

"I don't want an agreement. I want you," he replied. "And I'm not an asshole lawyer, yet. But I will be one someday." He knew Amanda appreciated humor in tense moments; he was trying his hardest to find some.

"Damn. I keep swearing in front of the baby," she said softly. "I'm a terrible mother."

James noticed that she didn't bother correcting herself, as if she didn't even realize that this baby did not belong to her.

And then James rose as if he were carrying a large barbell, his legs weak beneath its weight. He came closer, then sank again, sitting on the floor on his knees in front of Amanda. Amanda watched every move with her big, sad eyes that had seen too much to love this one again. He put his head in her lap. She reached out with one hand and gingerly touched his hair. He needed comfort. Who was she to keep it from him?

"Don't leave me," James asked, his words barely a whisper. Amanda patted his head, once, twice, then gently left her hand there. Though he said more, his confession never reached her. The baby's breathing was the only sound she heard.

The rumors at the plant, once numerous and unwieldy, had become one: GM was moving this sucker to Mexico. Gabriel and J.D. and the rest of the crew would be out of a job within a year. Gabriel tried his best to ward off this salvo: The management hadn't said anything to the union, had they? Wouldn't the union know already if it were true? To tell the truth, Gabe was sick of listening to J.D. bitch and moan about what was going to happen once he was out of a job. They all knew what happened in Detroit; many of them had families that started out in the once-thriving birthplace of the automotive industry that now looked like something out of a Mad Max movie. There was nothing in Detroit for the black man but burnt-out buildings and housing projects where kids daring to double-Dutch got shot up in broad daylight. Nobody had a job.

Gabe said nothing as his line took their break and drank their Cokes and ate their sweethearts' cold cut sandwiches and fried chicken and left-over enchiladas, and held court on the rumor that would not die.

"White man fuckin' us again."

"Yep. They holdin' out. That's what they doing."

"I got three kids. My wife don't work. What'm I supposed to do? Forty-eight years old. Ain't that a bitch."

"I am *two years* from retirement. Two damn years."

"It was too good to last. That's what it is. My luck ain't never been nothing but bad."

"Got that right." The joke is set up.

"Look at his woman." Guffaws all around.

"Shut th' fuck up."

"Tha's what they say. Here today, gone tomorrow."

Gabe got up from his spot on the bench away from the rest. He was tired of this. He didn't care anymore about the job. He didn't care anymore about anything. Almost a week since he talked to Amanda. He couldn't even start to say what he missed about her; he wouldn't be able to stop. He missed the baby, too. He missed the life he dreamed of having. Two days ago a packet came addressed to him in the mail from the community college on Vermont Avenue. His father had waited up to hand it to Gabe. When Gabe looked at the lined brown face of his father, asleep in his ratty armchair, the TV blasting nonsense to aging ears no longer able to get annoyed at the sound, his heart broke all over again.

His father had fallen asleep with the packet safely tucked under his arm, partially covering his round belly. Gabe could not tell him he changed his mind; he was not going to school after all. He could not tell his father his life had ended, and the person he was seeing standing before him, greeting him with a "Morning, Pops" or a light tap on the arm, was an impostor, a shell. Gabe had stayed up late as a child once, watching *Invasion of the Body Snatchers*, watching as folks were turned into zombies. That's what he was, a zombie. In the last week, he had lost ten pounds. For the first time in his life, he was having trouble eating. He'd taken to having angry conversations with himself. "What the fuck is wrong with you, boy?" he'd say. "Get it together." Then there'd be things like, "She's nothing but a woman, what'd you expect?" Or he'd try to convince himself to shop elsewhere. "Did you see that black-haired girl looking at you?" he'd say. "The girl with the big jugs?" He was even taking to memorizing some of the brand-new gangsta rap that was out—the brothers who called every girl a bitch or a ho and treated women like dogs. He wondered if he were capable of that—and promised himself he would set his mind to it. Someday.

It was all making him sick.

His pants bagged at the waistline and around his thighs, and he tightened his belt, and then tightened it again. And still he could not eat. His face hurt, and his mouth was curved down in a perpetual scowl, which frightened people; he could tell from the looks on their faces and the way they made space for him when he bought another six-pack or a newspaper. His tongue felt like sandpaper, his mouth dry as the desert. His forehead was suddenly lined by lack of sleep and bad dreams in which she teased him with cameo appearances, a smile on her lips. Her laughter throbbed in his ears, and then disappeared. In a week, Gabriel had become, suddenly, a man who no longer had anything to live for, and therefore had nothing to lose. Violence had replaced love in his heart.

"I said, 'What you think, big man?'" Gabe looked up to see J.D. smiling at him, his gold tooth catching the light off the lamppost. J.D. was measuring him, his baggy eyes showing concern behind the bravado of his shit-eating grin. He knew something was wrong. "You with us, man?"

"He don't care."

"He's single. He young. No kids."

"No kids? Dang."

"No girl." Sanchez smiled and wheezed. Sanchez was a muscled hulk of a man whose main contribution to any conversation was wheezing. A couple of the men were still laughing when Gabe suddenly turned around and whipped Sanchez up by the scruff of his short, thick neck and held his two-hundred-plus frame against the brick wall of the plant with one hand, the other clenched by his side, and the only thing that prevented Gabe from spending the next ten years in maximum security was J.D.

Moving fast, he swung his arm around Gabe's body and tightened his grip, and his words came fierce. "Let go, Gabe. Let go." Gabe, who saw nothing but gray, heard J.D. as if through a tunnel, and felt his hot, desperate breath on his shoulder; he suddenly opened his grip as if he had clutched a burning frying pan and dropped Sanchez, who fell limp against the brick, his knees buckling beneath him, his wheeze reduced to a gasp. No one said another word to Gabe.

Gabe sat on his motorcycle and drank from a large can wrapped in a paper bag and watched the house. He was on the hill across from her, his motorcycle parked on a spot that had been leveled for a condominium complex. Most of the time, the lights in the house would remain dim. Four o'clock in the morning, most people were asleep. But Gabe sat up and he watched, and he did not stop watching until the sun came up, and then he went wearily home, passing the bulldozers on the way down the hill.

Amanda lay awake from the hour of four to the hour of six every morning. She would drag herself, finally, out of bed at six and check on the baby, who would be, most times, cooing softly to himself in his crib, entertaining himself with his fingers or his favorite purple toy. During the past week, Amanda would gingerly slide around James's sleeping form, careful not to wake him. She hated him for taking back half her bed, the bed she had given to another man, a better man. But she hated herself more. When she looked at herself in the bathroom mirror in the morning, between the smudges and the toothpaste stains, she saw someone she was ashamed of looking back. Overnight, Amanda had become one of those women afraid to stand up for themselves; she had lost her opinion. She thought about why this had happened to her, this transformation. She had been so happy in those few moments with Gabriel, she had felt anything was possible.

And then it came to her.

"You don't think you deserve happiness," she said to her sad reflection. She thought about what she was doing, how she had allowed James back into her life, and added, hatefully, "And you might be right, you stupid, weak piece of shit."

She found herself sinking to her knees, praying to a God she professed not to believe in, not to trust. She prayed for strength. She prayed for conviction. Mostly, as in a warped, modern-day fairy tale, she prayed for Gabriel to come riding back on his trusty iron steed and take her and the baby away from this man, this house, this brother, this life. She looked at the pale figure in the mirror and felt physically repulsed, ill at her reflection. Her body could not forgive her weakness. Her body needed Gabriel. Her body was kicking her ass from the inside out.

James woke up to find Amanda vomiting in the bathroom. She was bent over the toilet, and in the brightness of day, he thought she looked too thin.

"You okay?"

She replied by vomiting more. He waited a moment as she caught her breath. She talked into the toilet, the sound echoing strangely. "I think I might have an ulcer."

"An ulcer? Is the job that stressful?"

"No."

"Maybe you should quit."

Amanda looked up at James, studying his profile in the mirror. She felt bile rise in the back of her throat. Her body did not like him anymore. She willed the bitter taste back down, promising she would call Gabriel that very day, no matter how ashamed she felt, no matter what he would say to her. She would take it like a man. The vomit went back down; the gagging ceased.

"I'm not quitting," she choked out.

"You'll love Boston."

"I love L.A." Not really. She just felt like saying it. Amanda would move out of L.A. in two seconds, if Gabriel would go with her. The thought cheered her for a moment before James spoke again.

"So we'll come back to L.A. When I graduate, I'll be able to get a job anywhere."

"I'm not quitting." And then Amanda started to cry.

"What's wrong?" James asked, concerned. He was hoping she wasn't crying over that guy.

"I'm worried about Val." Amanda realized

that she was, desperately worried about her brother. "James, he's over the deep end. I mean way over. He—you should have seen what he did. He . . ." She couldn't get the words out.

"What? What did he do?" James's voice got higher.

"You can't get upset—"

"Tell me what he did."

"He must have thought I was somebody else. He must've thought I was Patrice."

"Oh, God." The color drained from his face. "Did he rape you?"

"No, God, I mean, Valentin's sick, but please—he just kissed me. I mean, in that way . . ."

"What way?"

"That way that's not a sister-brother way, unless you're in a really, really screwed-up family."

"Amanda," he said, "I'm going to get you out of here."

"I don't want to leave; that's not the point. I just want my brother to get help."

"No. That's it," he replied strongly. "You have to save yourself." He looked at himself in the mirror, smoothed his hair. "You know, you really have to learn to be a little more selfish."

And James took her shoulders in his hands, cold from the ice water he splashed on his face every morning. He had seen Paul Newman do it in a movie once; what worked for the piercingly blue-eyed movie star would surely work for him. Amanda caught a glimpse of her backside in the mirror and remembered her butt-relative-to-happiness scientific method. With Gabriel, her ass had grown almost to extremes; she was considering naming it or finding it a separate apartment to live in. Or at least getting it a leash. The thought almost made her smile. But that had all changed. James was back and her ass had become a white girl's—flat as a board, and so bony it hurt to sit on anything unpadded for more than five minutes. Looking at it now, her sad small ass, she realized she had to save herself. She had to save her butt. But first she had to get James's icy hands off her shoulders. The baby started crying. Amanda smiled to herself at the amazing Madison's psychic skills. "Baby," she said, slipping beneath James's fingers.

At work, Joe could not stop staring at Amanda. Though to others she looked pale, a little thin

("You coming down with something?" he heard several ask), to Joe she was his personal Statue of Liberty. He hid his scrutiny of her every little move well, concealing his fascination behind lunch orders and requests for phone calls and questions about this memo or that one, instructions, demands, dictations. Anything to keep her in his sight. The funny thing was, Amanda did not seem to notice Joe in the slightest, no matter what he did, and he did *a lot*. It started with the Monday-morning meeting to go over the shows for the coming week. Joe talked openly about this guest ("The beautiful blond from *Sisters in Space*, what's her name, Amanda? She's stunning") or that ("The lead singer from that new band Garbage In, the one with the red hair and the nose ring; she's fascinating, don't you think, Amanda?"). He explored the possibility of shooting a week of shows in New York, to exploit Fashion Week, to shoot from behind the scenes of the fashion shows. The era of the supermodels was on the horizon ("I'd like to get that black model on the show. Who's she, Amanda, the one dating Tyson? Nineteen. Incredible body") and Joe wanted to catch that wave. At least, that's how he made it sound. Amanda just watched,

and took notes, and answered his inquiries politely, without a hint of disdain or sarcasm or
hurt. Or, truth be told, interest. It was driving
Joe fucking nuts; he couldn't smoke enough cigarettes; he'd have one in his mouth, one burning
in the ashtray, another on the way to the lighter.

Danny Markus, on the other hand, lapped
Joe's new, libidinous directives up like a hungry
dog. He had always thought Joe was too brainy,
too arty, a yuppie rebel in hundred-dollar khakis;
he'd no idea Joe had this more human—or even
refreshingly animalistic—side to him. In fact,
Danny got the feeling Joe was judging him when
Danny indulged in his numerous, multicolored,
tasty side dishes. Joe must have known about the
intern Danny just fired; the girl had not given
him a choice—the poor thing was in love with
him (an unfortunate and common happen-
stance), said something about wanting his baby,
and started threatening to tell his wife he was
sleeping with her. Danny, deploring messiness in
his life, whether in a desk drawer or in his assig-
nations, sent his faithful production assistant
with the pale skin and beady eyes to her dorm
room to fire her. A good thing he did, too; the girl
tried to kill herself by taking seven or eight Extra

Strength Tylenols before the PA could wrestle the bottle from her. Danny was very upset by her antics and relayed the message once again through his PA, dispatching him pronto to her hospital bed. Her sorority sisters were said to be quite upset with Danny, though several asked about a possible internship with the show.

The thing was, Danny Markus was a hungry guy; he always needed something on the side. The girl was one of many girls who couldn't understand; his wife couldn't understand, either, but at least never bothered him about it after the first two or three scenes. But now, Danny thought—now, more importantly, his producer understood. Now they could really have some fun. What was the use of living in Los Angeles as a television celebrity, amongst the most beautiful bodies and faces in the world, all clamoring for your attention, if you weren't going to take advantage of the good fortune? Danny couldn't help that he had to get married too young; his wife had gotten herself pregnant. Marrying her was the proper and, well, Minnesotan thing to do. But he was not going to punish himself for the rest of his life for being a good guy.

*　　　*　　　*

Patrice walked out of Union Station at eight-thirty that morning. It had taken five hours for her bus to get to L.A. from Vegas, but she had slept most of the way; when they pulled into downtown L.A., she was refreshed. She took a deep breath and smiled.

And wondered where she could score some dope.

Fourteen

It took Valentin twelve hours and eleven minutes to find out Patrice was back in town. And that was only because everyone knew not to bother Val before noon.

She had already slept with one of Valentin's friends, a guy who went to elementary school with Val, a real comer in the insurance scam business. Leo had hooked up with the Hungarian mafia in high school—their crimes were mostly nonviolent: office supply scams, car insurance scams, medical scams, anything with the word "scam" on the end. Leo's name had been in the *L.A. Times* more than once (when he was reading the paper). Leonardo Damanoff was always being investigated, and he was always getting off. Leo, who had a pad on Mt. Olympus with a pool and an indoor Jacuzzi and a wet bar, was doing all right. And seriously, it couldn't have happened to a nicer guy. But Val didn't like getting the phone call that morning.

"Yo, Val."

Valentin rolled over. It was eleven-thirty, half an hour before breakfast. Leo should know better than to call him this early.

"Leo. What up?"

"Val. You still pluggin' that girl?"

Valentin took a moment. Valentin wasn't plugging anybody; the fuck was Leo talking about?

"Leo. You callin' me this early to talk skank?"

"You know. Patrice."

Valentin drew a sharp breath in before he could stop himself. Oh fuck. What had Patrice gone and done?

"Haven't seen her. Why?"

"I've seen her."

Valentin tried to sound nonchalant. Hard to do with short breaths. He started to perspire. He stuck his hands under his armpits, the phone in the crook of his neck.

He had not yet gotten out of bed.

"Okay, what's the story? You want something? A dime, what?"

"Val, man, I'm into her."

Valentin closed his eyes. Leo fell in love faster than any man, woman, chimpanzee.

"Dude, are you saying you were with my bitch?"

"I'm saying, if you don't like her. Well?"

"Where the fuck is she?"

"Look, don't be uncool. That's why I was calling you."

"I'll be right over."

Valentin slammed down the phone. Eleven minutes later he was standing in Leo's yard, banging on every double-paned window he could get close to, when he realized he hadn't taken a shit that morning. Whenever Val got ramped up, a bowel movement was not far in the offing.

No one was answering except for the Senegal parrot Leo had picked up two years ago at an old pet shop on Ventura Boulevard. Val could hear it, even through the heavy wood door: "Cocksucker." Then it would make that caw sound. Then again: "Cocksucker." Leo had quite the imagination. And Leo had split.

Valentin kicked the front door. "Shit!" Valentin had made a mistake, he hadn't played it cool, and Leo scared too easily. Val knew he would scare easily—Leo was the kid who always confessed his crimes to the teacher while his friends, Val included, wouldn't spill if it meant having their prepubescent dicks cut off. They weren't sweet like Leo. "Did you throw the pencil, Leo?" "Yes, ma'am," fat little Leo would reply.

Valentin stood there a moment. And then he dropped his pants and left a morning dump right on the doormat, the one that said "Welcome" in bright yellow letters.

"Welcome this, asshole," Valentin said.

"Cocksucker," replied Fred the parrot.

Val laughed all the way back to Diego, and then went back to bed. Drifting into sleep, he almost forgot why he had gone over to Leo's in the first place.

And that's when he heard the soft breath and smelled the familiar, peculiar odor of pot mixed with L'Air du Temps and realized there was someone in the room with him.

Patrice.

"Where's my baby?"

"Nice to see you, too."

"Where is he?"

Valentin sat up and looked straight at Patrice. She looked pretty good, considering. She had gained a few pounds. Her hair was growing nice and thick. He knew the weight, which filled out her face, would be gone in a week, the hair would go anemic and patchy. Coke did that to girls.

He sorely wanted to touch her.

"Dammit, Val, where's the kid?"

"You don't miss me?" Valentin couldn't believe the words were coming from his mouth. They sounded so pathetic, so girly. What was he, a fag, now? But still he couldn't have stopped those words with a gun to his head, a knife at his throat.

"I want my baby back."

Now Val was mad. He knew she didn't give a shit about the kid, like she never gave a shit about him. Valentin was about to make a life-changing decision.

"This is important, 'Trice. Did you fuck Leo?"

"None of your business."

"Please—just—answer the question." See, the fucked-up thing about Leo was, he only liked to fuck girls in the ass. And the image slammed Valentin in the head like a fucking brick.

"That's my kid, asshole! *Mine!*"

And that's when Valentin knew he was going to kill Patrice.

He flew at her from his bed before her scream found life, and the look in her eyes told him she knew this was it. The last thing her blue, blue eyes would ever see was the face of her former lover, red with anger, veins popping on his neck, his bony fingers wrapped around her throat with the strength of someone who had waited a long time for the moment and would not let the moment pass.

She tried to tell him that once she had loved him but that girl had died inside of her a long time ago.

She did not close her eyes.

Valentin let go of Patrice's body and noted the clock. She had been in his room five minutes.

There were trails in Angelus Crest, in the hills past Pasadena, off the 210. People would drive up in their pickup trucks, old vans, and dump bodies, or bury them in shallow graves.

Valentin was glad there was no blood. That would have made it harder.

The doorbell rang, and Valentin looked out the window. A red Mercedes coupe, a chubby, hairy hand clutching a pair of aviator sunglasses.

Drugs never sleep. Valentin pulled his pants on, dropped a sheet over Patrice's body, and went to the door.

The guy was Iranian. Okay, Persian. He liked Persian better. The Persians were kings, the rulers of the Ottoman Empire. The Iranians were fucked-up fundamentalist towel heads with a hard-on for anything American.

It was 1985. No one wanted to be Iranian in L.A.

Sahid had a big face, a big gut, a big toothy grin, and fat hands. He was a rich kid whose parents sent him to L.A. to become educated at that illustrious (and expensive) playground for rich kids, USC.

Sahid was thinking about law school. Keep him here a little longer, drifting from club to club, from blond to blonder. He was also thinking about scoring a little blow for the weekend.

He smiled at Val. The deal was over. Val leaned back, hands shaking, wondering how he got through the cut without slicing his veins open.

Jesus Christ, he had just killed a person. Not

just any person. The mother of his fucking child.

Sahid smiled. "You come out with me this weekend? You want to go to Pips? Daisy?"

"Nah."

"Why 'nah'? I got girls. You should see."

"Busy. You know."

Val didn't have time to do normal things anymore. He was too busy blowing his money and his supply, and wondering how he would make up his debts. He was heavy into it with his best supplier. Heavy into it. Val closed his eyes and sighed, his small chest barely rising.

He opened his eyes and Sahid was gone. Val looked around, panicked. The money was there. He hadn't been ripped off. He heard footsteps. Sahid was down the hall, outside of his bedroom.

Val covered fifteen feet in two steps, flying over to his room. Sahid looked up, surprised.

"I'm looking . . . bathroom?"

Had he seen? Val looked at the sheet on the floor, then looked away. Had he seen?

"Over here."

Val turned him out of the room, into the bathroom, and leaned against the wall.

Was he going to have to kill this guy, too? He

could do it, he knew he could. Val looked at his hands. Skinny as they were, he could do it.

"I'll see you later. You think about it?"

Val looked up. "What?"

"This weekend, silly Val. This weekend."

Sahid slapped Valentin on the back and shook his head and walked out.

Valentin rushed into his room and slammed the door, stepped over the sheet, and looked outside. Sahid's expression hadn't changed. If anything, he looked happier. Bright eyed, bushy-goddamned-tailed. A guarantee of weekend sex in his coat pocket.

Valentin looked back at the sheet, and slowly walked over to it. The word "gingerly" popping into his scrambled brain.

And then he lifted the sheet.

There was no body.

Val ran outside—out into the yard, looking out toward the red Mercedes, brake lights barely visible.

Sahid was alone.

Val ran back into the house, breathing into the deepest forays of his lungs, and loud, loud like a train.

Where is the body? Where is the body?

Valentin looked at his hands. He looked at the floor. He touched the carpet, looked for her purse—her purse, it would still be here.

There was no purse.

He checked the bathroom, and then the entire house, the garage, the cabinets, the basement.

It took him two hours.

And then he knew.

He was losing his mind. Not figuratively, either. Not, "Oh shit, I must be losing my mind, I forgot where I put my stash." He was literally losing his mind.

Patrice had never been in his room that morning. She had never said those things to him. And lastly, and most significantly, he had never strangled her with his bare bony hands.

He had read about this somewhere. What happens to a person when they've done too much coke. Something about schizophrenia, about hallucinations.

And he knew. It was here. His madness had arrived.

And he knew something else.

He wasn't going to stop. He'd go full speed to the end of the line.

*   *   *

Gabriel did not learn what the letter *J* in J.D. meant until the day of the funeral. He stood in a long line of men in open shirts with wide collars and Jheri curls and women with flowered hats and ample bosoms and behinds dressed in the bright colors of Sunday best. Gabe stood in the hot Indian-summer sun with a moist brow and practiced what he was going to say. How he would make J.D.'s wife, now his widow, feel better.

He thought about the pension. J.D., one year, five days short of retirement, and they wouldn't give him a penny of it. Five kids. And then he realized he didn't even know his friend's first name.

J.D.'s wife, Loretta Daniels, in her forties, high cheekbones and a full, womanly body rounding out what must have been skin and bones in her teens.

Gabe whispered to himself, tried to keep his head low, his shirt scratching against his neck. He swore to himself he would not cry. J.D. would laugh if Gabe shed water at his funeral. "Pussies cry," J.D. would've said. "Real men get strokes."

Gabe thought about the girl he'd been crying

over since the day she could not look him in the eye. He hadn't cried like a human being. He cried like an animal, howling as though he were a wolf whose leg had been caught and twisted in the metal teeth of a trap, never to be released. He was never to be released.

And then Loretta looked up at him, her cheekbones lacquered in tears, and Gabe lost his voice, his practiced words, and as she hugged the big man to the fullness of her grieving body, his back heaved; his strength melted. He was ten years old again, skinned knees, all arms and legs, his mother protecting him from his stepfather's blows.

Loretta bent her mouth toward his ear and said, "Junior loved you, Gabriel. You know that."

He sighed. Deep.

"He's in the Lord's hands now," she continued, her voice deep, a warm blanket.

Gabe looked at her, her coal eyes shining. "Junior?"

"Yes, Gabe. J.D. Junior."

Gabe bit his lip as Loretta hugged him once more, then let him go as she turned to an older man wearing wide lapels, a powder blue Dacron suit.

Gabe shook his head ever so slightly, and walked away, head down still, eyes straight ahead. He was not one to laugh at a man's funeral.

Gabe got on his bike and rode three miles before he pulled to a dirt shoulder and laughed his damn ass off.

"Junior. Goddammed Junior."

Death had not come quick to J.D., and that stuck in Gabriel's mind and gnawed at his soul. Death had not come quick. Gabe should have known something was up when black crows spun circles overhead as he pulled his Ninja into the company lot; their laughter was so loud, their number so numerous that Gabe had commented to J.D., who had taken note of their mocking as well. Hell, even Stubbs, whose powers of observation were limited because he smoked half a dozen cigar-sized joints a day, mentioned the birds; even he saw something coming.

What they did not know, what no one knew, was that the chain used to hoist the engines coming down the line had a weak link. The chain was going to snap. Someone was going to get hurt.

J.D. died of massive head wounds.

Gabriel had been thirsty, had taken a moment

to sneak off to the water fountain near the foreman's office. Just a moment, when he heard it. The sound of lightning. Pop. And then the hollering. He ran over bodies to get to J.D. on the ground. An engine had flown off the hoist, knocked him back. His head had hit the cement floor. The blood was everywhere, and Gabriel flashed on Vietnam, on the book he had read about brothers watching brothers get blown to bits, tasting the flesh of their best friends as their heads exploded in front of them.

Gabriel tossed the engines aside as if they were candy and took his friend's head in his arms. Blood trickled from J.D.'s mouth. His lips parted and then came together. He was trying to speak. Gabriel bent his head toward J.D.'s mouth. His friend was dying. These would be his last words. They both knew it.

The world around them stopped. People were screaming now. Gomez was yelling in a hysterical, high-pitched manner, like a dog's yelp. A couple of women had fainted. The plant manager's voice rose above the din, calming people down. But Gabe and J.D., they were alone, eye to eye. It was as if the factory were a dance floor in an old movie and time had stopped for the star-crossed lovers as they danced their last dance. Gabe could hear only J.D.; could feel only his breath, shallow, against his cheek; could see only J.D., his eyes, the deep pores of his skin. They were alone, lovers locked in a final embrace against the backdrop of revolution.

J.D. whispered to him, "Lolo . . . my kids . . ." He closed his eyes.

The world came back.

Gabe would not leave his friend. He stayed with J.D. in the ambulance as the paramedics looked on, wary of the big man. He stayed with him in the cold hospital room on a basement floor. He stayed with him when his wife arrived. He stayed with him until a small Filipino nurse with a strong arm and warm voice told him it was time to go home. He did not stay with him out of obligation, out of guilt, out of pride. He stayed with J.D. because, in his state of shock, he wasn't convinced his friend was dead. He didn't want J.D. to be alone when he woke up.

Days later, the new rumor down the line focused on J.D.'s pension. Someone told Gomez, who told Rosemont, who told Washington that J.D.'s family wouldn't be picking up his full pension. Wife and five kids would be getting two hundred a month. J.D. had less than one year to retirement, and the motherfuckers at the top decided his family wouldn't be getting his pension.

Gabe sat on this into the night, this jagged piece of information that sliced into his heart. He did not say a word to anybody, just went about his business, a nod here, a catch of an eye.

At the end of the shift, Gabe waited, hunched in the dark recesses of the warehouse until he was sure all had gone home. The security guard, an old white man named Ernie with a bad hip and a worse case of hearing, would suspect nothing.

Gabe walked over to the Corvettes, the gold lineup. Reminded him of that dancing group, the Rockettes. Shiny, gleaming, flirtatious.

He opened the door of the one closest to him, ran his hands over the paint, admired it.

And started up the engine, the engine that he or J.D. handled, most likely.

Smooth.

He kicked it up. Drove the golden horse out the door and into the parking lot. Sixty. Seventy. Eighty.

Ninety miles per hour, spinning, turning. And that's when Gabe took the gold Corvette that was waiting to be picked up by a GM dealer in Wichita and rammed it head-on into a wall.

Gabe limped out of the car and onto his motorcycle.

Management questioned the night shift up and down the line but no one talked. They swore up and down, to a man, they did not see anything. The next few nights, though, there were several more pats on the back for Gabe than usual, more furtive nods. They were one, these men.

Days later, Gabe learned they would be closing the plant down for sure.

Amanda awakened in the middle of the night. The pain had come quickly and deep. She had cried out, but James had not awakened. She rubbed her eyes, caked with salt.

She crawled over his sleeping body and out into the hall and only then noticed the trail of blood following her, obedient black-red tears.

She pulled herself onto the toilet and sat there as a purple mass escaped her body, rejecting her in one violent shudder.

Amanda, dazed, focused on what would have been Gabriel's and her baby. Sweat bubbled on her forehead and weeped down her back and the world went metallic, the taste, the smell.

She woke up minutes later, her face to the ceiling, her body a pool of water.

She wiped the last of her baby from her legs with a dingy rag, and with it, her obligation to James.

She wrapped up Madison in his favorite blanket, and got into her lousy car, and drove empty streets to Gabriel's house.

It was four in the morning.

Gabe was just riding to the top of the hill opposite Amanda's house. He had been held up at work and so had not seen the lights of her car, the speed of her departure.

He sat and watched her house as he did night after night and thought about all the things he would never have a chance to tell her. And he wondered if she ever thought of him.

Amanda drove up the broken concrete driveway, weeds poking out between the slabs in green and vivid reproach. She took the baby out of his car seat, still sleeping, and went to the door. She had already knocked, after ringing twice, before she realized she was still in her nightgown, the dark brown spot on the back of the flimsy cotton angrily sticking to her skin, her regret plain to see.

Frank answered the door, finally. He heard the ring the first time, but honestly was too scared to open. "Who is ringing a doorbell at four in the morning?" he'd asked the dog with the spiked collar. Only someone with bad intent. But the dog with the spiked collar started whining and would not let Frank turn his back to the door, to whoever wanted in.

He looked at the girl. The white girl Gabe was killing himself over. This little girl who caused her boy to lose weight, to not smile anymore. To never laugh, even at his father's useless jokes. To not look in his father's eyes. This girl. Frank looked at her, and at the beautiful sleeping child in her arms, and neither said a word. And then he put his arm around her, and as he ushered her back into his son's life, he put to bed his anger.

"I'm sorry," Amanda said to Gabriel's father. He just shook his head. He didn't want this young girl apologizing to him. He sat her in his chair and watched as the child stirred and then fell deep asleep into her chest.

"I woke you up."

"'S all right. Wasn't dreaming anyway."

She looked around the living room, to the stairs. Frank caught the motion.

"He's not here."

Amanda nodded. She knew he wasn't there. He would have felt her in his house. He would have been stroking her hair already and telling her he loved her.

Frank saw the girl get smaller before his eyes. He knew then how much pain she was in, and saw it was the same as his son's. She had lost weight as well. The circles under her eyes belonged to someone much older.

"Please . . . tell him I miss him."

"I will."

The tear came and it was lonely and then it was joined by others and Frank sat there with the girl, and she cried usefulness into his old shoulder until the sun came up.

And Frank marveled at the sleeping baby and his peace, and thought he must be something special.

Fifteen

Joe Artuga used to dream in color, vivid dreams, every dream an animal, viciously alive.

Now he dreamed only in black-and-white.

The color was draining from him.

Joe Artuga was getting sicker.

Joe had called a doctor. His doctor was on his last legs himself. Joe had gotten his name, Vance Howard, M.D., from Danny Markus. Danny went to him because he never went to him, because he never actually had to meet him. Vance was a Hollywood doctor. If someone was famous enough (or close to someone famous enough), all the person had to do was give old Vance, or his loyal secretary, Pat, who was also Vance's loyal blue-haired mother, a call.

And Vance would prescribe whatever was needed, over the phone.

Sometimes people needed a lot of Percodan. Sometimes they needed to find an old, discontinued batch of quaaludes. Valium. Percoset.

Whatever it was, Vance would prescribe it.

Vance went to a lot of premieres.

And so Joe Artuga took the time to lay down his eighth, ninth lit cigarette and call Vance. Vance's mother answered, voice like a razor blade. Joe almost hung up. And then Vance got on. Barely audible. Whispering, really. Joe paused, then gave him his symptoms. Coated tongue, white patches on the inside of his mouth, night sweats, a sore on his leg that wasn't healing.

Vance coughed. A newborn's cough.

"You have a virus."

Joe could barely hear him. "A virus."

"You travel to any foreign countries lately?" Vance sounded like an obscene caller but without the joy.

"The Valley a foreign country?" Small joke; Joe thought he'd try. Vance either ignored this comment or didn't hear it. Maybe his hearing was as miserly as his voice.

"Antibiotics. I'll write you a prescription."

"Antibiotics don't cure viruses." ("Did they?" Joe wondered). Joe wondered a lot these days about what he knew to be true and what he knew to be false.

"I'll write you a prescription," said the downcast obscene caller.

"'Kay. How much—" But before Joe could continue the question, he heard a rustle as Vance covered the phone with his hand.

"Mommy!" Vance called. "Mommy, pick up the phone!"

Vance was nearing fifty, according to Danny. Joe looked at the phone and smiled. At least Vance had a relationship with his mother.

"That'll be one hundred and fifty dollars, Mr. Artuga," said the razor blade.

Joe Artuga got off the phone and flipped his cigarette back in his mouth. And then, like a hummingbird at an open rose, the briefest of thoughts flitted into his mind.

Who would care if he died?

Amanda had dreamed of the ocean, vast, deep blue, calm. She had felt the breeze, tasted its salt.

When she awoke with her head on Frank's shoulder, she knew why she had this dream. She had found safe harbor. She looked at the wall clock that somehow managed to still tell time despite its depressed appearance. Six-thirty.

Amanda looked at Frank, his old face relaxed into itself; soft, unwrinkled skin. A comfort zone. The baby cooed softly, playing with his fingers, fascinated with their patterns and form, the baby's face and Frank's somehow the same.

Frank's eyes had been closed until the warmth of Amanda's stare opened them. Frank awoke to the smile of a woman for the first time in fifteen years. And with the swiftness of breaking glass, he suddenly knew what he had been missing all this time.

Amanda didn't wait for Gabriel to come home. There was no telling, Frank said, as to when his motorcycle would find its way up the craggy driveway.

But she drove home lighter than she had come. Her truth had shown itself to her. The only thing she had left to do was to reveal it to James.

*   *   *

James awakened at 5 A.M. with a start. He looked over at the empty side of the bed next to him and the aching in his stomach told him what he had not wanted to hear. She was not his.

He threw his pillow across the room, the soft thud disappointing his sense of rage. He sprang up with the sudden urge to run. His legs twitched and his mind was too full to be contained in this small, sad room.

Five minutes later, James was hitting the pavement, one sure foot in front of the other, the high school cross-country racer inside guiding every step. Beyond the canyon was a small reservoir. Two miles there and back, another two around. Some people drowned their sorrows in alcohol, in drugs. James had tried both. He preferred running.

Twenty-three minutes in, the padding of his feet coalesced with the rhythm of his thoughts.

Amanda didn't love him.

He was going back to Boston.

He was going to graduate.

He was going to get a great job.

He was going to marry a nice girl.

He was going to fuck around on her.

Amanda didn't love him.

Someday Amanda would take him back.

He rounded the first mile of the reservoir and saw a famous soap opera actress, blond, skinny, all knees and elbows, walking with pink weights on her ankles, bulky sunglasses perched atop her chip of a nose.

He smiled, the charming young law student. She smiled back. Twenty minutes later he was in her gazebo overlooking the city, silently trying to pick out the block he grew up on.

His dick was in the actress's mouth, his hand around her aggressively blond head. He looked down, having finally spotted his old neighborhood, the familiar graffiti and cement walls, and then he saw her roots and pushed harder, causing her to cough.

James smiled, then heard a noise from inside the Spanish-style house. Recently remodeled, she had told him. She did it herself. "You can't trust interior decorators, especially if you're famous. They rip you off left and right." James thought she had done a pretty good job, although somewhat frilly—there was lace on every table, flowered upholstery in every room. It didn't occur to James that she was married until he saw the man, and the look in the man's eyes.

This was something she did on a regular basis.

James put his hand up, an awkward greeting. The man, disgusted, turned and walked back into the house, a tired walk. He looked about fifty, and James suddenly realized his new friend was older than he imagined.

He looked down at her hands. The skin was thinning, freckled, the nails manicured but with a yellow tinge.

James closed his eyes and leaned back and felt the sun on his face and prayed to God the old bitch would finish him off soon. He had to get packing.

Third night in a row. Patrice would never sleep again. She smiled, and then frowned. Pain seared through her mouth into her cheek. Patrice touched her face, the night coming back to her in a fragmented mosaic.

That pussy bitch Leo had left her on the corner of Sunset and Highland. They had hit a few of the nightclubs on the better stretch of Sunset, Carlos 'n Charlie's, the Body Shop, places where men would give Patrice all she wanted, and all she had to do was put out. A blow for blow. A simple formula Patrice was comfortable with, but Leo, apparently, wasn't. He had disappeared into the crowd at El Privado to fetch two gold margaritas and returned to find Patrice cozying up to the lap of a Persian guy, Sahid, a longtime customer of Val's.

Leo flipped out over the fact that Patrice's hand was halfway down Sahid's tightly zipped Sergio Valentes. No mean feat. He dropped the margaritas and grabbed her by the hair and dragged her into the valet parking lot and his Mercedes 190 convertible, which he didn't actually own.

Patrice had screamed at him and clawed his face as they drove east on the boulevard. Sahid was about to let her in on his stash, which was strong stuff, no doubt, and this asshole blew it for her.

That's when Leo drove up the curb on Sunset and Highland across from the crumbling facade of Hollywood High and ripped Patrice from his car, dumping her on the pavement in front of a dingy motor hotel. A vial dropped from her purse onto the cement, Patrice scrambling for it even before it hit the ground.

Now she remembered. Her face had hit cement.

Leo took one last look at her and sped away, north to Mt. Olympus. Patrice wondered what the chubby boy was crying about. She spit toward his retreating car, her saliva gray from smoke, and then sat for a moment on the cold, unforgiving cement, marveling that the vial had survived the spill. Then she turned toward the motel. She needed to make a phone call. She smiled at herself for a second, at her incredible stamina. She had not slept in two days. Maybe she would never have to sleep again.

She stood on stick legs and wandered toward the front office.

In the bright of bleak morning, Patrice grimaced. She touched her nose. Chips of blood in her palm. Patrice dug into her purse for her compact. The fact that her wallet was no longer there brushed past her like a breeze. Patrice's face had been her ticket to life's backstage. As she looked into the dusty compact mirror, she knew those days had closed to her like the pages of a bad novel that would never again be read.

She sniffed dust off the compact mirror, eager for leftovers.

* * *

Amanda returned home, armed with a novice's courage. She played the scene over in her mind like an overactive Gena Rowlands moll in a B movie. She, the heroine, was returning home to set her life straight. She was going to throw that man right out of her claptrap house and onto the earthquake-cracked asphalt. She was all set to tell James, "Sayonara!"—she laughed—"Later days. What don't you understand about the word 'Goodbye'?" when she realized his car was not parked in front of her home. Amanda, embarrassed in that someone-just-caught-me-singing-Motown-loudly-to-myself way, grabbed her bundle of Madison and gingerly opened her front door.

To the heroine's surprise, the not-quite-leading man was not there. For the first time in months, Amanda felt lucky.

Amanda called Mrs. Selby and dropped off the baby and dressed for work in a pantsuit her mother had left behind, unwrapping it from the dry cleaning bag like a Christmas gift. And then she drove, unhurried and unburdened, to work.

Today she would arrive early. Today she

would arrive the girl she was meant to be, the girl with the potential to be anything she wanted. Today Amanda would arrive armed with hope.

Nothing could ruin this day.

Val had waited and waited. He had spent hours crouched down on the backs of his bare heels like the pictures he had seen growing up of the Vietnamese soldiers. He had killed time in the twilight by counting blades of grass, by reciting the Pledge of Allegiance, by conjuring up every line, every angle, and every curve that made up what had been Patrice's face.

He had dressed in black, and more carefully than he had since his first date with Patrice, three years ago. He still remembered the first time he saw her. The straight blond hair, the upturned nose, the sculpture of the bones that was her pride and his torment. He had hated her on sight, sure that she would never look twice at him.

But she did, and he asked her out (screaming out the question, as they were at the balcony of the Whisky, watching Oingo Boingo's lead singer in a slam dance).

Val hesitated. A car drove past. A Bentley. A woman's laugh.

It was a buttoned-down shirt. Val almost laughed out loud. He had worn a buttoned-down shirt on his first date with Patrice. They drove down PCH to the old standby on the coast, a weather-beaten surf 'n' turf joint just past Malibu. Over a medium steak (his) and a Thousand Island–drenched salad (hers), Val talked, too much and too quickly, and Patrice listened. He could feel her eyes, wide and silver gray, picking up every nuance, every so-casual-it-had-to-be-studied gesture. He had wanted to tell her everything before she disappeared.

Val blinked. Was she high even at that moment? Even on their first date? Val mentally kicked himself. The first image of Patrice as clean, as uncorrupted, the image that had held him in its warm, seductive, soft grip—was that, too, false?

The morning after the unfinished steak dinner, Patrice wore that buttoned-down shirt, skirting the tops of her healthy thighs as she cooked him a breakfast of cold cereal and milk.

Val shifted his weight and sniffed and wondered where that shirt was now. Maybe he'd wear it to her funeral.

Lights in the driveway. Finally. Someone was home.

Val tightened his grip around the gun he had found after rifling through his sister's closet; he breathed. His pulse remained steady, even as the voices in his head screamed. He thought he heard his mother, calling to him in the moment before he jumped off their shake roof at that first house on Edgewood.

"Stop!" she had screamed. "Stop!"

Gabe awakened to the sounds of the large tractors lumbering slowly up the hillside, a parade of steel. He wiped their remorseless dust from his eyes and from the old, loyal letterman's jacket that had been his bed. He then rose, and with the arm of a natural athlete flung the heavy, empty bottle deep into the recesses of the canyon. And with it, his suffering.

Something had arisen within him with this new sun. He had drifted to the very edges of his torment and now was ready to return. He would not turn his back on the love that he felt, that he knew she had for him still—he would face up to his fear, not with a bottle but with a clear head and a strong heart. "A man does not retreat," he told himself. "A man asks for what he wants and does not fear the answer."

Today he would take the day off. He would shower and shave and pump iron. And listen to Miles Davis and Charlie Parker. And read. He would read.

And then he would go to Amanda and offer her whatever he was, and whatever he could be. And hopefully, that would be enough. Gabriel rode purposefully into the L.A. sunrise and the promise of a change.

It was the sound that had caught Val up short, perhaps because he had been alone for all those hours, nothing but headlights to break the silence. It wasn't the look of surprise on Leo's chubby face or the frantic wave of his hands as he tried to shield himself. It was the sound. The blast. In truth, Val had never shot a gun. After he blasted one into Leo's fat, contorted face, the report shocked him so, he had dropped the gun.

He picked it up, recovered, and drifted away.

Val was two miles from Mt. Olympus when he realized Leo had been alone. Patrice was still alive somewhere, in the city. He had to find her.

But first he needed to sleep. Suddenly Val, his eyes at half-mast, his face slack, was very tired. What he needed was a good night's rest. What was it his mother always told him? "Tomorrow will be another day, sweetie," she'd say.

"Fuckin' bullshit," Val said out loud. The gun agreed.

Sixteen

Even Danny's vicious demeanor could not break the back of Amanda's cheerful mood. Since this morning, a fog had raised from her view. Her footsteps felt lighter, even in her cheap shoes. Her ears could once again hear her favorite music (Prince, P-Funk, Marvin Gaye) on her favorite station (KDAY); she wondered where that music had been for these last months.

That afternoon, Amanda laughed out loud in a meeting with Danny and Joe Artuga and the writing staff, and the sound felt like a gunshot, so surprising it was to her.

The laugh made her jump, but no one else took notice of its unusual pitch. Danny went on with his monotonous diatribe, berating the talent coordinator for not aligning better guests, the A-list stars, on his sinking show (as though there were a choice), assaulting the writers for not providing "funny"—he said "funny" as though it were a noun.

"Carson has funny. Where's *my* funny? Why don't I have funny?" Danny whined, his voice spinning high and desperate.

Joe sighed, and finally spoke up, clearing his throat. "Danny, you liked these segments last week. Before the show went on, you were goddamned very happy."

"Shit, Joe," Danny retorted. "It's all shit. You know it and I know it. And that's why we're not pulling the ratings."

Joe scratched his chin, and Amanda stared at him without emotion and wondered when he had lost his baby fat. Skinny wasn't good on him—his head was too big to carry a gaunt, Mick Jagger/Keith Richards mien.

One of the writers, the guy with the glasses and newly graying hair, spoke. His voice came out muted, as though someone were stepping on his windpipe.

"You know what I think, Danny?"

"No. And you know what? I don't care. Because you know why? You're fired." Danny was on a roll. The writer looked from Danny to Joe to his younger partner, who slid his ever-present yellow writing pad the slightest bit away from him.

And then glasses said, in a much stronger voice, "Fuck you very much, Danny," and he got up to walk out. Amanda was impressed, until glasses tripped over one of the hard plastic chairs blocking the door.

His partner stayed.

"That was good, Danny. Very good," Joe stated in a way that made it wearily obvious. "You just fired the only funny guy in the room."

Danny was about to respond in poison when his mealy assistant knocked on the open door. "Francesca's here, Danny," he said, his voice drawing out the girl's name like too much syrup.

Amanda and the rest of the group recognized the treacly tone. It meant: "Your twelve o'clock blow job's here, Danny. Where do you want her?"

Danny didn't even bother with his usual fake good-byes as he slammed the door behind him.

Joe looked at Amanda with basset-hound eyes. "Maybe she's funny," Amanda said, her eyebrows arched high on her forehead in parentheses.

Joe laughed, and then, slowly, so did the rest of the hapless pen-wielding warriors at the hateful oval table, where many had died quiet deaths.

She left the station at a reasonable hour, having first called Mrs. Selby to see if she wanted anything to eat. Amanda was going to drop by the deli at Sunset and Laurel that charged way too much for sliced roasted turkey. Tonight, though, she didn't care what the damn bird cost, she was going to treat herself. She thought that Mrs. Selby, long a fan of watery coleslaw, would like something as well.

Joe surprised Amanda on the way out. He was standing outside, leaning against the ugly concrete soundstage, smoking a cigarette and watching the sky in a way that made Amanda slow, and then silence, her steps. Her mind flashed on the little girl in the Mary Janes who had been warned not to awaken her sick grampa from his nap.

"Grampa's not feeling well," her mom had told her back then, her womanly face bent so close to Amanda that all she could see was the red of her lipstick bleeding into the faint lines around her mouth.

"Nice sunset," Joe said, whisking the red lipstick away with his scorched voice. Amanda went and stood next to him. "Nice," she agreed.

"It's the smog," Joe responded, as if to himself. "Carbon dioxide, methane. Gives off the brightest color."

"Aren't we lucky?" Amanda replied. And Joe turned and looked at her and put his hand on her shoulder.

Amanda stared at him and waited, for in this simple gesture she felt he had something to say to her that was not glib, that was not clever, that would take its own sweet time.

"I'll see you later," Joe said. His mouth remained open, as though there were more.

"Okay?" Amanda replied. That was it?

"You be good," he said. And then his mouth closed, and his mustache twitched, and Amanda thought he might smile. But no; he took a futile tug on his cigarette, which had already given up its light.

"I'll do my best." Amanda smiled, and then she watched his slim figure as he shuffled away, one step heavier than the next.

Amanda's forehead pinched and she wondered why he seemed so down. By the time she realized Joe had probably been fired by Danny that afternoon, it was too late to call out to him.

She would call him that night at home, but only after she called Gabe. Amanda promised herself she would not put off her own happiness any longer.

An hour later, Amanda dropped the watery coleslaw off at Mrs. Selby's and escaped before being treated to the spectacle of seeing the old lady sharing the coleslaw with her hungry little dog—"One bite for you, one bite for me . . ." Amanda shuddered as she thought of it, and carried Madison, curled up and heavy with sleep, into her darkened home.

She stepped inside and felt for the light switch. She flipped it back and forth several times before the reality of last month's unpaid electric bill hit her, chastening her for her day-long good mood.

"Shit!" Amanda could find no better word. "Shit, shit, shit!"

Madison moved, and before he could inherit her crankiness, Amanda made her way to the living room and set him down on the couch.

"Val?" Amanda called out. She figured he was home, asleep; his car was in the driveway.

"Valentin?" Her good mood was still dancing inside her, undenied—for a moment, she was inspired to share her loot, her $7.95 thin-sliced turkey sandwich, with her big brother.

Perhaps it was the dark. Perhaps it was the echo of her own voice against the walls of the house. Suddenly Amanda felt a tremble in her chest. The world outside her front door was different from this place, her blacked-out living room. The world outside was safe. Here she felt something else. Fear.

She looked back at Madison, tucked into the corner of the couch that had long since lost its shape, and turned to make her way into the kitchen.

She felt for the phone on the wall, and almost laughed to herself. She was happy not to have its putrid olive green color inflicted upon her, for once.

She dialed Gabriel's number and surprised herself by praying for him to answer. She was already on ring number three.

"Please-God, please-God, please-God—"

"Hello."

Amanda breathed. Before she could speak, he was already talking.

"Amanda, is that you?" he said. He hoped he didn't sound too pathetic.

"Gabe," her voice shook. "I was going to call you tonight. Then I came home . . . I hate to ask you—"

"I'm coming over," he said. "Ten minutes."

"Ah," Amanda smiled. "You know you can't make it here in ten."

"Watch me," he said.

Amanda hung up the phone, holding on to it like a prayer. Tears sprang to her eyes, she felt so relieved—panic was not something a person like her should do alone, she thought, mocking herself. She took a deep breath and turned toward the living room, her hand brushing over the kitchen counter.

She knocked over a box of cereal. "Damned Val," Amanda cursed as she bent over to pick up the scattered Froot Loops. She thought about leaving the mess there for Val to clean up, and then she smirked to herself. "That'd be one long-ass wait," she said to the Froot Loops as she gathered them in her hands.

She put the cereal in the sink and washed it down, and reached in the dark for a damp dish towel to dry her hands. The towel was tossed to the side, over a hard object Amanda had trouble placing in her mind as she ran over it with her fingers.

And then she picked it up. A gun.

Her breath caught in her throat, choking her as she almost dropped the thing. She almost screamed, but not in fear. She was angry. Valentin had left a gun out. The baby, his baby, could toddle around, could reach up, could play with his goddamned gun.

Amanda made the decision right there and then to move out. She was going to take what little money she made and move to a crappy little apartment and take the baby with her. She was not going to expose Madison to his father's lifestyle anymore.

"Lights are out." Val's voice cut through the dark. Amanda turned toward him; she could see the outline of his body, could feel him move . . .

"Val, I'm taking the baby tonight. I don't think it's safe here—" Valentin was up against Amanda, his cold hand at her throat, before she finished.

"You're not taking my kid anywhere."

Amanda tried to pry Valentin's hand from her

neck; the picture of who he once was, the tanned, smiling boy with the puka shells and shock of blond hair, was torn from her memory.

"Val, you're hurting me." Amanda thought of Madison, asleep on the couch. "Let's just talk about this."

"I am through talking, bitch." Val breathed into her ear. "I am so through talking."

And then Amanda knew. Her brother was going to kill her, with his bare hands, his only son in the next room. Her only nephew would grow up knowing his aunt had been murdered by his father in the next room.

Amanda brought her foot down, the cheap soles, hard on Val's bare foot.

He howled in pain and released her.

Amanda reached blindly through the dark and made the decision.

And just as Valentin flew back at her, ripping the air to get at his baby sister—

She pulled the trigger.

When he looked back on the moment, Gabriel couldn't remember exactly when it was he knew the game was up. The house was dark, yes, but that in itself wasn't fatal. He walked in, saw the baby playing by himself on the living room floor, and scooped him up with one hand. In the other hand, he held three daisies, plucked from a neighbor's garden to be put to good use.

And then he walked into the kitchen, illuminated by moonlight, and for the worst moment of his life, he thought he had lost her forever.

Amanda was sitting, legs flung out before her, her back against the kitchen cabinet. Gabe thought she must be dead, her eyes glassy and unseeing.

But then he saw Valentin, and the gun in her hand. And he knew what had happened.

Gabriel put the baby in his crib. He had only a few minutes to set things right.

But at that moment, just when the situation couldn't get any worse, Gabe heard a car drive up, a door slam.

It would be the last person he wanted to see.

Seventeen

In the kitchen, Gabriel reached down and took the gun from Amanda's limp hand. He wiped her prints off on his flannel shirt. And then he gripped the gun, shooting off one bullet into the wall, away from where the baby was sitting up in his crib, plucking petals from a daisy.

The doorbell rang. Gabe ignored it.

The moon behind him, Gabe looked at the hole in the wall and poked his finger through. If he looked hard enough, he thought, he could see the rest of his life there, down that black hole.

And then he saw words, something someone had written, scratching sentiment into the wall in a child's scrawl.

The words, the chicken scratch, said: "Here 2 day gone 2 morow."

The doorbell rang again. "Amanda?" He heard James's voice. "Are you there?" And then, "Open the door."

Gabe sat down, his knees shaking, and put his big arms around Amanda and brushed back her hair and waited. And the faint wail of the siren came, and Gabriel knew for sure it was crying for him. Gabe hoped the cuffs would not cut too deep, as his wrists were quite large.

He heard the front door open. In a second, James was standing above him, staring at the macabre scene, Val's vacant stare.

And then it came to James.

"Did she do this?" he asked the big guy.

Gabe just nodded. He stroked Amanda's cheek. He wanted to bring her back. If only he had gotten there earlier.

"I should have been here," Gabe said, softly. "I should have been here."

The sirens were getting closer. They were seconds away when James, the poor immigrant with the fast mind, made his proposal.

James had a prof at Harvard—a guy who specialized in self-defense cases, a guy who fancied himself as a man against the system who saw James, this kid who came from nowhere, in the same light.

"No. I'm taking the rap for this," Gabe said. James was speaking fast, but Gabe understood every word.

"Okay. You take the rap. But my guy gets you off."

James heard the cop cars pull up. "I'll help you. I'll testify on your behalf. Her brother was a goddamned creep."

"Enough of that shit," Gabe said. James backed off Val.

"I'll get you off, but the deal is—"

Gabe waited. The cops were about to break the door down. They were yelling now, yelling for someone to open up.

"You never see each other again. Ever."

"She doesn't go to prison," was all Gabe said. It was all he wanted. Madison needed her, and Gabe couldn't live with any thought of her behind bars.

"This guy doesn't give a shit about himself," James thought. This was truly amazing.

"No one goes to prison," James assured him.

And they shook on it, sealing the deal just

as they heard the words, "Get your hands up!"

A few miles to the west, Joe Artuga slipped in a pond of his own sweat on the floor of his bedroom and lay there into the dawn, crying out but once. As there was no one to hear.

Eighteen

The nineties. Everyone was going somewhere and getting there fast. Except, it seemed, for Amanda Cruz. Her life had been reduced to a series of repeat experiences. Jog around the reservoir at 6. Kids up at 6:50. Car pool at 7:25. Drop-off at 8:05 (if she's lucky). Starbucks at 8:20. Gelson's at 8:45 . . .

There were times Amanda would take a class at the local college—a creative writing course here, a watercolor course there. She would walk in and look around the classrooms and see faces like hers, and hair like hers, and nails like hers, and she'd think, "This is what I am. Just another housewife desperately seeking avenues of self-expression in the hopes that I don't just *explode* one day." Then she'd suppress a scream,

smile pleasantly, and take a seat next to a
woman who could've been her twin. Amanda
had found an outlet in the creative writing
courses, until the day James "discovered" a
couple of her more recent pieces in the drawer
of the faux-antique cherrywood desk in their library; evidently, James did not appreciate her
biting take on suburban life in southern California. Especially as the cranky attorney husband in the stories was ever-so-slowly balding.
"This shit," as he called it, "is not funny." He
yelled this as he ran his hands nervously
through his fading gold curls, each strand holding on for dear life.

Amanda could seldom remember what day it
was, except on weekends, and that was only because her husband was home from the firm.
James would get up early, eat the oh-so-healthy-
and-dull breakfast that Amanda had made for
him (scrambled egg whites, no yolk, dry wheat
toast, no crust, decaf coffee) and head off before
the sun to the Encino golf course to spend time
with the lawyer pals he had worked with all
week long, twelve hours a day.

So today was Saturday. Saturday morning, to
be exact.

Oh, the list. There was always a list on Saturday mornings. Amanda had been using lists for almost ten years now. Her life was spelled out on tiny strips of yellow paper. Her orders came on tiny strips of yellow paper.

On occasion, James would even request sex on tiny strips of yellow paper.

Grocery shopping. Basics.

Shoe repair.

Soccer uniforms. (Soccer season again! Ugh!)

Car wash.

Amanda would tackle the grocery shopping last. Secretly, she loved grocery shopping. The promise of new things, even in perishable packages. And her favorite store, Gelson's, on Ventura. You could eat off the white-tiled floor.

But then, one could eat off the floor of Amanda's home. Even under the dog dish.

Amanda had awakened that morning to James's silence. And then she remembered last night. The lawyer dinner party. Did she really run out like that, like her French silk La Perla panties had caught fire? She tried to recall the conversation she was having before the incident.

"Where are you vacationing this year?" someone asked. It was the skinny woman with the collagened lips. Amanda could not look at her without staring at her mouth.

"Mmm. I think Maui," Amanda replied.

"Maui? Maui is lovely, but please, the mosquitoes."

"Maui doesn't get mosquitoes," the opinionated woman with the blond hair and freckled hands said. "Kauai is a mosquito nightmare."

"Oh yes, stay away from Kauai."

"Mental note—no Kauai," Amanda said. She wondered what they would think if she suddenly stuck a fork in her eye. Amanda laughed, too heartily, causing James to throw her his famous look, perfected over years of cohabitation: James's head would tilt downward, his eyes would glaze over, the eyebrow over his left eye would engage. This meant, "Amanda, dear, cut the shit out," or, "Amanda, say one more word, and I mean *one* more, and you're looking at an entire week of silent treatment." Amanda excused herself just as the conversation at her end of the table was veering into interior decorating and whether we had finally seen the end of the faux antique. She knew she would not be strong enough to curb her wayward tongue.

In all these years, what Amanda referred to later as "the dinner party years," she had noticed something about the majority of the women she knew. They talked about car seats, they talked about manicurists, they talked about where to find a good nanny (not too cute but not too ugly, not too Spanish but not too British, not too smart but not a moron . . .).

But they did not talk about love.

Amanda thought about Gabriel from the moment she opened her eyes at dawn and looked out at her celadon and eggplant bedroom (as the J. Crew–impaired interior decorator had labeled the theme colors of the Cruz master bedroom— Amanda just called it lilac and light green) to the hour at night when she would slide between Egyptian cotton sheets, her head resting on a down pillow. For a long time, she carried him with her every day, like a stolen locket, hidden to everyone except herself. She reasoned that thoughts of him would dwindle away, until one day she wouldn't be able to conjure up his face or perhaps even remember his name. That day never happened.

Amanda, sitting in her bathroom, smiled despite the trouble she knew she was in.

But really, could James blame her for running out?

Of course he could, and he would. If he hadn't made partner within five years, he would have blamed her. If he hadn't been able to buy the house he wanted in the most suburban (read: white) area of Los Angeles, he would have blamed her.

If their daughter's reading scores weren't at the top of her class in her exclusive private school, he would blame her. James didn't even have to say anything. Amanda could see it in his eyes, could feel it in what was not said.

But she was grateful to him, and her gratitude had turned her into a prisoner.

She owed James. Didn't she?

Amanda looked at herself in the mirror. On the outside, she was the perfect suburban housewife. Slender (she had taken up running and tennis at James's behest—and now could trounce all the partners and their wives, until James put an end to her streak; he feared retribution from the firm). Attractive, still, but not overwhelmingly so. Her hair was cut into a sort of soccer-mom pageboy that all the "girls" preferred. Girls, that is, who were in their thirties and forties and long ago lost any semblance of innocence, along with their baby fat. The breasts that James had bought for her (after the baby, he pronounced them a bit too saggy) were exactly between a B and a C. They would be this shape until long after the rest of her body had turned to dust. Silicone never dies.

Perfect. All too perfect.

She couldn't have hated herself any more.

Every single day around three, Amanda would take the gun that James had purchased for her birthday (for protection, of course) and hold it up to her head, and wonder for a moment what it would be like to be without pain.

Her daughter would be better off without her—in her darkest hours, in the afternoons when she felt most useless, Amanda felt certain of it. Her husband definitely would be better off. He could even trade in on the sympathy he would get—maybe marry a sweet girl who could follow his orders better. For James seemed tired of Amanda's distance; even though it was a deal he'd brokered, he'd thought he could win her affections back. In the first couple of years of marriage, James had tried to be what he thought she wanted—attentive, gentle, patient. But Amanda knew that beyond his change in behavior was a stronger need to control. And she knew that someday he would stop trying; and she knew that she would never love him in the way he wanted.

But Madison wouldn't be better off. And Madison was everything that mattered to Amanda. Madison reminded Amanda that there was something good and real in her. Madison was her one true thing.

James knocked on the door to her bathroom. He always knocked. He was, above all, polite. Except, of course, when he was angry enough to smash his fist into a wall. Except then.

Amanda looked up at him and smiled. She wondered if he approved of her new lipstick, momentarily eager to uphold her end of their bargain. She had bought the salmon-colored tube with him in mind.

"I want to talk to you," he said.

Amanda turned briefly to the small television set that kept her company as she spent part of her mornings making herself presentable for a world she did not approve of and would never be accustomed to. She switched it off, just missing Danny Markus's unmistakable grin as he plied sparkly wares on the QVC, rambling on in his best Richard Dawson impersonation about the virtues of cubic zirconium.

"I want to talk to you," James had said.

"I'm sorry about the dinner party," Amanda said, automatically.

"Fuck the dinner party," James said. "This is beyond some stupid dinner party."

"Hey, they're your friends," Amanda replied.

James waved off her response. He was growing impatient with her. Waving was his way of showing impatience.

"You are not being supportive of me," James said. "You don't respect me the way other people do."

"I'm not being supportive? I stuffed those goddamned game hens myself—you try doing that."

"Oh, stuffing game hens. Now that's difficult," James replied, so sarcastically it felt like a slap. "What else is difficult about your life? Ah, let's see. Manicures? Tennis? Shopping?"

"You're the one who insisted I stay home." Now Amanda was getting pissed. "You're the one who begged me not to go back to work."

"Your 'work' was ridiculous," James declared. "I mean, who would slave all day on some stupid show no one's going to watch anyway?"

"It was a start." Amanda felt defeated, again. This was an argument that, like a broken record, had been played over and over again in their marriage. She was even sick of it herself. But ten years ago, in that shitty little job, in that shitty house, with her shitty little life—that was the last time she knew herself.

"Whatever," James said. "Listen, I think you should know. I want a divorce."

Amanda looked at him. "What's the punch line?" she asked. She knew she shouldn't have, but she just couldn't help herself.

"The punch line?!" he yelled, his voice going up an octave. "The punch line is I've been seeing someone! That's the punch line!" James was on the verge of hysteria.

"So I guess that terribly gifted new paralegal you're using is working out fine, huh?" Amanda replied calmly. ("Oh Amanda," she thought, "you are such a bad girl.")

James turned color and stormed out, leaving several broken perfume bottles in his wake. Amanda sat there and thought about the look on his face, and it dawned on her that she had never seen that shade of red before.

And then James came back to finish off what he started. Amanda figured as much, which is why she hadn't moved a muscle.

"And don't think you're getting any of my money!" he screamed. "If you try—I'll tell everything! Everything!"

"I don't want any of your money, James," Amanda said.

"And I get Tildy," he said. And with that last blow, he finally left her in peace.

She was just sorry he had taken first strike.

Amanda remembered the day she hired the private detective. Tildy had just taken a hunk out of Madison's hand with her sharp little teeth, and Madison had come running into the kitchen bleeding, very upset.

James was in the kitchen, sharpening their special set of German kitchen knives, the best in the world.

"Daddy!" Amanda heard Madison wail.

"My God. Madison, what happened?" Amanda could hear James was on top of the situation. She slowed her pace from the upstairs bedroom.

"She bit me! Tildy bit me!"

"I'm sure she didn't mean it. Come, sit up here."

Amanda watched from behind the door, genuinely touched, as James sat Madison up in a kitchen chair and sprayed Bactine on the wound and bandaged him up. She had willed herself to stop taking over as James performed a fatherly duty on this boy. She did not want to interrupt.

"How's that feel?" James asked.

"Good," Madison said, wiping his nose.

"Good. That's a brave boy."

And then James bent down toward Madison, face-to-face, and peered into his huge brown eyes and said, "You know I'm not your daddy, right, Madison?"

Amanda's heart skipped a beat. She wasn't sure what she was hearing.

"I know," said Madison. He was so small.

"You know your daddy is dead," James said calmly.

"Yes." Madison squirmed.

"We need to figure out a name you can call me. . . . How about Uncle James? How's that?"

"Okay." Madison looked away. He started pulling at the bandage.

"Great. Okay, big guy."

Amanda wanted to sink one of the new German kitchen knives between Jimmy's shoulder blades, but only by accident. One homicide was enough for any family.

The word "daddy" had really come into force in the family since Tildy was barely one, and she used it so often that Madison had started calling James "Daddy" every time he could—as though he were testing the waters.

But James had never adopted Madison, and Amanda knew why. It wasn't because he was preserving Val's memory—it was the thought of this child with Val's genes and Patrice's genes mixed into some sort of wretched stew. He couldn't bear it.

Minutes after being silent witness to this scene, Amanda set out to find the man she had not stopped thinking about every day for ten years. First, she called every Williams in the greater Los Angeles phone book. This lasted several days. "Hello, is there a Gabe or Gabriel Williams at this number?" was repeated so often she woke up saying the words. Thank God, she thought, panicking as she looked over at the snoring mound next to her, that James was such a heavy sleeper.

She drove around the old neighborhood with the cracked sidewalks, under the guise of looking for new lawn furniture (knowing, in James's opinion, that this would be a worthy use of her time); she scoured the streets for the Ninja she knew would be considered an antique; she talked to neighbors who remembered the old man, Frank, but not where he'd gone; she even learned to use the Internet, for crissakes, after being told anyone could find anything on the Internet. Even a lost love.

After months of this nonsense, of hiding credit card bills from James, of babbling in her sleep, of tripping over old sidewalks, Amanda realized she was having an affair with a ghost. If she was really serious, she would put what little money she had saved where her mouth was. So she took out the yellow pages and called the first private investigator whose name she put her finger on, and Henry Goodstein came on the line. His gravelly voice gave her instant solace. She knew she had found a friend.

Henry told her it would take two, three

months at the most to find her friend. He was never wrong about these things.

The drive to Gelson's had gone by so fast, Amanda wondered how she arrived, what streets had brought her to the crowded Saturday-morning parking lot. And then she realized. Everything in the last decade of her life had been done by rote. She could drive to Gelson's from her house with a blindfold on and a half bottle of California chardonnay in her bloodstream, no problem. The little girl who liked to stand out in the rain in her Mary Janes had not drawn outside the lines in ten years.

Now James had threatened a divorce, and he wanted custody of their daughter, Tildy. But not custody of Madison. He was not his child, after all.

And he would not necessarily be in the mood to share the money he had made in his law firm.

Amanda, before she married James on a rainy September morning, had agreed to a Faustian bargain. After James and his professor had gotten Gabe swiftly released on a self-defense argument (Val had, after all, just murdered his old friend Leo), Amanda was obligated to stick to her agreement with him. What else, she would ask herself over and over, so many times that the question greeted her with every morning—what else could she do?

Gabriel had told her in no uncertain terms, and James had further convinced her, that if she went to jail, even for a short period of time, there would be no one for Madison. The child would wind up in a foster home. Or worse—with Patrice's parents.

James offered her a "better deal." And for better or worse, she took it. But now, as he made clear to her that very morning, James was not above blackmail in order to keep Amanda in line, in order to keep her from taking any of his money.

James had threatened to divorce her a few times in the past, but this time was different. This time, she knew he meant it. Amanda should have pleaded and begged for forgiveness. The old Amanda would have. Instead she just sat before her bathroom mirror and listened. She knew in the end he probably didn't have the guts to divorce her. But she surprised herself.

She didn't care.

*   *   *

She parked her suburban soccer-mom four-
wheel monstrosity in a compact spot and looked
over at Madison, sitting beside her with his
Gameboy; she playfully tugged at his cheek,
knowing this annoyed him. He looked up and
smiled, the cocky smile his father once had.

Amanda had tried to track down Patrice several times over the last ten years. She had always
been one step behind Patrice—had been yelled at
by more screwed-over landlords than she could
count. And finally, Amanda had given up the
search for Madison's real mom, secretly happy
she had never found her.

There was a time, two years earlier, when
Amanda had stopped by a Sav-on in San Pedro.
She and Maddie were on their way back from a
day trip to San Diego, and Madison had needed
something for the sore throat he had developed
by yelling at killer whales. At the checkout
counter, Amanda looked up from Maddie at a
woman whose cat eyes, though dry lines had
formed around them, belonged to Patrice, but
whose face had been blurred. The nose was flat-
tened, the lips and teeth slightly skewed

Amanda had done a double take, had opened her mouth in an unconscious greeting, but the woman looked away quickly to her cash register and did not look up again, even as Amanda took Maddie's hand and briskly walked out onto the sidewalk, and did not dare look back.

She loaded up the groceries into the back of the suburban and wondered if this was one of the last times she'd be making this run. Were her days at Gelson's numbered? Would she no longer be able to afford the produce that was polished and stacked so neatly, the apples lined up like naval academy cadets at a graduation ceremony? Horrors, would she have to shop with the mortals? She smiled and tipped the lanky boy in the red apron $5, as she did every time (even though he argued every time), and turned to follow Maddie into the car.

The sound, a deep rumble. It surrounded her—she felt encapsulated in its warmth. The parking lot seemed to vibrate under her feet, sending a charge through her chest and into her throat. She felt an ache; and she thought, ruefully, this is what a heart attack must feel like.

She shook the carefully highlighted strands of hair from her eyes.

And looked up at Gabriel.

"Girl, I think you got a little skinny," he said, his helmet sitting to the side of his lap, under his arm. Amanda, trying desperately to keep her balance as her legs threatened to buckle under her, didn't hear his words right away. Her eyes were too busy taking in what she had seen only in her mind for ten years. His lips were the exact same tawny color, same full heart shape. A decade of waiting melted away.

"You are Amanda McHenry?" Gabe was trying to make a joke, make light of this ridiculous situation. He had spent all these years getting his life straight, in a big way, in anticipation of this moment. After the trial, and after the plant closed, Gabe had gone on to college. First to a two-year, and then on to Cal State–L.A. He had worked construction along the way, always remembering those lonely times on the hill, watching the lights of his only love's house.

Gabe had received his general contractor's license a couple of years ago, and as the southern California real estate market rebounded, so did he, with a vengeance.

Gabe had found a place to live that would do him proud the first time she came to see him, the first time he cooked dinner for her, the first time they made love again. Every move he made, he did with her in mind.

He had that swimming pool, and he had that great, big backyard. Gabriel was missing only one part of his recurring dream. And finally, after all this time, she was standing right in front of him. The call had come that very morning at the office, the trailer he used on site, from some old guy with a gravelly voice, a voice that very much reminded him of his father's father.

"You Gabe Williams?" the voice asked. Gabe could hear him, even above the jackhammers.

"This is," Gabe said warily. He thought for a second that the guy sounded like a parole officer. Which one of his men, he thought, was in trouble this time?

"Jesus Christ, boy, where you been?" the gravel said. Gabe didn't know whether to be more pissed than curious, or more curious than pissed.

"I got somebody who's looking for you," continued the gravel.

And Gabe leaned back in his chair and listened, and hid his face in his hand as tears rolled down his cheeks and over his lips. He didn't want his men to see him cry.

Amanda cursed her muteness, and still could not find words to answer his, and Gabe looked at her, eyeing her warily now. She felt him trying to read what was going on behind her tortoiseshell sunglasses. She took them off, her manicured fingers shaking, and showed him the meaning behind the color of her eyes, and hoped that he would understand what she could not yet say.

She also knew, once she started talking, she would not stop.

Amanda smiled as she realized this defining moment, the moment she had been waiting for for over a decade, was happening in a supermarket parking lot. God had a warped sense of humor—could there be a less romantic spot?

She became aware of Madison in the car, waiting, not knowing that his future had changed. And she thought of Tildy and the question of custody, and realized that when push came to shove, James would not expend the time, the energy.

She would fight him, and she would win.

"I am," she finally said, "I am Amanda McHenry."

Gabe tried his best to control the tear from spinning in his eye and spilling onto his cheek; he tried to stop the heaving shoulders that would surely give away everything. If these tough years had taught him anything, it was that there was a God. And Gabe had prayed day in and day out for this moment to come. And here it was, and he was not going to blow it. He opened his arms that had remained empty all these years, laying his heart bare.

"Rescue me," was all he could finally say to her.

Amanda didn't remember dropping her purse, that salmon lipstick rolling away into Saturday-morning parking-lot traffic. What she would remember always, and what she would tell her children, and her new friends who didn't care for tennis, and the neighbors who actually talked to her about things she cared about, was this.

He came back for her and she was there.